PRAISE FOR JAMES MACMANUS:

Midnight in Berlin

'Based on real events this gripping, atmospheric thriller brilliantly captures the malevolent mood of the Nazi capital on the eve of World War Two.' – Roger Moorhouse author of *Berlin at War*

'A remarkable novel which totally grips.' – *Daily Mail*

'As pacey as any modern thriller... a vivid portrait of an entire city seething with intrigue and danger.' – *The Times*

Ike and Kay

'The fascinating dramatisation of a true story... a deeply emotional read.' – *Daily Mail*

'Highly readable... successfully combines intimacy with an awareness of the wider picture.' – *The Sunday Times*

'Offers a convincing picture of three crucial years of the Second World War.' – *The Times Literary Supplement*

Also by James MacManus

Ike and Kay
Sleep in Peace Tonight
Ocean Devil: The Life and Legend of George Hogg
Black Venus
Midnight in Berlin
The Language of the Sea

THE WOMAN WITH WINGS

Leabharlanna Poiblí Chathair Baile Átha Cliath
Dublin City Public Libraries

JAMES MACMANUS

ENDEAVOUR QUILL

AN ENDEAVOUR QUILL PAPERBACK

First published by Endeavour Quill in 2019

Endeavour Quill is an imprint of Endeavour Media Ltd
Endeavour Media, 85-87 Borough High Street,
London, SE1 1NH

Copyright © James MacManus 2019

The right of James MacManus to be identified as the author
of this work has been asserted by them in accordance with the
Copyright, Design and Patents Act, 1988.

All rights reserved. No part of this publication may be
reproduced, stored in a retrieval system, or transmitted in
photocopying, recording or otherwise, without the prior
permission of the copyright owner.

ISBN 978-1-911445-76-0

Typeset using Atomik ePublisher from Easypress Technologies

Printed and bound in Great Britain by
Clays Ltd, Elcograf S.p.A.

www.endeavourmedia.co.uk

For the next generation:
George, Willa and Sonny, Zalie and Aoife

The Company of Birds

Ah the company of the birds
I loved and cherished on earth
Now, freed of flesh we fly
Together, a flock of beating wings,
I am as light, as feathery,
As gone from gravity we soar
In endless circles.

Sasha Moorsom (1931-1993)

CHAPTER ONE

The eagle turned, raising one wing against the updraft from the mountain below, its talons tightening on the rabbit. The animal struggled, kicking out in its dying moments, forcing its captor to adjust the final approach to the nest. It was a young animal, too young to know the danger when a sudden shadow masked the sun. The eagle slid through the wind sideways, losing height and speed. Hundreds of feet below, three beaks craned from the nest. Primaeval instinct told them that food was at hand.

Below the nest, on a narrow ledge carved into the rock face by time and weather, the bird could see four splashes of white on the grey-green canvas of the mountain. She knew them well; they came here every nesting season in the spring, to observe her young.

In the dark old days, men with guns would shoot her kind – white-tailed fish eagles – bringing the birds thumping to the ground or splashing into the river with stomachs ripped and feathers torn by heavy shot.

Those men, mostly gamekeepers, knew where to find their prey; for the eagles hunted for food along riverbanks and over sheep pastureland. They were easy targets and once brought down, the bodies of the birds would be stripped of their finest feathers and left to rot.

But not now. The eagles were safe to roam the mountains and seashores of the Hebrides, breeding, hunting for prey, riding the high Atlantic winds with partners that remained lifetime allies in the sky.

One hundred feet or so from the nest, on a narrow ledge, they awaited the approaching eagle. Each watcher fingered a switch, which was on a lead to the digital camera strapped to their helmet. The group of four had climbed 2,000 feet that morning for a rare chance to capture the moment that Britain's largest bird of prey, hunted to extinction in the last century and returned to life in this, brought food to the nest.

Their timing was perfect. The watchers had arrived within camera range of the nest as the eagle was about to return with food for her young. The group of four tensed, knowing what was going to happen. The eagle would land beside the nest and, holding the rabbit in its claws, would tear the creature to bloodied shreds with its powerful beak. The strips of flesh would be held over the nest, forcing the eaglets to push upwards. The highest, and thus the strongest, would be rewarded first. Eagles, like every other animal in the wild, learn early that life is a struggle for survival.

This was the photograph for which they had tumbled out of bed early that morning, snatching a breakfast of coffee and biscuits at the hostel before walking a mile to the foot of the mountain. A two-hour climb had followed; up the western slopes before the group crossed to the east side, looking back over the mainland. They had inched along a narrow path to within range of the nest. Below, the mountain dropped away in a long steep fall through scree and bushes to the valley beneath.

The nest had been built, rebuilt and returned to every spring for the past thirty years. The eagles chose the site both for shelter from the west winds, and because no predator could make the final climb up sheer rock to the cleft where, every year, in the cold month of April, the eagle laid her eggs – at least two, never more than four. In the warmth of a nest woven from twigs, ferns and even small pieces of driftwood plucked from the sea, the eagle would sit and incubate the eggs until the young chicks broke free from their shells.

The eagle was coming in fast now, long wings beating the air with a rhythmic, almost musical sound that increased in tempo as the bird thrust her head up and leaned back, pushing the clawed feet forward to slow the descent and allow safe landing.

For the chicks in the nest, and for the birdwatchers crouched below on a narrow ledge, this was the moment they had waited for. There were just four in her bird club, as she called it, and Alison felt almost maternal pride in seeing the others so tense, excited and expectant as they waited less than fifty feet from the nest.

Alison had trawled the internet for months, seeking three like-minded young professionals in the London area to make up her group. In various chatrooms she had posed the same question: "Why would anyone want to spend precious weekends waiting for hours on end, often in considerable discomfort, for a fleeting sight of a rare bird?" She had answered the question: "Those long hours in some of the most beautiful parts of the country just watching and waiting are a form of meditation. You empty your head of all that fuzzy brain clutter that piles up during the week. It's like great poetry. It explains yourself to yourself."

She had received many responses. She weeded out the usual eccentrics and perverts. Most of the suitable replies came to nothing when Alison made it clear that birdwatching trips meant whole weekends away, sometimes travelling to the far reaches of the country.

She finally chose three young people, both for their enthusiasm and because they were only dimly aware of the pleasures and frustrations of birdwatching. She deliberately limited the number to four, arguing that any more worked against the stealth and guile required to get close to rare birds in the wild. She was going to teach them; watch while they marvelled at the shimmer of a woodpecker's green-gold wings as the bird shrugged off water with a silver sprat in its beak; share with them the once in a lifetime sight of a hen harrier, its grey-brown colouring lost in the dusk, flying like a ghost to its nest in the winter wheat of an upland field; listen with them to the musical notes of a song thrush hidden in thick bushes, whence its soft "seep, seep" floated upwards through the branches.

She was left with Nick, Xanthe and Douglas. They were all in their late twenties, roughly the same age as herself. She helped them buy the right clothing and binoculars. At first, they came out of curiosity – and then she watched with pleasure as their interest turned into obsession.

She had spent many weekend hours with the group, mostly within a day's drive of London, where they all worked. Nick was a tall, gangly accountant with a lopsided grin that seemed to slide off his face when he smiled, which he did a lot. It gave him the innocent look of a schoolboy. Xanthe, his girlfriend, worked in hospital administration. Christened Elvira after her Victorian great-great-grandmother, she had changed her first name by deed poll to one whose origin and pronunciation were totally obscure, which is why she chose it.

Finally, there was Douglas: bespectacled, round-faced with a beaky nose and small ears that made him look exactly like a barn owl, which he claimed to have been in a former life. Always elegantly dressed, even in camouflage clothing, and indiscreetly camp, Douglas had several times tried and failed to interest the group in night-time owl watching expeditions. Alison had voiced the general opinion that staying up all night, on the off chance of seeing a common bird they could neither film nor photograph, made no sense.

Here they all were, standing precariously on a mountain ledge, waiting for the golden moment she had always promised them, the sight of the rarest bird in Britain on the nest with her chicks, close up in their camera lenses. No one had demurred when she told them of the three-day trip to the Isle of Skye off the west coast of Scotland. It meant taking a day off work and a long, tiring trip. They had been birdwatching together for two years, and this is what they had worked towards.

From the nest came inchoate cries for food; the watchers waited, expectant, excited, hopeful that their cameras would capture an image of power and beauty that would win awards, grace exhibitions and maybe make a spread in a national newspaper.

It was not the first time Alison Spedding had climbed this mountain or seen this particular eagle. She had been here the year before, and the year before that, without ever finding the perfect image that now presented itself: a white-tailed eagle, its seven-foot wingspan at full stretch, showing a feathery fan of white and grey on the underwing; the brown coat of the clawed rabbit streaked with blood, its eyes bright and alive, held now just inches from three straining beaks, and all against a background of distant mountains and a molten silver sea.

Back in the office her photographs and, more importantly, the video would win praise from her colleagues, perhaps applause from those who attended the talk she hoped to give in the staff canteen. There might be an interview in the company newspaper, perhaps even a kind word from the chief executive herself. It was a big company in which she played a small and insignificant part within the IT department.

Small and insignificant. That was Alison Spedding. Even among her own birdwatching group, few could say they knew her well. What they knew of her lay in the efficiency with which she organised their trips and circulated information about weather, transport and lodgings, which meant, as Xanthe remarked more than once, that they didn't really know her at all.

Alison was always quiet and said little even on those evenings when the group sang folk songs backed by a badly played guitar, and passed the whisky bottle around after the traditional supper of sausages, black pudding and locally-baked bread. Their trips always ended like this. First, they would watch their videos and look at their photographs of the day's birdwatching on their laptops. Then the whisky bottle would come out. Alison would drink as much as any of them, but always in an absentminded way while tapping away on her laptop or flipping through images on her camera.

Xanthe suspected that no one really knew Alison. She had few friends and seemed to prefer it that way. At the age of thirty-two, with a slender figure, mouse-brown hair, a long oval face that framed a prominent nose and a thin-lipped mouth over a small but dimpled chin, Alison knew she was not attractive in any conventional sense. "You're never going to be good-looking," her mother had told her, "but remember, it's character that counts."

The remark stayed with her. She did not resent it. Her mother had been hurtful, but had meant well. In any case, Alison told herself, good looks didn't last; character did. And if character meant strength of will, then she had character. She'd settle for that.

Alison stepped back as the eagle beat powerful wings to brake the descent before landing. Three beaks craned from the nest. She looked down, checking the distance to the side of the ledge. She was standing at the back of the group. Below, the valley floor could be dimly seen through small bushes that cloaked the mountainside.

She turned back and pressed the remote control in her left hand. The head camera was on and the video running. She raised her head and shuffled sideways to ensure her helmet was at the best angle. The eagle landed. The curved beak turned red with blood as it rose and fell on the rabbit.

Alison felt one foot slip. The rock beneath her feet was mossy. It had rained overnight and the moss was damp and spongy. She tensed her body and leant into the mountain to counter the clutch of the valley below. The eagle continued to feed her chicks, seemingly unconcerned by the presence of strangers nearby. Alison slipped sideways as her boots lost their grip. With no more cry of alarm than a loud "Oh!" she tumbled over the edge and disappeared.

Fixated by the presence of the eagle, the three remaining watchers did not connect the gasp of alarm with the disaster that had befallen their group leader. It was Xanthe who turned, realised what had happened and screamed. The eagle lifted away from the nest.

It took an hour for the group to clamber down the mountain. No one spoke. There was no chance of calling for help. Mobile phones did not work in such a remote area. To raise the alarm and call in the mountain rescue team, they had to get back to the hostel where they had spent the night. It was no more than a wooden hut with a large communal room that was also the kitchen, and three bedrooms. A radio receiver and a tall mast ensured contact with the emergency services and the rescue helicopter on the mainland.

The trio said little to each other as they reached the base of the mountain. "Are you all right, are you OK?" were the only words spoken. Then, they turned towards the hostel. Shocked into silence through sheer disbelief at what had happened, they half-walked, half-ran down the dirt track.

When they talked about it later, they discovered a shared reaction. They had all felt suddenly displaced. A comfortable routine had been broken, the accepted norms of life had changed. The group travelled the country a few weekends every year seeking to photograph birds, both rare and common, indigenous and foreign, at well-known breeding and migratory sites. That had been an added dimension to normal lives. The trip to Skye, to see the largest and most wondrous of British birds, was the reward for all that hard work. Now, it had turned to tragedy. Life wasn't normal anymore.

Shattered by the death of their group leader, Nick and Douglas ran ahead and arrived at the hostel first. They kicked off their boots, pushed open the door and walked straight into the communal room.

Alison was sitting on a stool beside the kitchen counter. Her helmet was beside her on the bar. She was ghostly pale. There were bloodied scratches on her face and a rip in her jacket.

She turned and gave a slight smile as the two men came in. They stopped, speechless. Nick found his voice first.

"Alison, how did you get here?… Are you all right?… You fell… We thought you were dead!… What happened?"

"I don't know," said Alison. "I just fell and then must have lost consciousness. I came round and I was here. Mrs M made me some hot chocolate. She said I needed the sugar."

"But you fell off the mountain! " said Nick. "I mean… ?"

The old cliché was true, thought Alison. The man was lost for words. She finished the sentence for him.

"…how could I have survived? Good question. I don't know, but here I am. I'm fine."

Nick walked over and gave her a hug. Alison held him tight and began to cry. He stepped back.

"We must get you checked out. Mrs MacLeod, can you radio for a doctor, please?"

Mrs MacLeod, known to all as Mrs M, presided over the hostel as matron, mother and nurse. She was of indeterminate age with craggy features that looked as if they had been hewn from rock. Deep lines ran from cheek to jaw, grey hair was scooped back in a bun. The overall appearance was of a woman who had been weathered in the wind and rain on a remote mountain top. In all her years she had never seen any Scots folk come and climb the mountain of Skye to watch eagles. In her view this just proved how canny her countrymen were, compared to the strangers south of the border.

"There really is no need," said Alison, wiping away tears with a handkerchief and blowing her nose. "Look at me! I'm fine. I just want to get some rest. I'm sorry I spoilt the day for you. Did you get the pics?"

She picked up her helmet and slid off the stool. Xanthe came through the door in a rush, then she stopped and stared. Her mouth opened without utterance. She bent double, breathing deeply.

"She survived, look at her, she's here with us," said Tim in a weird voice raised almost to falsetto.

"I can't believe it! Are you all right, Ali?" said Xanthe. It was a stupid question. Alison was evidently all right. She was alive and standing in front of them. Everyone in the room began to move silently, in slow motion, at least that is how it seemed. That is what shock does, the doctors say. It freezes the conscious moment while the mind tries to catch up with what has happened. And in this case, what had happened was neither real nor explicable. The flesh and blood presence of a woman who had fallen to certain death was both surreal and inexplicable.

Xanthe walked over, put a hand on Alison's brow and turned her head to look at the scratches.

"Can you remember what happened to you?"

"No," said Alison. "It's all a blur. One minute I had the bird in focus, the next I…" She began to cry again. Xanthe hugged her.

"The bushes and saplings must have broken your fall. You're a very lucky woman. No pain, no broken bones?"

"No, I just want to sleep. Forgive me, I am really sorry to have spoilt everything for you… ermm… did you get the pictures?"

"Never mind the pics," said Nick. "You go and lie down. We'll get the doctor."

"I don't want a doctor!"

Alison was suddenly angry. The room was closing in on her. The faces of her group merged in kaleidoscopic patterns and their words became a long buzz.

"Look, I've told you. I'm fine. Now please, leave me alone."

They watched as she walked quite normally through the door. A buzz of chatter broke out behind her. She heard Xanthe say, "She's in shock but she's fine. She's had a bad fall and been very lucky. That's all, leave her be."

Then there was Nick's voice. "She can't have…"

The rest of his words trailed away unheard as Alison opened the door to her room. She stripped to her underwear and lay down on the narrow camp bed. It sagged beneath her, a reminder that the joys of birdwatching did not include comfortable hotel bedrooms.

Two flies circled the room's solitary lightbulb. She tried to make sense of what had happened. But it didn't make sense. The mountainside had not been sheer but, even so, how had bushes and small saplings broken a fall of over 2,000 feet? How had she survived without any serious injury?

She ran her hands over her stomach and thighs. She didn't feel bruised. She looked at the ceiling and watched the flies as they flew in lazy arcs around the lightbulb. There was no discernible purpose to their flight. She closed her eyes. Sleep would help. She would make sense of what had happened later.

She thought of the eagle with wings powerful enough to lift a new-born lamb from its mother's side, or so they say. She had captured the bird in all its ferocious beauty. Those images would be edited into the film she was making... a film of...

She sat up slowly and rubbed her eyes. She swung her legs off the bed and thought for a moment. Keep calm, she told herself. Stop thinking what you are thinking. Move slowly. Concentrate on the camera.

She crossed the room to a small table and picked up her helmet. She slipped the SIM card out of the head camera and breathed softly over it, a ritual remembered from school days. A magician called Mr Bonzo always entertained them at the end of term Christmas party. They loved his act, especially when he held out his empty hands for inspection, closed them, breathed on them and then held up a little bird. He threw it into the air and they watched as it fluttered away. Pure magic. They had all squealed with delight.

She sat down, opened her laptop and pressed the power button. A green light blinked at her. With a short cable she connected the laptop to the camera.

With two clicks, the video played. There was the eagle on its final approach to the nest, the majesty of the bird captured in every frame, then the beating of wings as the bird landed, the rabbit being ripped apart, the chicks straining upward with open beaks, then a flash of blue sky and a blur of greenery and suddenly...

Alison played the video again, not once but twice. After the blurred images the footage became clear, showing the mountainside and the valley floor below. There were dark shadows moving slowly over the heather and bracken.

She tried to grasp what she was seeing. She replayed the film a third time and slowed it down. The shadows were probably a hundred feet or so below the head camera. They were the shadows of wings. The dark outlines moving over the ground were clear.

She lay back on the bed and took several deep breaths. The flies above continued their aimless flights to nowhere. Their existence was as improbable as the fact that now faced her.

No bird had cast those shadows on the ground.

CHAPTER TWO

They gave her a lift to the bus stop the next day and said goodbye, the men shaking her hand, looking at her strangely, and the women hugging her close and telling her to see a doctor the moment she got back to London.

The bus trundled past mountain and moorland for two hours before reaching the mainline station. Alison stumbled off the bus, feeling drugged. She had a strong black coffee with plenty of sugar at the station café. The London train was on time. She still felt exhausted and slept almost all the way until the train arrived, late at night, at Euston station.

A taxi took her to her small flat in Highgate, north London. It was almost midnight and she was due at work the next day. She made herself scrambled eggs, drank a glass of red wine and went to the bathroom. The heat and steam of a hot drenching shower, together with the wine, normally gave her a good night's sleep.

She lay between the sheets, unable to stop thinking of the eagle, the rabbit, the chicks, the mountain, the sudden lurching slip and then the fall and... She got out of bed, took the SIM card from the camera and went into the kitchen. She took a strong pair of scissors and placed the card between the twin blades. She paused. Whatever had happened on that mountain had been a dream, or maybe a nightmare. The SIM card was a tiny sliver of technology that held either a lie, a fantasy or an impossible truth.

She held the SIM card up and breathed over it. She put the scissors away. She wrapped the card in foil and put it in the deep-freeze section of her fridge, alongside an assortment of frozen fish fillets, milk and ice cream packs.

She told herself she was going to forget the whole episode. She was going to go back to work the next day and allow the balm of office routine to wash away memories of a nightmare. The nightmare in which she had ruined the greatest photographs any of her group, or indeed any birdwatcher, would ever take of the white-tailed eagle.

*

As befitted one of the world's largest advertising agencies, Foxglove's head office in London was situated north of Oxford Street in the fashionable Marylebone district. The six-storey building was clad in silver and black glass panels, set at angles to project shifting beams of light onto passers-by. The effect attracted attention, which was the point. The business of Foxglove demanded attention, from a global audience, and its London headquarters were designed to do just that, in microcosm.

The creative genius that lay within was announced by a large aviary, so designed that it arched over the main doors inside the entrance. The aviary contained a range of birdlife, creating the impression for visitors and staff alike that they were walking through a giant birdcage as they entered. The cage had a transparent plastic floor to catch droppings while allowing visitors and staff to look up at the colourful display of blue tits, robins, thrushes, sparrows and other domestic birds.

Carved in gold letters high on a black granite wall behind the reception desk in the lobby were the words, *we fly high to serve and inspire.*

The chief executive, Tamara Morgan, was fond of repeating the company motto at staff meetings, which only served to inspire various ribald variations. As usual, Alison gave a visible shudder as she walked under the aviary, hoping that her disgust at the distasteful display of captive wildlife would be noticed by others.

The cage was an obscenity, an affront to anyone civilised enough to believe that wild birds belonged in their natural habitat, not caged for decorative purposes in the foyer of a large office building. She had organised a petition calling on management to release the birds, but her colleagues showed no inclination to oppose an initiative personally endorsed by the chief executive.

She took the lift to the third floor, punched the code into the numbered panel on the door of the IT office and went to her desk. She and her colleagues told themselves that this was the beating heart of the company. Without constant support from Alison and her team, the digital systems would collapse – and the business with it.

"Good morning, Ali, how was your weekend?"

Jed was a sallow youth in his mid-twenties with a wispy moustache and a ponytail of greasy brown hair held back in a clasp. Whatever the season he wore the same shabby clothes: drainpipe jeans, a scruffy T-shirt and black trainers.

His head was poised on a long neck with a prominent Adam's apple, and the neck was in turn attached to a gangling frame whose arms and legs seemed to work independently of each other. His nose was misshapen, as if someone had tweaked it at birth. Unkind colleagues remarked that he looked as if he had been put together in a hurry by someone working with Plasticine. The eyes belied this shambolic

15

appearance. They were cat's eyes, yellow-flecked irises around dark pupils. They changed colour, the yellow turning to gold and the pupils to pure black, according to mood and light.

When Jed looked at someone, they stayed looked at. That was his little joke, although no one thought it funny. His colleagues thought him weird, but took care not to mock him openly. Jed rarely talked to them and when he did, there was just a faint impression of menace in his mildewed appearance. He spoke in a deliberately low voice that resembled the half-heard tolling of a church bell at night.

"Fine thanks," said Alison.

"See any of those eagles you were after?"

"Yes," said Alison, opening up her desktop computer and wondering how Jed knew where she had been that weekend.

"You must have got close, looks like one scratched your face."

Alison ran her fingers over the scratches on her cheek. They were not deep and would fade in a few days.

"Do me a favour, Jed."

"Sure. Anything."

"Shut up. I'm busy."

Jed got up, stretched and flipped his drink carton into a bin.

"They've got eagles in London Zoo, you know," he said.

He ambled away, leaving behind the unmistakable aroma of someone who had slept in his clothes over the weekend and not bothered to wash. Jed didn't care. He knew the rules didn't apply to him. He parked his Yamaha motorbike in the basement car park supposedly reserved for executives. No one rebuked him or told him to park the machine elsewhere. The bike was immaculate and gleamed with polish. The joke in the office was that Jed spent more time cleaning his bike than he did cleaning himself.

Tamara Morgan insisted on a smart dress code for her staff, on the grounds that looking chic was part of the company image. "You're all part of the message. I don't care if you're with the beautiful people on a beach or out of your mind in a wine bar, you've got to look good, make clients believe in you. That's how we sell advertising."

This did not apply to the information technology team, who could slouch around in their pyjamas as far as anyone was concerned. No one understood what they did or how they did it.

The IT team spoke a language impenetrable to the outsider: algorithms, satellite circuits, digital vortex beams, cable suppressors, micro encrypts, OpEx files – the vocabulary of the internet was designed to reveal its mysteries only to a chosen few.

All the staff, from Tamara Morgan and her executives down to the lowly team on the reception desk, knew that the magicians of the IT department kept their secrets to themselves. Only they could repair, restart and otherwise fix those essential gadgets of the internet age: laptop computers, desktops, mobile phones, PlayStations and all the rest of the digital wizardry. They were the plumbers of the internet, digging deep into the digital bowels of a company and fixing the pipelines through which the communications flowed to and from the outside world.

The IT staff switched roles within their department every three months to broaden their experience. For some weeks Alison had been assigned the job of sorting out the technical problems of the senior executive team, their personal assistants and, as so often happened, their families.

On Monday mornings there was usually a backlog of requests relayed by personal assistants – that was the smart new name for secretaries – for technical help. But Alison's first call that morning was different, and an unwelcome surprise. Would she report to the company doctor immediately?

Dr Sampson was an imposing middle-aged woman who split her time

17

between a private practice and two days a week at Foxglove. There, she usually dealt with cases of alcoholism, work-related stress and emotional crises caused by the breakdown of relationships. It was boring work, for which she was well paid.

She looked forward to her first case that morning; she had never had anyone referred to her for falling down a mountain before. She motioned Alison to a chair, looked at some notes on her desk and said in a voice of motherly concern, "How are you feeling?"

"Fine. But may I ask why I am here?"

"I gather you had a serious fall over the weekend."

"Who told you that?"

"Miss Spedding, there is no need to be so defensive. I am here to help you. A member of your birdwatching group called the human resources department. He was worried about you."

"And who might *he* be?"

"I can't say."

"Who was it? Surely I have a right to know?"

"I gather all of your birdwatching group were worried. You fell from a great height, apparently, and survived."

"Frankly, I resent being here on the basis of third-party gossip."

"We're not dealing with gossip, Alison. You fell a great distance – I believe the drop was some 2,000 feet from almost the top of a mountain."

"Yes, that's true, but I've told you, I'm fine."

"Apart from those scratches?"

"I have no memory of the incident, Dr Sampson. I assume the scratches came from bushes, which broke my fall."

This was a classic case of a patient in denial. Such patients typically resent medical opinion and reject advice. Dr Sampson adopted the brisk tone of a hospital matron.

"Alison, my job here is the welfare of the staff in this company. I think you would agree that it is not usual for anyone to survive such a fall without serious injury. Undress and lie down over there, please. You may keep your underwear on."

The examination showed no internal injuries, nor even bruising consistent with a fall in the way Alison described.

"You are very lucky. If you did indeed fall in the circumstances you describe, I would say your survival is miraculous," said Dr Sampson.

"Thank you, doctor."

There was a Post-it note on her desk when she got back. Kennedy Doxat had called in person. Would she go and see him at once? Alison was puzzled. Doxat was the company's creative director, the man who dazzled big corporate clients with campaigns to sell everything from toothpaste to passenger aircraft. Why would he call in person when he had his own executive assistant to handle such matters? And in any case, what was the urgency?

She had never met Doxat but well knew who he was. Everyone in the company knew Ken, as he liked to be called. "Kennedy Doxat, call me Ken," he would say on first meeting with clients. They were usually surprised that he chose to shorten such an impressive first name to something so mundane, but that was Doxat. He liked to surprise people.

Doxat was Foxglove's Mr Style, a nickname he had created for himself and which he encouraged staff and, rather more importantly, the trade press to use. The three-day stubble was kept in careful trim, the full head of almost certainly dyed blond hair was swept back to fall just over the collar of the inevitable silk shirt, almost always in a shade of blue to match the colour of his eyes. He wore linen suits, dark blue in winter, cream white in summer, with a matching triangle of handkerchief peeping from the breast pocket.

The only day he wore a tie was on 11 November, in memory of his father, who had been killed in the second Gulf War. The tie was dark red. On that day he would wear a similarly coloured carnation. He would go out to lunch at Wiltons, an expensive restaurant in Jermyn Street – in fact, one of the most expensive in London – and not return that day.

Doxat always ate alone on these occasions, although he insisted the table was laid for two. He also asked that a glass of wine and a balloon of brandy be poured for the absent guest, and placed on the table.

Throughout the meal waiters would observe Doxat talking to the empty place in front of him. Stranger still, he seemed to listen to replies from across the table. Waiters would regularly refresh Doxat's drink and watch as he made a gesture, as if asking the absent guest whether he wished for another glass.

Doxat would nod to the waiter and another glass would be placed alongside others at the unused placement. Towards the end of the meal he would rise to his feet and raise his glass in a toast. He would drain the glass, reach across the table and drink every one of the glasses lined up opposite him. After this, he would sit down and use a napkin to wipe his face. Regular waiters who observed this scene over the years knew that he was crying.

The bill for a single lunch was always well over £1,000 and would be presented with a detailed receipt as a business expense. The chief financial officer, a bald-headed boiled egg of a man called David Shortfield, would refuse payment. Doxat would receive an email, demanding to know why the company should cover the cost of an outrageously expensive solitary lunch that included a £500-plus bottle of Cheval Blanc claret and brandy of such rare antiquity that diners were usually only allowed one glass each. Doxat always had two.

The row between the two executives took the form of extravagantly insulting emails that inevitably reached the desk of Tamara Morgan. She would summon the chief financial officer and sympathise with him. Doxat was a cross they simply had to bear. His outrageous business expenses would have to be treated as legitimate claims and repaid.

Morgan liked to expand on this theme at such meetings. Doxat, she would say, was a man who moved through life blowing up the bridges behind him. He cared for nobody and never looked back at those he had used – and often abused – on his corporate ascent. Image meant everything to him, in both his personal and professional lives. Behind the image there was only darkness.

Morgan's senior colleagues were familiar with these views and most of them felt the same way. They were aware that Morgan was often on the point of sacking Doxat, and many of them urged her to do just that, but she always drew back.

The annual altercation over the expensive lunch always ended the same way. Morgan would hold a brief meeting with Doxat and assure him that the chief financial officer was an uncultured idiot who did not understand the value to the company of a bottle of Cheval Blanc 1996.

This would be Morgan's little joke, but Doxat never laughed. He just smiled at her, said nothing and left. Tamara Morgan always felt belittled by these meetings. Doxat never appeared to accept her authority or recognise her commanding role in the company.

The phone on Alison's desk rang.

"Mr Doxat is waiting for you," said a woman's voice.

She turned to see Jed looking at her.

"Hurry up," he said. "You don't want to keep the boss waiting."

*

"Come in!" The bellowed response to Alison's knock was, like everything else about Doxat, louder than necessary.

Alison walked into a large office that was centred on an oval glass table, behind which Doxat sat in a high-backed black leather armchair. A desktop computer sat on the table. A TV screen on the facing wall showed a news channel with the sound off. A white orchid stood on a glass side table beside a framed portrait of a man in uniform. It was unlike every other executive office she had seen. There was no clutter, no bookshelf, no in-trays, not even a wastepaper basket to be seen.

"Good morning, Mr Doxat," she said.

"Ken, please," he said. "Take a seat."

Alison sat down. Doxat lent back in his adjustable chair, knitted his hands together as if in prayer and looked at the ceiling.

There was a long silence. Alison looked at the door, wondering whether they were waiting for someone else to join them.

"How can I help you?" she said, finally.

Doxat allowed the chair to tilt forward and placed both hands on the desk.

"I have a problem," he said.

"That's what I am here for," she said. "I'll fix it if I can."

"This is between you and me, although I suppose everyone will know soon enough."

"Know what, sir?"

Doxat frowned at her.

"Sorry, Ken," she said.

Doxat leant forward and looked at her. There was another pause. Alison wondered whether this theatrical performance was designed to intimidate her, or just the eccentric behaviour of a powerful man in a very large office.

"How long have you been with us, Miss... um..."

"Spedding."

"Spedding, of course."

"Three years."

"And you like the job?"

Alison shifted uncomfortably in her chair.

"Yes, but why do you ask?"

"They say you're the quiet one, keep yourself to yourself."

"*They*, Mr Doxat? Sorry... Ken?"

"Never mind. You seem to be someone who can keep a secret."

Alison felt a tremor of alarm. She had read somewhere that dogs can sense a coming earthquake minutes before the eruption. That's how she felt. She didn't want to be given secrets. She just wanted to fix the man's computer or whatever other web-related problems he had.

"I think that rather depends on what the secret is," she said.

"Well said." Doxat pushed the chair back, got up and paced across the office.

"I am going to share information with you, and you alone. This must remain confidential. Am I clear?"

"If you are asking me whether I will treat this matter in confidence, of course I will," she said, adding the mental rider that she was not going to do what several of her colleagues had done, namely agree to remove pornography from a desk or laptop and delete it from the hard drive.

"Good," said Doxat. He walked to the window and stared out at the grey murk of an autumnal London morning. Seen from the back, Doxat's suit was creased and crumpled. It looked as if he had slept in it. She wondered why someone so careful with his appearance wore linen suits.

Doxat spoke while still looking out of the window. The effect was that of a disembodied voice speaking from outside the room.

"I will be leaving the company shortly," he said. "I need someone to set up my IT comms at home. Someone I can trust."

Alison shifted in her chair, trying to think of something else to say beyond the obvious questions – why was he leaving and why her?

"I'm sorry to hear you're going. You're... um..."

"...well known, well liked, the laughing cavalier of the company?"

"Something like that."

"I have been let go, released from my duties, offloaded, told I am surplus to requirements. In short, Miss Morgan has fired me."

Alison was amazed. This was the second most senior executive in Foxglove, a man praised for his contribution to the company's profits. She fumbled for a response.

"I am sorry," she finally said.

"And surprised?"

"Yes."

"So you might be, and so am I. For legal reasons I won't go into, I have to be out very soon. I have to clear my desk and all my effects tonight. That is why I need someone to set me up at home as soon as possible."

Alison tried to think clearly about what was being suggested. She knew everyone else would be amazed at the news, and so was she, but what did it mean?

"May I ask why you are leaving? It seems extraordinary," she said.

"A £50,000,000 hole in the budget – entirely due to an exchange rate movement, but that doesn't matter. It was just an excuse."

"I see."

"I doubt whether you do. Anyway, I want you to fix me up with digital comms at my home. This is a private assignment, and you will work in your own time. Of course, I will pay you. I am told that you know all the kit I will need and about the backup data, cyber-security and all that stuff."

Alison was nervous. She felt like a fly in a web watching an approaching spider.

"I do know what is required, yes."

"So that's OK?"

Doxat was looking at his watch. He was probably late for another meeting. Alison pursed her lips and found herself clenching her fists. The arrogance of the man was astonishing. He was treating her as if she was just another item on the conveyor belt of business that passed across his desk every day.

He had assumed that she would agree, and the meeting would close with her swift departure. Well, it wasn't going to be like that. She looked at her watch. She had been in the office just nine minutes. Within the company Doxat was well known for making quick decisions and showing scant regard for those who questioned or delayed him. When dealing with clients outside it was a different matter, or so everyone said.

"I am not sure I am suited to this task," she said.

"Of course you are. I am told you are one of the stars of the department."

Flattery was just another form of coercion. It was a familiar business technique. Praise, even obviously insincere, meant people would work harder for you. Her nerves gave way to defiance.

"What if I say no?"

Doxat stopped fiddling with papers on his desk and looked at her in surprise.

"Why would you do that? I am asking you to do a very simple job. You will be very well paid. No one here need know anything about it – if that's what's worrying you."

"It's a reasonable concern, isn't it? If you are leaving the company so suddenly, I assume there has been a major problem. It can hardly just be the exchange rate, can it?"

"What are you trying to say?" snapped Doxat.

"I just think it might not be wise for me to get involved."

Alison did not know who was more surprised by this statement. Doxat had sat back in his chair and was staring at her as if a complete stranger had walked into his office and lit a cigarette. Alison dimly wondered why she had been emboldened to talk like that to such a senior executive. She looked at the carpet and waited for a response.

Doxat got up, walked round and sat with his backside on the desk. He leant forward, placing his hands on his knees.

"You're absolutely right," he said. "I admire that."

"I just want to be sure I am doing the right thing."

"Of course you do. Let me help you here. You know, as do your colleagues, what I have done for this company. If you ask them whether you're doing the right thing in helping me now, I think you know what the answer will be. I stress, my departure has nothing to do with my work. It has come as a great shock to me. This is a personal issue between me and Miss Morgan. I am asking for your help, that's all. I need the skills you have. I am counting on you."

He spoke slowly, with conviction, looking not at her but at the floor as if contemplating the blow that had befallen him. She saw a glimmer of the persuasive charm that had captivated major clients. She wondered why they fell for it. Everything about this man was synthetic.

"Let me think about it, " she said.

"I would love to give you time to do that," he said, "but they are about to cut me off from all my comms here, and I'm leaving shortly. I really, *really* need your help to get up and running at home."

There was nothing synthetic about the pleading tone in Doxat's voice. "All right," she said.

Doxat looked up and smiled. He put a hand on her shoulder.

"You won't regret this. Thank you. And between ourselves?"

"Of course."

Alison took the lift to her office, at first wondering whether she had made a mistake and then becoming certain that she had. She had fallen for the charm of a good-looking man who had cleverly presented himself as the victim of brutal management. She realised why Doxat was so popular with the staff.

Like everyone else at Foxglove, she was aware of the annual row over Doxat's expenses – just as they all knew all about the solitary lavish lunch that led to it. Doxat made no secret of his yearly visit to Wiltons and was well aware that his secretary circulated all the details to those interested. It became the focus of canteen gossip for days. Doxat didn't give a damn. He made little effort to disguise his contempt for Morgan and her colleagues. That's why the staff liked him so much.

He would regularly eat in the staff canteen, the only senior executive to do so, and take a seat at one of the communal tables. There, he would ask people about their jobs and listen to formulaic descriptions of life in various departments: marketing, finance, legal, human resources, public relations, creative, design and all the smaller cogs that turned the wheels of a big advertising agency.

Initially, these canteen visits disrupted lunch for anyone unlucky enough to find themselves next to such a senior executive. The usual mundane gossip about the weather, the food, that morning's commute and someone's new engagement ring were not possible when Doxat was at the table. But after a while, he became accepted as part of the canteen routine. Staff young and old welcomed him at their tables and returned his questions with queries of their own. These were variations on a single theme: what exactly did he do?

"People will tell you I am in the persuasion business. I am not. I am in the dream business," Doxat would say. "I sell wealthy clients dreams, and they pay us a lot of money to make those dreams come true."

The second question, always put by one of the bolder spirits at the table, concerned money: just how profitable was the company? At this point Doxat would give a short tutorial. The company was riding a boom in advertising that had increased profits threefold in five years.

The global headquarters in New York, of which Foxglove was a subsidiary, were very pleased. When Doxat said this, what he meant was that New York was very pleased with *him*. He left his canteen audiences in no doubt that New York saw him as the coming man in the company.

Alison returned to her desk. Jed watched her sit down and walked over.

"What did he want?"

She sighed.

"All right. Just tell me to mind my own business."

"Mind your own business."

"Maybe it's my business, too. After all, I do work here."

"Jed."

"Yes?"

"Do me a favour…"

"…and shut up. OK, OK. But be careful, Alison, that man is dangerous."

He made a pistol of his right hand, pointed it at her, said "bang" softly and wandered off. Alison wondered whether she was taking a risk. The chief executive would not thank her for helping out a colleague she had just fired.

*

In her sixth-floor office, Tamara Morgan dictated a brief note to New York detailing the reasons for the dismissal of her creative director. She knew they would understand. Doxat was not popular across the Atlantic.

Occasionally, New York summoned executives from subsidiaries all over the world to attend a three-day conference in a lavish resort on the California coast. At the most recent event, Doxat had given a presentation that left no one in any doubt that he was largely responsible for the profit surge at Foxglove.

It had been the final morning of the conference. Doxat had been introduced to an audience of several hundred executives and their partners gathered in a huge marquee by the ocean. The comforting sound of the waves, added to the early morning start and hangovers from the revelries of the night before, induced a number of those present to close their eyes and sit back as if to contemplate the talk that would follow. Doxat woke them up.

"The first thing to understand about advertising is that the client knows nothing," he said. "The client thinks he knows what he wants, but he doesn't. So never ask the client what he or she wants. You will always know better how to sell the product. But to get the maximum fee, treat your client like a woman."

Here Doxat paused and looked slowly over his audience with a slight smile. He went on.

"Woo her, seduce her, persuade her that you are hers and she is yours. Find out what she really, *really* likes – no, not sex, ladies and gentlemen, that comes later, besides we sell advertising, we don't sell our souls – opera, a helicopter ride to the races, a big pop gig, whatever turns her on, then shower her with extravagant gifts and make her think she is the only woman in the world. Finally, you make love to her. Then she is yours. And the account will stay with you as long as she has money in the bank."

This crude and racy analogy enraged Tamara Morgan and the wives present, and did not sit well with the grandees in New York, but they slapped Doxat on the back all the same and told him he was doing a good job. Doxat made money for Foxglove. Morgan was forced to join the backslapping and congratulate her creative director on his talk. But a line had been crossed. He had upstaged her in front of the most senior figures in the New York office, including the Great Man.

If Doxat made the company profitable, Tamara Morgan gave it the style and social grace that impressed boardrooms, both in the City of London and across Europe. She dressed as befitted one of the few female chief executives in the city. Unlike other women of her status in the business world, she did not employ a personal dresser to help her select the latest fashions to be found in the big department stores, especially Harvey Nichols and Harrods.

Every month on a Thursday evening, she visited one of the stores with a woman friend. If she bought anything, and that was not often, it was usually another of her trademark trouser suits. These, and the large hooped earrings she favoured, were delivered to her home in Chelsea the next day. They were never returned. Tamara shopped carefully, with an eye to price as befitted one who had risen far from a background of poverty and poor education.

As an ambitious young woman, she had faced the usual challenges from a male world quite unconscious of its misogyny. The fact that she had left school at fifteen and began her ascent making tea on a weekly local newspaper added weight to the story, or rather the myth, that she had created for herself. Her time spent in lowly tasks on the paper was crucial to this story. She allowed it to be known that it was then she had discovered a passion for journalism. The chase after a good story was excitement in itself, but the real pleasure came in confronting authority with its own failings. That's what she told people. And that was what made her stand out from the corporate crowd. She was different. She had fought her way to the top. She liked that.

But it wasn't true. Tamara Morgan had experienced the same privileged education and wealthy background that had eased so many other corporate executives into the leather chairs of the boardroom, smart tables at expensive restaurants and occasionally into the comforts of a company jet. The private school, an MA honours degree and business course MBA had placed Tamara Morgan on a well-trodden route to success.

Morgan did not deny her background; she simply chose not to reveal it. Her occasional remarks about the story of her early years and a refusal to discuss her personal life allowed others to create the myth for her. It helped that the one arresting moment in her life had arisen from her work on a newspaper. It was a fortnightly university paper of which she became editor by default. No one else wanted the job.

She introduced a lonely hearts column, published awful student poetry and ran reviews of local bars and restaurants. Soon, students and local businessmen were soliciting her support and asking favours. She found the influence that a small student rag could wield, seductive. This was what power felt like, she realised: the power to please or displease, to confer or withhold favours. It was a moment of complete clarity in her life. From then on, she knew exactly what she wanted to do.

Tamara Morgan and Kennedy Doxat were alike in many respects. Both were somewhere in their forties and highly secretive about their past and present lives. There were rumours of divorces with children in the background and new partners, but nobody really knew. Morgan

31

never gave interviews to the press and, while Doxat rejoiced in such exposure, he was careful to reveal nothing of his private life.

They were spoken about as the twin pillars on which the edifice of Foxglove rested. Doxat and Morgan worked well together although, as anyone who observed them in the weekly executive meetings could see, they loathed each other.

Doxat presented himself as a flamboyant outsider. He was described in the trade and financial press as the man who put a splash of bitters into the company cocktail, giving it a sharp flavour, a bright colour and the aromatic appeal of an exotic perfume. Doxat enjoyed the description, not least because he had made it up himself and discreetly disseminated it to his preferred columnists.

He frequently mocked ideas from colleagues and challenged orders from the chief executive. Famously, he once brought a full-size sex doll into an executive meeting, and introduced it as the second smartest person in the room. Everyone laughed nervously, except Tamara Morgan.

Her views on her creative director could be summed up in a single word: impossible. Doxat was a child delinquent in a man's clothing – insubordinate, rude and ungovernable. Now he had paid the price.

She had fired him. Good riddance.

CHAPTER THREE

The dappled brown colouring of the bittern was just visible among the muted green-gold of the reeds. The bird stood completely still, its giant beak pointing skywards. The bittern had sensed the presence of strangers on the banks of the reedy river that threaded its way through the Norfolk Broads on the east coast. This was bittern country, but only the most patient would be rewarded with sight of the bird. Once alarmed, it adopted the classic defence of stasis, standing motionless, allowing its colouring to melt into the surrounding reed beds.

Alison had been the first to see one of the rarest and most secretive of Britain's marshland birds. Through binoculars she had picked out the slight change in the pastel colours of the reeds. The camouflage of the bird was almost perfect, but a slight breeze caused the reeds to shiver, exposing the tell-tale change of colour – and there was the fully grown bittern, one of only a score of such birds to have returned after near extinction at the hands of wildfowlers.

"Got you," whispered Alison, as she tightened the focus of her binoculars.

"Where?" whispered Nick.

"Get the branch poking into the river from the right bank and then move right." Around her in the hide, the three other watchers focused their lenses. "Beautiful camouflage," whispered Nick. He reached for his long-lens camera and began taking pictures.

"Shh!" whispered Alison. The bittern had turned its head towards them. The faint click of the camera shutter had carried on the breeze to the bird some 150 feet away.

The large wings opened, the neck and head retracted, and the bittern rose slowly from the reed bed and headed upriver. The shape and movement of the bird in flight, with its bulbous chest, V-shaped breast, trailing feet and long pointed bill, all held together by powerful wings, lacked the grace of smaller waterfowl. But Alison saw in the wing beats of such a rare creature a majestic defiance. Shot to extinction a century earlier, the bittern was slowly returning to its natural habitat, its booming voice once again heard over miles of fenland.

Happy with the sighting and with their photographs, Nick, Alison, Xanthe and Douglas drove to a local pub for an early lunch. They had been in the hide since dawn with only chocolate biscuits and a thermos flask of tea to sustain them. They were tired and hungry, but happy.

Normally, there would be excited chatter over the sighting of such a rare bird. They would discuss which photographs to put up on their website. To see a mature bittern in flight against the background of river and reeds was an occasion to treasure and would create much admiring comment in the online birdwatching chat groups. They would talk of selling the photographs to one of the popular bird-watching magazines and maybe even try to get a mention on the BBC's wildlife programme.

But this time, the first since the Scottish trip, the atmosphere was muted. It was as if one of the group had revealed a serious illness and no one wished to bring up the subject.

"Your face looks much better," said Nick.

Alison touched her cheek and looked at her friends. This was her opening, a chance to lay to rest the mystery they had talked about behind her back. She knew they wanted her to say something about what had happened in Scotland. They wanted an explanation. She didn't have one.

"Yes, I feel fine now, thanks," said Alison. "Shall we order?"

They ordered beers and fish and chips and sat outside on a bench waiting for someone to broach the subject that had pushed the bittern to the back of their minds.

"Did you see the doctor?" asked Nick.

"I meant to talk to you about that. Did you call my HR department?"

Nick bit into a piece of heavily battered fish and ate it slowly. "I did it for you, Ali," he said at last.

"You really had no right to do that. I wish you had told me," she said.

"You seemed to be in denial," said Xanthe, softly. "There could have been internal damage."

"Be fair, Ali," said Douglas. "You don't just fall off a mountain like that and go to work the next day. It doesn't make sense."

Alison knew they had discussed these remarks in advance. She accepted that the group had reason to be worried and curious about what had happened in Scotland, but she resented their interest. It was an intrusion. They should mind their own business.

"It doesn't make sense to me either," she said. "I fell a long way down through all that scree and those bushes, and here I am. I was lucky, that's all. I cannot remember what happened to me and I can't explain it, but here I am."

"It's amazing – how did those bushes break your fall? I mean, there have been small rock falls from that mountain and they have gone straight to the valley floor," said Nick.

"And how did you get back to the hostel?" asked Xanthe.

"Questions, questions, questions!" said Alison, putting her hands to her head as if in pain. "Look, if someone told me the hand of God had reached out and plucked me from the mountain and put me back in the hostel, I would kneel down now and offer a prayer of thanks. But I don't think that's what happened."

There was a silence. They ate their food.

"What did the doctor say?" said Nick.

"There's nothing wrong with me. I had a full examination. Now look, guys, let's not beat our brains out about this. This morning we saw a mature bittern both in camouflage and flight. When did anyone last get that on film? There's your miracle. What are we going to do with the pics and video?"

The group returned to the bittern, unsatisfied that Alison's fall remained a mystery but thankful to be able to agree on the rare beauty they had seen that morning.

The birdwatching weekends took place every month and usually ended in excited chatter about what they had seen, and plans for future trips. This time was different. Alison felt relieved when she got into the car for the drive back to London. They had barely discussed what they saw that day. She cheek-kissed the men, hugged Xanthe and told them once again not to worry about her. She was fine.

She told them that she would upload the bittern pictures to their website that night. Nick would pitch an article with photos to a bird-watching magazine, and Douglas would contact the BBC's Wildlife programme. At any other time this would have called for a celebration supper of curry and cold beer sometime in the week ahead.

Nobody had suggested such a meeting, this time. Everyone was glad to go their own way. Alison resented the sudden distance that had grown between them. She smiled grimly in the car. She had started this group and had done more than teach them the art and craft of birdwatching; she had imbued them with a passion for a wild world they had never known before.

They didn't understand, of course, just how deeply she felt about that world. She found something beyond satisfaction, almost a sensual pleasure, in the solitude of birdwatching. Admittedly, it was a deeply selfish pastime. Waiting in a hide, hidden behind an upturned boat on a lonely stretch of shore or even, as had once happened, squatting in the attic of an old windmill, she had no need to consider, or talk to, anyone else. She talked to herself, of course, all the time, long whispered conversations and not just about the beauty, character and the habits of the birds that were framed fleetingly in the focus of her binoculars.

You're a sad, lonely, old spinster, she would say to herself. "All you have in this world is an adoring father, a boring job and these lovely friends in the skies. As for men, forget it. When I feel like it, I make my own pleasure – it's so much easier and less stressful."

She would like to pretend these conversations were a communion with someone deep inside her, an inner self. They weren't. They were just a way of dealing with loneliness. She would admit to a certain sadness at her isolation from those around her. It was not that she shunned company. It was just that when you are waiting at dawn for a skein of pink-footed geese to fly over a seawall into tidal marshland, and finally catch the moment when the birds, in almost perfect V formation, splash into the water raising curtains of silvery spray, the pleasure is all the greater for not being shared.

And that was the whole point. Alison did not really want to move with a crowd of fellow enthusiasts. Monthly weekends with Nick, Xanthe and Douglas reached the limit of her desire to spend time with other birdwatchers.

She had read in online discussion groups how members of bird-watching clubs described an experience close to spiritual satisfaction in their communion with birds. Some said they longed to be a part of the world inhabited by winged creatures that had been on Earth long before man rose to two legs on the African savannah.

Alison had not been brought up to be religious. Sunday church had never been a family ritual at weekends, but she vaguely understood how some people found solace in the belief that there was a guiding authority in their lives. If others found deep meaning and satisfaction, not just in the study of birds but in actually wishing to become such creatures, was that not also a kind of religious experience?

She found her solace in studying creatures whose largely benevolent behaviour contrasted so sharply with the horrors of human history. Sometimes simplistic, obvious truths are the most potent, and Alison would occasionally explain her interest in birds by pointing out they did not, on the whole, wage war on each other or plunder the resources of the planet to the point of exhaustion.

She once mentioned this to Jed, who retorted in his usual contrarian Welsh way that without mankind on the planet, birds would hardly have survived. They were two interdependent species, he said. The point was arguable, but debating with Jed was futile.

She knew some people in the office thought her birdwatching weekends a mark of eccentric, insecure and antisocial behaviour. While seated in the ladies' lavatory one morning, she had heard herself described along these lines with the added opinion that what "that Spedding girl" needed was to put a smile on her face and find a decent boyfriend who would give her "a jolly good seeing to".

She was not worried about such gossip. Despite her mother's unkind remark about her looks, she knew she was attractive enough. She had gone out with several boyfriends and enjoyed the nights they spent together, but no relationship had ever flowed from these encounters.

"I never feel you're with me," one young man had said to her. "You don't seem connected."

"Connected to what?"

"Well, I don't know, the world maybe."

She had sworn at him and left. The fact was that not many young men liked spending weekends hidden away for hours in a hide with nothing to do except peer through binoculars at a landscape that was usually empty of what they had come to see. Alison accepted that the presiding passion in her life had left her with hardly any friends.

Her solitary nature had been a lifelong characteristic, remarked upon by her teachers in regular school reports. She did well in her exams, and the term-end reports always spoke of her as a clever girl with an imagination that enabled her to "look round corners," as her history teacher put it.

Her shyness had first expressed itself in a stutter that left her tongue-tied in primary school. Puberty, and the move to the anonymity offered by a larger secondary school, eased the stutter. She wore her shyness like a cloak, concealing a young woman who felt more comfortable in a dream world populated by the characters and fantasies in the books she had been reading since childhood.

She had read *Alice in Wonderland* at the age of ten and perfectly understood why Alice had decided to take the risky step of following the White Rabbit down the rabbit hole. Alice had not been surprised by the sight of a white rabbit hurrying past her, saying he was terribly late. It was only when the rabbit pulled a watch from his pocket that Alice was stirred into action. After all, she told herself, rabbits did not usually carry watches.

Like her near namesake, Alison found magic in that moment. Her father had given her the *Alice in Wonderland* book, not as a special present for Christmas or a birthday, but out of the blue at teatime one day.

"You'll like this story," he said, "it's all about you." Alison was very proud of that. Her father had obviously seen in his daughter something of the wide-eyed wonder and adventurous spirit of Lewis Carroll's creation.

"There is only one way to go in this life. Your own way." Her father told her this more than once as she watched the adored man fade to a husk, his mind and memory seeping away.

If you asked Alison how such a clever, personable girl found herself spending most weekends birdwatching all over the country from the shores of the east coast in autumn to the mountains of Scotland in spring, she would probably tell you it all began with her father and a young blackbird with a broken wing.

She found the bird hopping around helplessly in the back garden of the family home in south London. It was just after Easter, and that morning the weather was cold with the threat of rain. She picked the bird up, took it inside and wrapped it in kitchen paper. The little creature flapped and struggled but Alison held it tight, feeling the very beat of its heart, or so she told herself. Unlike most girls her age – she was then thirteen – she had never had the usual run of pets: mice, hamsters and rabbits. She preferred her books and could trace the trajectory of her reading, or being read to, from Winnie the Pooh to Harry Potter.

Her father had carefully unwrapped the paper, examined the bird and said it had a broken wing.

"It must either have fallen to the ground on an early flight or been attacked in a tree by a grey squirrel. It won't live, darling, so best to put it out of its agony."

One look from his daughter changed his mind. He fetched a nose dropper from the bathroom, rinsed it out and watched as she fed the bird on warm milk. She decided her blackbird was male, named him

Arthur and built a nest using paper waste from her father's shredding machine and a small cereal bowl.

The nest was placed in the thorny tangle of a budding rose bush in the garden. Alison twisted the stems back and crosshatched them to create a platform. This was the only time her father had objected to the enterprise, pointing out the damage to his rose bush. He once again suggested that the bird be put out of its misery.

"This may make you very happy, doing all this," he said, "but I am not sure the bird likes it. Set him free, let him take his chance in the wild."

Assailed by her protests and being a kindly man, he relented and watched as his rose bush was transformed into a bird sanctuary. Arthur thrived. He did not have a broken wing at all. He grew quickly on a diet of milk and chopped-up worms, until the time came when Alison believed he was ready to fly.

She took him carefully from the nest, held him in her cupped hands, felt the shiver of his wings and the beating of his heart beneath the feathered breast and raised the fledging bird high above her head.

Arthur did not move. He was several months old by her estimation and well able to fly. With a pang of guilt, she tossed him into the air then watched the frail body fall, wings flapping feebly, to the ground. She returned him to the nest and twisted the thorny rose stems even more tightly around the bird. Orange-rimmed eyes standing out against a glossy blue-black coat stared at her bleakly.

The next morning Arthur was gone. There was not a clue as to how he had manged to flee the nest, not even a feather to suggest he had found some difficulty in wriggling through the thorny bars of his cage. Arthur had flown when he wanted to, not when commanded.

She saw him again, sitting on a branch in the park, looking at her before flying away. He looked strong now and well able to hold his own in the wild. Then he was on the garden fence, chirping a familiar song and, once again, this time at a bus stop, pecking crumbs from a sandwich. Every black bird she saw was Arthur. The broken speck of a fledgling had grown to spread its wings and fly into her head.

And that is how it had started.

CHAPTER FOUR

When it was announced that Kennedy Doxat was to leave the company, Alison pretended to be as surprised as everyone else. There was talk of nothing else in the staff canteen and in the surrounding bars where people gathered after work. The general view was that Doxat had been poached by a rival company. Lurid stories went around of how Tamara Morgan had offered large sums of money to retain his services and, when he refused, had flung herself weeping on the boardroom table, pleading with him to stay.

Staff enjoyed these fantasies because they rationalised what seemed to most people utterly incomprehensible. Everyone knew that Doxat was the genius who brought in the big clients. He had not been modest about his achievements either at regular presentations to the small circle of his peer group or the occasional companywide meetings of the staff.

Doxat's colleagues on the senior management team, and especially Tamara Morgan, added to their long list of complaints his egoistical behaviour, which showed none of the team spirit deemed so important to the company's morale and success. The fact that Doxat chose to share confidential information about budgeted profits, sales targets and competitor analysis with the general staff was a further irritant. But there was nothing they could do.

The rumours around the reasons for his departure increased when it was learnt that there was to be no formal farewell, no office leaving party, no final speeches from his fellow executives, no parting gifts from his many admirers, nothing but an empty office and a tearful personal assistant.

Kennedy Doxat left the building without a word of farewell. He was rumoured to have flown by private jet to an apartment he owned in San Sebastian in northern Spain. Others placed him aboard a chartered yacht in the Pacific, and still others swore he had been seen in a nightclub in New York.

Tamara Morgan issued an all-staff statement saying that Mr Doxat had left by mutual agreement. She wished him well in his career and thanked him for his contribution to the company. His successor would be appointed shortly. The unwritten postscript to this bland statement was that everyone should get back to work and forget their former creative director.

Alone in her office, the chief executive breathed a deep sigh of relief. She was pleased that the departure of such a senior and very difficult colleague had been handled so well. She told herself she had every right to get rid of such a disruptive influence in the company. Privately, and with less assurance, she admitted that there was another reason.

She had long and bitterly regretted what happened in San Francisco at the end of a corporate conference some years ago. She and Doxat had made well-received conference presentations. She was his boss and he her likely successor. Both were ambitious rivals, but they forgot their differences over celebratory champagne that night. What followed had been a mistake, a very bad mistake, a mistake fuelled by too much drink at the closing party, fatigue and the undoubted physical attractiveness of the man. At business school they had hammered home the lesson that mistakes were the key to success. Analyse and learn from your mistakes, they had been told over and again. She had learnt from her mistake. She had learnt to hate. It was a very satisfying emotion.

The sense of relief on the executive floor at the sacking of a much-disliked colleague was as evident as the dismay in the canteen. Alison was the only person who knew why Doxat had departed so suddenly. She enjoyed her secret all the more since she was about to meet and work with the man who had caused such an eruption in company routine. There was another reason: Jed seemed to be as much in the dark as anyone else.

She requested two days' annual leave and reported at 9.00 am to an elegant house in the leafy suburb of Dulwich, south London. Alison was surprised that Doxat lived in such an area. Dulwich regarded itself as an oasis of cultured gentility surrounded by a sprawl of urban decrepitude and described itself as a village. The main road, bordered by an old pub once frequented by Charles Dickens, a row of cottage shops and stately eighteenth-century mansions, supported this description.

Dulwich took itself and its history very seriously. Elderly residents would happily tell visitors of a golden age in the late sixteenth century when riches acquired through bear-baiting, brothels and theatres along the Thames allowed the entrepreneur Edward Alleyn to buy large tracts of land south of the river.

As if to make amends for the sordid origins of his riches, Alleyn, a great actor and close friend of William Shakespeare, or so Dulwich liked to believe, acquired 5,000 acres on a gentle hill overlooking the smoky city. There he placed his wealth in a trust, which in turn funded a school, almshouses and what would finally become the first independent art gallery in the country.

This richly textured backdrop to their daily lives gave residents of the village a sense of permanence and security as they looked down on the ever-changing scramble of the capital below them. *People move to Dulwich, very few move away*, was the local saying.

Doxat seemed the very last person who would choose this particular corner of London as his home. A man for whom style and image were the guiding lights of a life lived feverishly for the present seemed out of place amid such reverence for the past.

Alison's first impression confirmed this view. Doxat lived in a large detached house in whose front garden colourfully painted gnomes, very much in the Disney tradition, had been placed around a stone plinth topped, not as one might have thought with a snow queen, but rather a stone sculpture of a seated nude woman facing the house. On closer inspection Alison realised it was a copy of the Little Mermaid statue in Copenhagen. Doxat either had a weird sense of humour or very poor taste. Probably both.

Wondering what the neighbours made of these ornaments, Alison rang the bell. It was 9.00 am on a Monday morning, the first of her two days' leave. She had told Jed she was taking time off to look after her father. An insolent smile told her he knew this was a lie.

A young woman, duster and polish in hand, opened the door and showed Alison into a large front room that extended through to the kitchen at the back. The kitchen looked as if it had been installed straight from the manufacturer's showroom. Fitted appliances in black cladding rose from the tiled floor to a ceiling in which recessed lights shone brightly.

Doxat was sitting on a bar stool at the centre island, drinking coffee and talking on his mobile phone. Alison was struck by how strange he looked. Dressed in a T-shirt, shorts and canvas slip-on shoes, he looked very different from his flamboyant Foxglove persona. He glanced at her and went on talking. Alison looked through floor-to-ceiling plate-glass windows at the back to a long, well-kept garden. The call ended.

"Coffee?" Doxat said, gesturing to a stool. "Have a seat."

They talked for ten minutes, during which time Doxat's phone chirruped with incoming texts almost continuously. At the end, he gave her a credit card. The arrangement was simple. She was to buy all the equipment she needed to restore his communications. The study on the first floor was the media hub of the house, but she was to make sure that all landline and mobile phones, laptops and PlayStations were fitted with devices to detect and block bugging. The fee for the two days' work was to be £2,000 in cash.

"Is that OK?" he asked.

"Yes," she replied. The fee was a great deal more than she had expected.

"Right," he said, "the house is yours – go anywhere you like. Galina will show you anything you want."

"Galina?"

"The cleaner. Comes from Ukraine. Doesn't speak much English. Good kid. Hates the Russians."

With that, Doxat turned back to his phone. In the hours that followed Alison could hardly recall a moment, except for brief interruptions when she asked a question, when he did not have the device jammed to his ear.

Galina was nowhere to be seen. Alison looked around the living room for clues to the man who lived seemingly alone in such a large house. The floor was highly polished and made of very expensive wood. There were no bookcases, no books and none of the usual framed family photographs.

A sofa, coffee table and chairs were the only furniture apart from a large-screen TV that occupied most of one wall. The sole intimation of artistic taste lay in a series of abstract paintings that lined the remaining walls. Alison thought them prime examples of meaningless modern art.

She had drunk too much coffee that morning. She walked into the kitchen and waited patiently for a minute while Doxat remained hunched over his phone. She gave him a little hand wave. He looked up, faintly irritated.

"Where's the loo?" she asked. He pointed a finger at the floor and went on talking.

She went downstairs. The lavatory contained none of the family memorabilia usually found in such places. The rest of the basement had been turned into an exercise area with a range of machines that would have equipped a commercial gym.

Galina appeared and showed her to the upstairs study. The staircase was lined with framed sepia photos of a mother and young girl seated in various poses in a studio. The woman wore a long wasp-waisted dress with a tight bodice, while the little girl looked like everyone's idea of Alice in Wonderland. A Victorian family portrait, thought Alison. Maybe these were Doxat's distant relatives. The office joke was that Doxat had arrived on Earth fully formed from planet Ego. Maybe he did have a family and a past after all.

The study was in complete contrast to the room below. Bookcases lined the wall. Two white orchid plants in glass vases stood on a side table. An hourglass with red sand, two anglepoise lamps and three framed photographs stood on a cluttered desk.

The first of the photographs showed a middle-aged woman who looked remarkably like the Victorian lady on the stairs. The similarity was unmistakable. This was probably the little girl on the stairs, grown up. The second picture was of a girl aged about ten in school uniform, looking shyly at the camera. There was no doubting the parentage of the girl. She looked exactly like Doxat. The final photograph was of a handsome young man in military uniform. Again, the family resemblance was inescapable.

That morning, Alison shopped in town for new laptop and desktop computers and the two mobile phones he said he needed. All his old equipment had been company supplied and thus returned. By the end of the day Alison had connected the new equipment and installed the encrypted software to ensure confidentiality of communications.

Doxat had hardly said a word, beyond telling her to help herself to tea and coffee in the kitchen. She had brought sandwiches for lunch, and Doxat nodded his assent when she asked if she could eat them in the kitchen. He never moved from the room throughout the day and paid little attention to her, speaking quite openly on the phone in long conversations frequently punctuated with the phrase "that fucking bitch".

The main theme of the phone calls seemed to be that the fall in company profits for which Doxat had been blamed had nothing to do with him, and had been used as an excuse for his sacking. Doxat told various callers that he was going to sit back and enjoy watching mounting debt and mismanagement bring Foxglove down.

Alison listened discreetly to these calls while taking rather longer to eat her sandwiches and drink her coffee than was necessary. The relish with which Doxat repeated the accusations and insults throughout the day spoke of a childish desire for revenge without thought for his former colleagues. Alison felt uncomfortable. He spoke openly in front of her, as if they were conspirators with a shared secret.

She was listening to a mission of revenge by a man whose wounded pride hurt much more than the loss of the perquisites of executive power: the personal assistant, the chauffeured car, the nightly choice of invitations to cocktail parties, the opera, gallery openings.

It was just after 6.00 pm when Doxat finally turned his phone off. Alison was seated at the kitchen counter drinking yet another cup of tea. He looked at her with surprise, as if he had forgotten what she was doing there.

"I've finished," she said. "Can we talk?"

He listened as she took him through the new equipment and showed him how it all worked.

"God, I am going to miss having you around," he said. "Any chance I could call you if I need to, I mean when these things go wrong?"

"I don't think I could do that," she said. "Apart from anything else, we work shifts and I am not always there. You need to find a local IT expert. There must be plenty around here."

Doxat smiled. "I don't think Dulwich does digital," he said. "How about a glass of wine?"

She did not reply for a moment. She was tired and had eaten little for lunch. It was a long haul back to north London and she should get going.

"I think I'd better—"

"I'll Uber you back," he cut in. "There's some decent pâté in the fridge and a nice light rosé. You look as if you could do with a glass. Sit down, I'll fix it."

The offer was tempting. She sat down and watched as Doxat took the pâté and wine from the fridge. She wondered if anyone ever said no to this man. He poured the wine, handed her a glass and raised his to hers.

"Thanks, Alison," he said. "You've been a great help."

She sipped her wine and nibbled small biscuits loaded with pâté. Doxat had taken great care not to break the biscuits while spreading it. She watched him do this with some amusement. It seemed odd to spend time over such a trifle when he had spent the entire day planning a strategy of revenge. He had placed a plate of pâté in front of her then swung round and looked into the garden where lights had come on, illuminating various small trees and shrubs.

After a silent minute or so she said, "Those photos on the desk – is that your daughter?"

"Yes," he said, without turning around.

"And your father?"

He turned around.

"Yes, that's him. Well spotted. He was a captain in that photo. Became a colonel. In the tank regiment."

"Can I ask your daughter's name?"

"He was killed on the approach to Baghdad. Last week of the war. 1991. Bled to death before they could get him to a field hospital. Only fifty-four."

The finality of the statement ended the conversation. The silence was broken by the only words Alison could think of.

"I'm sorry," she said.

Doxat stared into the floodlit garden.

"Security," he said suddenly and swung back to her.

"Are you sure this kit is secure, you know, from hackers, trolls and listeners?"

"Nothing is foolproof these days, but you've got a pretty safe system here now."

"And where does the company think you have been today?" he asked.

"I took annual leave."

"And did you tell them why you were taking leave?"

"No."

"So, what are they saying about me in the office?"

The questions irritated her. This man assumed too much. She didn't wish to discuss anything to do with the office. Despite the money, she began to regret undertaking the task. The house, like its owner, was strange, empty. Something was missing, something hidden behind the empty art on the walls and the books in the study. The photos were the only clues that an emotional life lay behind the dyed hair, the thee-day stubble and the fashionable clothes. Doxat had not told her the name of his daughter. She wondered why.

"They're surprised."

Doxat laughed. "So was I. Anyway, enough of that. I won't need you again. I have decided to go to Spain. I've got a place there. I'm going to write a book."

He left the room and returned with a brown envelope.

"Two thousand," he said. "Thank you again."

"But I have only been here one day."

"Take it," he said. It was a large amount, and she left feeling gratified at the reward for such simple work but puzzled at how such a man could turn his back on a world he had dominated for so long.

The legend Doxat had created for himself was that of a man who could move markets with a single slogan or an inspired image. Unlike most corporate legends, Doxat's achievements were real – the evidence was there for all to see in the company's balance sheet. He could get a job anywhere in London or New York. Yet he was going to an apartment somewhere in northern Spain. Alison had dimly heard of San Sebastian as a mecca for gourmets rivalled only by Barcelona. He would soon be bored.

CHAPTER FIVE

As the drama of Doxat's disappearance receded, the social life of the office resumed with the usual carousel of birthdays, baby days wherein the new-born are brought in to be admired, and gossip about who was ill, who was having an affair with whom, and collective sorrow about those suffering from serious illnesses, mostly cancer.

These were the distractions from the tedium of the workplace routine. Only a few were privileged to work at the creative end of the company, forging the campaigns that would place jars of Marmite on tables in China and persuade the gullible to buy a new model of the perfectly good car they had sitting in their garage.

Alison's work had not changed. She moved as before through the executives' offices, improving defences against data theft, fixing the intricate backup systems and reassuring senior execs that they were not as technophobic as their inability to master simple actions might suggest.

Her work occasionally involved confidential company data, and she had been required to sign a document pledging not to reveal such information. With that status, the HR department occasionally called on her to look at inappropriate emails sent by staff and check up on those who spent too much time using their office computers to log on to social media.

She was proud of her expertise. Technology promised a new and ever-changing future. The impossible one week became possible the next – in the speed of change lay the allure of the anarchic science of the internet, which conferred power on those who understood even a fraction of its workings. Alison felt that power. When she entered the offices of senior executives it was as if she held a light sabre in her hand.

The boyfriend who told her she was not connected to the real world was probably right. She *was* connected to a world in which belief is continually suspended and the new becomes the old within days. She enjoyed her very small role in the revolution of digital technology. It challenged one of the beliefs with which she had grown up, that she had been taught at school and which she had accepted as an absolute truth.

Science can explain the history of the world and predict its future. There is a rational explanation for everything around us because we live in an age of reason. These were the conventional ideas knitted into a web of belief with which she had been equipped for life by her teachers and friends.

It wasn't true. Alison knew that science may explain where we have been but not where we are going. Her father doubted even the first statement. She could hear him say that *might* was the most dishonest word in the vocabulary of science. How many learned papers had been written by distinguished historians saying that ancient man *might* have built Stonehenge to worship the sun? It was a pointless statement, he said. The mysterious circles of granite blocks on Salisbury Plain was one of her father's favourite subjects. He used Stonehenge as an example of how many mysteries of the ancient world lie beyond the reach of science.

Alison had taken a different path to the same conclusion. She had spent countless hours on the Wash on the east coast or in the far north of Scotland, and even in Norway, noting the flights of small birds on their annual migrations. Satellites track these huge flocks southbound from the western hemisphere in the autumn, but still cannot explain fully how they navigate and endure their journey.

When asked, as she frequently was, to name her favourite bird, she would dodge the question and say that she favoured certain birds when found in their natural setting. Thus, in London her favourite was the sparrow, in Scotland the white-tailed eagle and in America, which she had visited twice on birdwatching trips, it was the bar-tailed godwit.

At this point her listener would look blankly at her: a bar-tailed godwit? Most had never heard of the bird. She would explain that the small wader – weighing only eight to ten ounces – was a migratory champion. The godwit carries with it on its annual seven-day flight south from Alaska to South America the greatest mystery of the avian world.

The bird is known to fly nonstop, without pausing for sustenance and aided only by light tailwinds, for 9,000 miles. Scientist and nutritionists hold that no bird can make such a nonstop flight and survive. Yet tiny tracking devices reveal that the godwit does not break its journey to feed or rest.

The flight north is even more unlikely, taking nine days because of headwinds. Every year the godwit makes the flight south in the autumn and returns to its breeding grounds in the spring. No one has ever worked out how the bird does it.

Perhaps it was that sense of mystery, of a world unknown, that first imbued a shy schoolgirl with a fascination for birds. Perhaps it was Arthur's escape from his cage of thorns. Alison did not know. But she did know that contemplation of the unknown and delight in the unsolved mysteries of the avian and human worlds was drawing her back to the foil-wrapped SIM card in her deep freeze.

Every time she opened the fridge the guilty thought occurred to her that she had cheated herself. She had denied what was so palpably evident in the video clip. *You are thirty-two years old*, she told herself. *You delight in the mysteries of the avian world. You explain to befuddled middle-aged men and women that the technology of the internet is not like a piece of new furniture – it is a living organism that will eat us all alive unless we understand the mysteries that it throws in our faces.*

And yet you, my difficult, delightful self, are a hypocrite. You preach the need to grasp a world beyond science and reason as if it were a divine gospel, yet you do nothing about your own secret, either a truth or a fantasy born of a bad dream, who knows, that lies among the frozen food in your refrigerator."

*

It is said that Parliament Hill, on Hampstead Heath in north London, is so-called because Guy Fawkes and his fellow conspirators intended to gather there on the night of 5 November 1605, in the hope of watching and celebrating the explosion that would destroy the Houses of Parliament and kill King James I.

That enjoyable myth has been handed down over the centuries and entertains the tourists who climb 300 feet to the top of the hill. They are rewarded with a view that sweeps from the high-rise offices of Canary Wharf in the east to the panorama of central London, where the sturdy tower of Big Ben and its four-faced clock commands centre stage.

In the shadow of Big Ben, the Houses of Parliament pay graceful tribute to the Victorian taste for gothic architecture. Unscrupulous tour guides happily describe these as exactly the same buildings that Guy Fawkes intended to blow up on that fateful autumn day.

The Hampstead hill slopes gently away to the south and more steeply to the east, where it falls into a wooded vale where fishing ponds can be seen through a screen of trees. Large three- and four-storey mansions line the flanks of a hill beyond which climbs to the glory of a high-spired church at one end and the dome of an observatory at the other.

The heath is open day and night, and a summer dawn always brings the sight of weary revellers, disappointed or otherwise by the night's activities, plodding or staggering homeward down the hill. Alison arrived just before first light, as the sky over London turned to a misty grey and the tall buildings along the Thames began to take shape. Soon the dog walkers, the joggers and other early risers would climb the hill, admire the sunrise and continue across the heath.

She drank hot coffee from a flask. She was dressed in running shorts and a blouson, her hair was tied back in a ponytail. She looked around and saw nobody. She had been here the day before at this time and worked out that there was a brief moment of solitude to be found on Parliament Hill at exactly this time. There would be no witnesses.

She turned east towards the steep slope, finished the coffee and threw the flask in a bin. She needed a new one anyway. She took several deep breaths and looked around. At the bottom of the hill to the south an old man was making his way slowly along a zigzag path towards her. He had his head down and was using a stick to help him on the climb. A black Labrador panted behind him.

Alison raised her arms, looked at the rim of the rising sun in the distance and ran forward,s flinging herself into the air. The ground dropped sharply away below her. She held her arms out and pushed her head and neck forward. She felt a rush of wind on her face and closed her eyes, waiting for the uplift. *It's happening*, she thought, feeling the lift of flight and the surging excitement of knowing that she had left the ground and was flying. The thought flashed through her mind that even a short flight would take her straight into the trees. She dared not look at the ground below or at her outstretched arms.

In dreamy disbelief at what was happening to her, she looked only at the golden orb of the sun taking shape in the distance. So it *was* true. This is how she had survived the mountain fall in Scotland. She hadn't fallen, she had flown. This is why the others had looked at her so strangely that morning. In their startled eyes she had seen their incredulity at her survival. They gazed at her as if she was an alien from another world. They had been right, hadn't they? She had again proved what she had shown in Scotland, that she had the power of flight. The dazzling thought struck her that the air, the clouds and the sky were now her sanctuary, a safe haven from the anarchic terrors of life on earth. Birds had found freedom in flight millions of years ago, and she too could now exult in the liberation gifted by her wings.

The fall was swift and sudden. She crashed heavily to the ground, curling up to soften the impact and clawing at the grass as she rolled down the hill for a few yards.

She lay there for a few seconds in a foetal position, her knees to her chest, gasping for breath. She got to her feet slowly, breathing deeply, and brushed herself down. She felt bruised, but much worse she felt ridiculous, embarrassed and ashamed.

Why on earth had she believed she could do this? She hardly dared admit to herself what "this" meant. She had somehow succumbed to the crazy belief that she could lift herself from the hill and float free like a bird over the trees. For a second or less perhaps, just milliseconds of time, she had believed that. She had desperately wanted to believe it because… well, because what? Because there was no other explanation for her survival in Scotland. Because within her subconscious mind, a dream had somehow assumed the shape and colour of the real world.

She looked around. The dog walker had reached the crest of the hill and was looking down at her. He must have witnessed her moment of madness. And it was madness, a painful and rather obvious discovery that she was not a bird and could not fly.

She could imagine the old man in his local pub, telling his friends that he had seen a grown woman flinging herself into the air down a steep grassy slope.

"Are you all right?" The reedy voice of the dog walker floated down to her.

"Fine, thanks."

"New kind of yoga is it?"

Alison would have laughed if she had not been feeling so stupid.

"No, I must have tripped."

"You want to be careful with that yoga stuff, much steeper than it looks on that side."

"Thank you."

She turned to leave the scene of her humiliation. That's exactly what it felt like, the chastening indignity of confronting one's own stupidity. Then she stopped, turned and walked back to the point where she had flung herself into the air. She looked down the hill. The marks where she had fallen and clawed the ground showed on the turf. She paced forwards slowly and deliberately counting the steps out loud. She reached the point of her fall and looked back. Fifteen paces were about thirty feet, measured by a woman's stride. There was no way she could have hurled herself that far. Gravity would have pulled her to the ground long before the point at which she fell. She walked back to the top and paced the distance again. Fifteen paces, thirty feet. It didn't make sense. Unless, of course…

She took the bus back to her flat, looking at the sane, ordinary, rational people around her. Almost without exception they were fixated by mobile phones, many with cheap headphones that leaked tinny music to the very few people around who chose to read a newspaper or, rarer still, a book.

Perhaps they were not sane after all, but captives of a digital world that would empty their minds and leave them just as mad as she was. And she *had* become mad, had she not? How else to explain what had happened on the hill?

When she got home, she found her flat as neat and clean as usual with everything exactly as she had left it. The only sign of disorder was an unmade bed, a welcome reminder of the real world. It was too early to go to work. She undressed and lay on the bed, pulling the blankets over her, hoping for sleep from which she could awake and look back on the whole episode as a bad dream, a nightmare.

Her mind flitted like a butterfly between memories of the old man on the hill thinking she was practising some strange new eastern ritual, to Jed laughing at her in the office when he found out – and somehow he would find out, he always did – to Doxat sitting alone in his huge house, plotting revenge.

She showered and saw the beginnings of bruises on her arms and thighs. Strong black coffee and a usually forbidden breakfast of fried eggs (organic), mushrooms (organic), toast (gluten free) and marmalade (low sugar) provided a portal to sanity.

Her food shopping was conditioned by ingrained strictures of healthy eating. She had no idea what made an egg organic. She would ask the Indian man who ran the organic grocery shop. He would have the answer. But there was no answer to why she had left the warmth of a bed in the familiar surrounds of her flat and flung herself off a hill.

She opened the fridge door, took the SIM card out of the deep freeze, cut it into quarters and threw them into the bin.

CHAPTER SIX

If there had been any other entrance to the office, Alison would have taken it. As it was, she was forced to arrive and leave beneath the arched cage of captive birds. Tamara Morgan had initially demanded that the birds be drawn from all over the world to underline the global nature of the company, but this proved impractical. She was told that tropical birds would not survive being caged in the foyer of a large London office.

It was widely supposed that she had refused to accept the advice and insisted on having colourful and exotic hummingbirds, macaws and the like fluttering overhead in the foyer. Like many things said about Tamara Morgan, this wasn't true. Envy breeds malice. Her striking looks, elegant clothes and the power she wielded within the office invited malign rumours. They clung to her like ivy, spawning countless vicious stories about her private life, affairs, drug taking and so forth, all of which were untrue. There were a few people at Foxglove who suspected that behind the onion-like layers of carefully crafted imagery lay a decent woman who was deeply insecure about her commanding role in the company. Nobody listened to them.

In fact, a number of tropical birds were initially introduced into the aviary but quickly withdrawn and returned to pet shops. The idea of greeting visitors with a showcase birdcage was not even her own. Kennedy Doxat had come up with the idea. Tamara Morgan thought it a ridiculous waste of money when the plan was costed, but as usual Doxat got his way.

The favourable press coverage when the aviary was formally opened before an invited audience of journalists persuaded Tamara that the idea had been hers. In the cavernous entrance to a great advertising agency, wild birds could be seen flying in relative freedom, safe from the perils of life outside. The imagination behind such a living work of art surely sent a message to clients and rivals alike.

New York had congratulated her. The office aviary was seen as a triumph of corporate branding, sending a powerful message of flight to a better future to all those who entered the doors of a great company. That at least was the plan. After the initial excitement, the Royal Society for the Protection of Birds had complained about the treatment of wild birds and threatened legal action. Visitors were seen entering the building with lowered heads. The caged birds began to die off. Social media began to hum with snippy comments.

Tamara consulted New York, revealing the whole idea had originated with Kennedy Doxat. New York wasn't interested. All that mattered were the numbers, and the numbers were good. Profits were rising. Morgan was told to fix the birdcage problem any way she chose.

In what she regarded as a press relations masterstroke, Tamara Morgan assembled the staff outside the office one spring morning and, before an invited group of journalists, watched as the wild birds were released into special cages to be taken to London Zoo. The aviary remained, however, populated now by birds long accustomed to domestic use, such as budgerigars and canaries. They were just as colourful and much smaller than those that had departed, but Alison looked at their beaky bodies and colourful plumage with distaste.

"Feeling a bit sorry for them, are you?"

Jed had sidled up to her in the foyer.

"Would you like to be stuck in a cage like that?" she said.

"Why not? " he said. "It's a life of luxury: free food, someone cleans house for you, and sex whenever you want it."

Alison looked at him. Jed was smarter than usual. The plain white T-shirt was clean, his jeans had been washed recently and the baby face had lost its fuzzy moustache.

"Come and have a drink," he said.

Alison looked at her watch. It was past seven, and the main rush home had tailed off.

"No thanks."

"Go on. I've got something important to tell you."

"Like what?"

"Like come to that nice wine bar around the corner and I'll tell you."

Only Jed would have described the Dark Side bar as nice. The outer door led to black curtains that parted to reveal a long, narrow room barely lit by four candle-shaped lights behind the bar. Seamus the barman did nothing to alleviate the gloom. He was not Irish, as the name suggested, but spoke with a West Country accent that thickened to the point of being incomprehensible after a few drinks. He was not allowed to drink on duty but ignored the rule.

Alison sipped chilled rosé from a tall glass. She had developed a taste for the wine ever since Doxat gave her a glass. She wondered vaguely how he was getting on with his book. Jed drank lager from a bottle. For the first time in the years they had worked together, she looked at him properly. There was something different about him. She had not seen him out of the office before.

In fact, she had never really seen him *in* the office. Jed was a cartoon character at the edge of her vision, an ill-dressed colleague with revolting personal habits, not least picking his nose or sneezing into his hands and wiping the snot on his jeans.

She spoke to him as little as possible, and he seemed to feel the same way about her. If they had anything in common, it was their fascination with the outsize ego of Kennedy Doxat – but then that was true of everyone on the staff.

"Want a refill?" he asked. He was looking right at her. She noticed his eyes, the unblinking eyes of a cat.

"Maybe," she said. "First, what's the secret?"

"You're going to have to be really nice to me if I tell you this."

"Depends what it is."

Jed took a pull from his beer bottle and waved to a waitress, holding up two fingers to indicate another round.

"Our saintly chief executive has pulled your file up from HR. It's on her desk."

"How do you know?"

"Do you mind if I tell you that's a silly question?"

He is right, thought Alison. Jed had the rat-like ability to slide into secret places in the company's digital archives and read encrypted files. Compromising emails, text messages long assumed deleted were all there, revealing love affairs, financial skulduggery, personal triumphs and tragedies; all the private particulars of a great company's staff laid bare.

"When was this?"

"Couple of days ago. I thought you might like to know."

Alison thought quickly. There was no obvious reason why the chief executive should take an interest in her. There was another round of redundancies coming, but that was such a regular feature of corporate life that few but the closest friends bothered to go to the farewell parties on Friday nights.

She was not going to be sacked, neither was she going to be promoted. In any case, a chief executive would not get involved in such mundane matters. Why then had Tamara Morgan called for her file? There was nothing on that file anyway, just a few dates of employment, salary details and the personal information demanded of a low-grade, anonymous employee. Alison felt her cloak of anonymity had slipped open.

"She won't learn much there."

"Maybe not, but she's asked HR to arrange a meeting with you."

"You're joking!"

Alison looked straight at Jed, eye to eye, seeking the sudden smile that would tell her this was a joke.

"Scouts' honour. You're going to get the call tomorrow morning."

"Bollocks! This isn't funny, Jed!"

He was smiling now, showing a row of buckled teeth. The smile illuminated a pale, high-cheekboned face with that squint nose and soft amber eyes.

"I'm just helping out a colleague."

"Like hell. When did you get so interested in my welfare?"

"I didn't. I was checking out some HR files and I came across the info."

"Confidential information that is supposed to be encrypted?"

"That's right. It made me curious. Why is all-mighty Ms Morgan so interested in little Alison from IT?"

"Little Alison from IT needs another drink. What are you having?"

They drank for an hour and talked in a meandering conversation loosened by alcohol. Alison wanted to forget about Tamara Morgan and the supposed meeting. Jed had got it wrong. He was such an unlikely character that it was hard to believe anything he said. He told her he was an orphan given up for adoption by an unknown mother in Swansea. He was proud of his Welsh heritage, he said, and mocked the pretensions of other Celtic nations.

"The Irish would pick a fight with a paper bag and the Scots have fallen in love with their own mythology; they think bagpipes, kilts, sporrans, haggis and a splash of North Sea oil can make them a real nation."

Alison laughed. Wickedly untrue but not a bad joke. He told her he had spent six years in a council care home and watched other children leaving to live with foster parents. His turn never came. He was lucky. The stories he heard from fostered children were frightening. The local council looked after him well, schooled him until he was able to get a job and live on his own.

"So you've always been on your own? That sounds kind of sad," she said.

"I have never been lonely. I'm not the type. Come on, let's eat."

They walked across Oxford Street into Soho and ate at a small Vietnamese restaurant. Alison talked a little of her own life. She told him of her stammer at school, and the frustrations of being trapped in a classroom all morning being taught things she knew already. Jed, by now quite drunk, asked where "the bird thing" came from.

This surprised Alison. Normally on such occasions, men would probe in ham-fisted fashion about boyfriends, lovers, girlfriends, anything to indicate that they might be lucky enough to have found a single woman who would sleep with them. Jed just seemed interested in her birdwatching. Tough. That was a private world shared only with fellow enthusiasts.

Jed persisted, finding various ways to repeat the question in spite of Alison's polite rebuffs. She was suddenly tired. She didn't want to talk about birds. The CEO of Foxglove wanted to see her in the morning, apparently. She wanted to go home.

"Come back to my place," said Jed. "I've got some great jazz, early Dizzy Gillespie." It was raining, a light spatter of drops heralding a heavier shower to come. They were standing under the awning of the restaurant. Alison saw people along the street checking their mobile phones, waiting for an Uber. Jed slid his arm around her waist and tried to kiss her. She stepped away.

"I don't like jazz," she said.

"How about early Elvis?"

He turned his hand into a mike and began singing an early Presley song.

People walked past without a glance. The rain began to fall more heavily. "Thank you, Jed. It's been a good evening." She offered him a cheek and said goodnight.

Jed did not appear in the office the next morning, which was not unusual. Alison reviewed the events of the previous evening and decided to ignore everything he had said. She didn't think he had been lying. He may have been telling the truth. It was hard to tell. It was hard to know what to think about Jed. He was different from anyone she had ever met.

He called himself a techno-anarchist, but beneath the crafted image of an uncaring outsider lay the scar tissue of a wretched childhood. It had all come out after a few drinks. The baby face had crumpled and the cat's eyes clouded when he talked of his young years.

"Alison! You haven't logged on yet! What's the matter with you, girl?"

The head of department was looking down at her.

"Sorry, I was distracted," she said.

"Well, un-distract yourself. The boss wants to see you."

"The boss?"

"Her very self. In her office in an hour."

"Why?"

"How do I know? Smarten up and put some lippy on."

She looked at Jed's desk. So he had been right. She wished he was there. She went to the ladies, combed her hair, put on some lipstick and tried to unscramble the thoughts in her head. Tamara Morgan would hardly call her up to the executive sixth floor to fire or promote her. She was too insignificant and, anyway, that was the job of the bastard head of department or the HR people.

Maybe she wanted some technical help. She was reputed to have at least three mobile phones, one reserved exclusively for dealings with New York. Or perhaps she wanted to come birdwatching? Alison gave a little laugh, then put her hand to her mouth as two other women looked at her. Jed would enjoy the joke. Somewhere at the back of her mind an absurd thought formed. She pushed it away.

Tamara Morgan had two personal assistants, both of whom sat in a glass-walled office through which visitors had to pass to reach a much larger office, again with glass walls, although here they were lined with venetian blinds. Everything was glass, but the view was disappointing. The sixth floor was not high enough to command an inspiring panorama of London and provided only a vista of grey-slated rooftops rising and falling in waves parted by an occasional church spire.

Alison was told to take a seat in the outer office and offered a drink of water. She accepted, grateful for the small kindness. She looked around. She was curious rather than nervous. She had worked at the company for three years and only ever seen Tamara Morgan on the occasions when she swept through the lobby en route to her chauffeured car.

The staff newspaper frequently carried photographs of TM, as she was known, lunching in the office canteen, but Alison had never seen her there. The more she thought about her summons to the top floor, the stranger it seemed. Her curiosity gave way to the ominous feeling that this was not going to be a pleasant meeting. She breathed in through her nose and out through her mouth several times to relieve the growing tension.

The trick on such occasions was to think of three things that make one really happy. Allow imagination to banish reality and turn those three subjects over in your mind; squeeze the juice out of them as if you were squeezing a lemon. She had come across that advice in a medical column in a newspaper. She thought of the next birdwatching trip to the tidal flats along the Thames estuary on the Kent coast. It was to be in the middle of September. In the crisp early autumn weather, local and migratory birds would be plentiful on the shingle foreshore and the tidal mudflats of the coastline.

She counted them off in her head, her mind turning into an aviary of winged creatures. Sand martins would be on a stopover to North Africa along with wheatears and yellow wagtails, all small birds feeding to gain strength for the long flight south and all planning the shortest Channel crossing to France. Away from the seashore, in rough grassland split by deep drainage sewers there would be tree sparrows, distant and much shyer cousins of their city brethren, plump little corn buntings and maybe even turtle doves with pink mottled plumage and green under-feathers.

"You can go in now." The voice brought Alison back from the estuary marshes. She stood up.

"Thank you," she said and walked through into the office of the chief executive.

Morgan was tapping away on a computer at an expensive executive desk with leather inlay. A round white-faced digital clock on the desk gave a small click as Alison entered. Four chairs were placed around a glass table piled high with books and papers. The only other furniture was an easel, holding a sheet of art paper on which various graphs had been drawn in red crayon. The room felt unoccupied, as if it was a hotel conference suite. The clock clicked again, recording another passing minute.

Tamara Morgan smiled a welcome and got up.

"Thank you for coming, do take a seat. Coffee or tea?"

"Neither, thank you." Alison sat down.

Tamara Morgan dispensed with the usual pleasantries about the weather, the problems of commuting due to the latest rail strike and such like. Alison was relieved. She wanted to hear why she was there.

"I have excellent reports of your work, Alison," said Morgan.

"Thank you, Miss Morgan," said Alison

"Please, call me Tamara. "

"Of course. It's a nice name," said Alison and wished she had kept her mouth shut. What was nice about the name Tamara? It sounded like a card game, a version of canasta perhaps. Either way, it was pretentious.

"Nice?" said Morgan, looking at her half-smiling.

"Well, it's unusual."

"I suppose it is. I have never really thought about it. My mother chose it because it was the name of a great friend who died in a car accident."

Before Alison could think of a suitably anodyne reply, Morgan picked up a file from her desk and said briskly, "You have been a good servant of this company."

The description jarred. It implied a relationship that Alison did not recognise. She wasn't anyone's servant. Why couldn't this woman just get to the point?

"I have asked you here because I have a highly confidential task for you, and I wish our conversation to remain between us alone. Do you understand?"

Alison did not understand but nodded.

"Yes," she said.

"As you know, Kennedy Doxat left the company two months ago."

"Yes, I do know that," said Alison, surprised and slightly alarmed.

"The point is that we have asked him to come back and resume his position as creative director."

"Really?" said Alison, even more surprised and wondering what this had to do with her.

"Yes. We have made him a very generous offer, which he has agreed to consider."

There was a pause as Tamara Morgan looked down at papers on her desk. She shuffled a few around, seemingly finding it difficult to continue. The digital clock moved forward two minutes before she spoke again.

"As you know he is living in Spain."

"I had heard that."

"The offer is contained in these legal documents, which he will need to consider and sign. As I said, it is a very generous offer and we are confident that he will be back with us shortly."

Alison realised that there had been a terrible mistake. Tamara Morgan had got the wrong person. Maybe there was someone called Spedding in the legal department or at the very least in corporate affairs. None of this concerned her.

"Miss Morgan, I think you may be talking to the wrong person. I work in IT."

"Tamara, please."

"Sorry. Tamara."

"I know where you work, Alison. I am telling you this for a very good reason."

Alison remained silent. There was nothing to say until this woman realised her mistake.

"I want you to go to Spain and take these documents to Mr Doxat.

I want you to hand them to him personally and bring them back once he has signed them."

"I don't understand," said Alison, now totally confused. "Why me? Surely a courier would be more—"

Morgan cut her off.

"It may surprise you to learn that Mr Doxat has asked for you personally and will accept no one else as the intermediary."

"What! Why?"

"That is what I want to ask you."

"I have no idea. I hardly know Kennedy Doxat."

"Forgive me for asking this," said Morgan in the smooth, confidential tone that a doctor might use when questioning a patient. "Have you had any kind of relationship with Doxat?"

Alison felt a blush of anger colouring her cheeks.

"Absolutely not."

"But you went shopping for him. You bought all the equipment to set up his home internet systems. You put in all the cyber-security. You spent the whole day with him at his house. That implies some kind of relationship, doesn't it? "

That was supposed to be a secret. The rat-like Jed must have found out somehow. She would give him a swift kick in the crotch when she next saw him.

"That was a private, professional arrangement."

"Doxat has had one or two casual relationships with young women on our staff. I am sure you are aware of that."

"I am aware of no such thing, Miss Morgan."

It was a lie, of course. It was well known that Doxat, apparently a divorcé although no one was quite sure, had dated several women on the staff. Jed knew all the details.

72

"And if you are implying that I have had any such relationship with Doxat, all I can say is that it is untrue, and I resent the suggestion."

"Calm down, Alison. I am merely trying to understand why Doxat demanded that you, and you alone, travel with these documents."

"I have absolutely no idea, and may I say that what you have just told me is a complete surprise."

"That makes two of us, Alison. He says he will trust no one else to undertake this mission – and you have no idea why?"

"No," said Alison, feeling rather as her near namesake did when she fell down the rabbit hole and found herself in Wonderland.

Tamara Morgan stood up and smiled.

"I know this is all a bit of a shock and you resent my questions. Fair enough. Let us have tea."

She walked to her desk, pressed a switch on the intercom and said, "Tea for two please, milk and sugar for me." She turned to Alison. "How do you take yours?"

"Straight black, no sugar," said Alison.

Tamara Morgan smiled.

"Then you shall have yours straight black, no sugar, Alison. Now, where were we?"

They talked for another ten minutes, during which time the tea was brought in by an assistant who whispered audibly that the next appointment was waiting. Morgan's mobile phone buzzed three times with text messages, and rain began to drizzle down the windows.

The interruptions were ignored. The rooftops of London vanished into a grey mist. Emboldened by the surreal conversation and her apparent importance in the company's affairs, Alison asked why Doxat did not simply return from Spain, consider the offer and sign the documents if he wished.

"Because he likes playing games," said Morgan.

She told Alison that Doxat had demanded both legal and verbal assurances to guarantee his return. The verbal assurances could not be expressed in writing, for legal reasons. Alison Spedding was to convey the assurances to Doxat and do so word for word. She was then to forget what had been said.

Alison felt more than ever that the White Rabbit was going to walk through the door any minute.

"And what are these assurances?" she asked, hoping that this would bring the meeting to an end.

Morgan rose from her desk.

"Just tell him what I am about to tell you."

Alison waited while Tamara Morgan bent over her desk, as if seeking inspiration from the shiny leather inlay. She straightened up.

"Just say that I promise that this company will honour all the legal undertakings we have offered in these documents which I have signed."

Alison waited, wondering whether there was any point in a statement that could have no meaning in law.

"Is that all?" she asked.

"Tell him I look forward to working with him again. I welcome his return. Have you got that?"

Alison said she would repeat the words faithfully to Doxat. She was relieved to find herself being ushered to the door.

"Remember to tell him what I said," said Morgan. "Your plane tickets and a briefcase with the documents will be on your desk in an hour. I suggest you go first thing in the morning."

As they shook hands at the door, Tamara Morgan said briskly, "We must do everything we can to get our talented colleague back with the team here. I know you will be very helpful in that respect."

Alison knew nothing of the sort.

Tamara Morgan watched her leave and sat down at her desk, wondering whether she might risk a quick cigarette on the smoking deck on a lower floor. It was not a good image for the staff, but then this had been the most difficult day in the office she could remember – and there had been quite a few.

She laughed to herself at that thought. She had been through some tough times, and life wasn't going to get any easier when Doxat was back. She had had no choice but to offer him the deal. New York had insisted. He would look at her in meetings with that knowing smile that took her straight back to that night in California.

When she thought about that night at all, and she tried not to, she wondered why on earth she had given such a hostage to fortune. After too much champagne, Doxat had suggested a nightcap. She had agreed, and somehow they found themselves in her suite drinking tall glasses of iced lemon-flavoured vodka.

What followed was her seduction as much as his. They both wanted each other. It was as simple as that. She dimmed the lights, he poured the drinks, they raised glasses to each other to toast a successful conference, and then by mutual but unspoken consent they collapsed onto a long leather sofa. There was no small talk.

Buttons were unbuttoned, zips unzipped, clothes shed onto a thick shag-pile carpet. The accidental lovers never made it to the bedroom. She did not like to recall what had passed for lovemaking that night, and consoled herself with the thought that Doxat had somehow spiked her drink.

Worse still, and much more embarrassing, she had tried to turn the drunken fling into an affair. She had sent him a text the following day inviting him to join her for dinner in her suite that night. He replied with a smiling emoji.

A carefully chosen meal was prepared and arrived on a trolley at the agreed time. She wore a black satin dress with long-drop pearl earrings and embroidered slippers. The lacy underwear matched her dress.

While turning in front of the dress mirror, Tamara Morgan had briefly wondered whether it was sensible for a woman in her position to have... what? A dalliance, an affair, a tryst, whatever, with a senior colleague. She did not know her creative director well, although she did know that, like her, he was divorced.

She suspected there were other similarities. Doxat was an alchemist. He had turned the base metal of a lowly career as an ad salesman into gold, and gilded himself with the sheen of success. Tell people what they want to hear and they will believe you. Doxat well knew that old trick. That is why his halo shone so brightly in the company and beyond. Tamara was sure it was a deceit, but she could hardy criticise. She too had carefully created her own myth: nothing had been given to her in her career, no one had helped her, every promotion had been fought for. She had used charm, cunning and good looks to take everything she had achieved. Others on their career ascent used sharp elbows to shoulder aside rivals. Tamara Morgan used her claws. That was what people believed – and what she had almost come to believe herself.

The skilfully created image of a strong woman from a hardscrabble background had won admiration and helped her rise. She looked in the mirror and saw a warrior woman who had shed her past as a snake sheds its skin. Here she was, one of the youngest chief executives in London and certainly one of the few women in that role. Her conference presentation had won praise, her hotel suite overlooked the Pacific Ocean and the vintage champagne would soon be the right temperature. She was well set to entertain the man who would become her lover.

She turned again and admired the black dress. It fell to just below the knee and was a tight, but not immodest, fit. If she was making a mistake then so be it. She was in control. Doxat was highly ambitious but then, so was she. He was attractive and available. And she was lonely. That was the truth. That was what business did to those at the top. To be equally honest, she was in need of good, hard-driving sex. The do-it-yourself-variety had its merits and fairly obvious limitations. She needed a man. Doxat would keep their secret. She was sure of that.

The waiter whipped the cover off the trolley and opened the champagne. The pop and fizz as it was poured into a flute was the overture to the evening. The Veuve Cliquot chilled in an ice bucket while Sinatra sang softy on the multi-speaker audio system.

An hour later the trolley was back in the corridor, the food untouched, but minus the champagne. Tamara never forgave herself for trusting Doxat, nor him for humiliating her.

Neither had spoken of, or alluded to, their brief liaison. The memory of that night lay awkwardly between them, the unspoken resentment on her part matched by the knowing and slightly superior look in his eyes.

And now he was coming back.

CHAPTER SEVEN

Alison decided on a new look that morning, because life was suddenly different. For some incomprehensible reason she was being sent to northern Spain to meet a man she hardly knew. She put on a red dress, red shoes and decided on a black handbag. She would take the documents in the combination-locked briefcase she had been given. She could not decide whether to take her light fawn raincoat.

It was early summer in Spain, and the weather reports said the North Atlantic coast would be warm, without a chance of rain. Then again, it might be raining when she got back to City Airport in London. She decided to leave the coat. She had all she needed. She would be back that night.

A quick look online the previous night had told her a great deal about her journey and destination. The early morning flight to Bilbao, the nearest international airport, would take ninety minutes and was likely to be full. From there she would take a thirty-minute bus ride to San Sebastian along the coast. She had been given the address of an apartment Doxat owned on the seafront.

Like all tourist destinations, San Sebastian promoted itself alluringly on its website. It certainly had an interesting history. The architecture of the city centre was modelled on that of Haussmann's nineteenth-century Paris and spoke of a time when the city was a popular royal resort. That's what the website said: "The architecture of the city speaks of a long royal history." Alison liked the wordplay. She looked forward to hearing grand buildings whisper of a time when kings and princes stayed in luxurious seafront hotels while their mistresses were installed discreetly in nearby apartments.

In the 1930s, the Spanish Civil War ended that era, but the temperate Atlantic climate, so much more pleasant than the foetid heat of the Mediterranean south, helped restore the city's fortunes. Film and music festivals, glorious beaches for surfers, sunbathers and naturists and, of course, restaurants to rival those in Barcelona made San Sebastian the cool capital of Spain. Then there was the location. The website described it as a stunning seaside setting and showed a number of photographs to make the point.

On the plane, Alison reviewed the day ahead. She was to go straight to the apartment, deliver the documents and repeat the strange statement she had been given. Doxat would sign the documents, and she would return to Bilbao to catch the evening flight back to London. She suddenly regretted that her visit was going to be so brief.

Her task sounded so simple; surreal but simple. A straightforward mission that meant she would be back in London that night. Best of all, she knew now why Doxat was being asked to return. She did not know, however, why he had asked for her. It seemed very strange. Except for a brief conversation over a glass of rosé, they had scarcely talked when she had set up the computer network in his house.

She wanted to get back to her normal, boring life. Nothing had been quite the same since the fall in Scotland. That mystery remained, but she had pushed it to the back of her mind. All she needed to do now was to get Doxat to sign the papers, report back to Tamara Morgan and then resume her role in the IT department.

She shifted in her window seat and wondered whether another Americano would raise her caffeine levels to dangerous heights. She sipped water instead and looked down at the scratched blackboard of the sea below. The pilot announced ten minutes to landing. The "fasten seat belt" sign came on. She thought back to the strange conversation with Tamara and wondered again how she had known of her brief work for Doxat.

Alison had not believed Jed when he had denied all knowledge of leaking the information. It didn't matter, because she desperately needed to tell someone about the extraordinary meeting she had just had with the CEO. Jed was the only person she could turn to. She had invited him to join her for a drink the evening before her flight, in the same wine bar as before.

Jed mistook the invitation and ordered a glass of house champagne each. Poor Jed. She looked at him, all spruced up in a clean T-shirt and a new pair of jeans. He had been hanging around her desk recently. Now he really thought that the suggestion of a drink meant she was going to change her mind and listen to Dizzy Gillespie in his flat.

"Jed, what do you know about the company finances?"

"What do you mean?"

"Don't stall: revenue, profit and loss."

"Why would I know anything?"

Jed was like jelly. He slithered into every corner of this company, sliding under the cracks of locked doors and into the digital vaults where the true secrets of any company lie.

"Because you know more about our business than the bald boiled egg."

"You'd better not let him hear you call him that."

"Everyone calls him that. Come on, Jed, we're friends."

"Why do you want to know?"

"Never mind."

"OK then. Let me tell you why you want to know. They're sending you to see Doxat in his Spanish hideaway because they want him back. You know why?"

"No, tell me."

"Because the big brands are pulling out: Golden Wings, Zenith Bank, World Wheels car hire and several more. These are big boys with big money. The company is looking at a big black hole in the budget. New York is not happy."

There was rich satisfaction in his voice. He was enjoying the power conferred on those who have privileged information to impart.

"I don't get it. Was Doxat that good? I mean, how much creative brainpower does it take to sell a new brand of scotch into the American market? Stick a bagpipe on the label and say it's a hundred years old and you're away."

"Wrong. It ain't that easy. The major clients loved Doxat, and not just because he gave them the numbers. He worked them, played them, made them feel loved, honoured and obeyed. This is a man who put the ooze into schmooze. He made his creative ideas theirs. He reinvented flattery and took it to a new level. On top of all that, they loved the numbers. They got the sales they wanted and more."

"So why fire him?"

"Oh, Alison! Too many questions! Let's just say there were two sides to Doxat. Flattery of the clients and contempt for his colleagues. There is only so much humiliation dear Miss Morgan and company can take."

"That's been the case for years – why now?

"Enough, dear Alison."

81

Jed was irritated. This was not the cheerful get-to-know-you-better drink he had hoped for. His evident irritation pleased her. This was the first time she had seen him like that. He was such a know-all.

"Just get on that plane and bring him back."

"While you stay here reading encrypted comms from New York? You know you could go to jail for that?"

Jed laughed. "It's a digital world, baby. No one has secrets anymore."

He blew her a kiss, slid off the bar stool and left her with the bill.

*

The plane landed with a thump, and twenty minutes later she was on the bus to San Sebastian. The background information in the airline magazine told her this was Basque country, famed for a rootless language almost impossible to learn and, of course, Guernica, scene of one of the worst atrocities of the Spanish Civil War and certainly the best known.

San Sebastian offered no immediate clues to the fact that it had been besieged during the war. On one side, a rumpled rug of green hills blurred into the distance, while on the other a rough sea broke into lines of sugar-white waves on long sandy beaches. Alison checked the address: Apartment 6b, 22 Avenida Zurriola.

Doxat opened the door almost as soon as she pressed the bell. The janitor on the desk downstairs had obviously announced her arrival. He looked very different from the ill-dressed, angry figure she had met in Dulwich. He was deeply tanned, and his face had the silken sheen of expensive moisturiser. He wore a blue polo shirt, unbuttoned to reveal a hint of blond chest hair, white jeans and leather sandals.

"Welcome, come on in," he said.

She walked into a high-ceiled hall that led to a large living room, in turn opening onto a broad terrace. The view was amazing, a long crescent of golden sand bordering a grey-blue sea sprinkled with yachts and small boats. The website had been right. The city really was a splash of gold among the emerald hills of the Basque country.

Doxat looked at his watch.

"Well done, you're on time – want some coffee? And here, let me take that."

She declined and kept tight hold of her shoulder bag and the briefcase.

"Just water, please," she said. It was 11.30 am. She'd been up since six, had little for breakfast and was hungry. She vaguely wondered where and when she might get lunch.

If Doxat signed the documents, she could be free in an hour and find a nice restaurant on the front, where the airline magazine had said there were many tapas bars.

"Take a look," said Doxat, waving an arm at the terrace. He vanished into the back of the apartment. Alison walked onto the terrace and looked out. The airline magazine had been right. This was an amazing city, a beach resort carved out of the sea. The front followed the crescent beach for half a mile in either direction, giving way to rocks and cliffs at either end.

It was midweek in September, but there were still plenty of people on the beach, sunbathing swimming, surfing. She took out her mobile phone to take a quick snap, stepped back and almost fell over. She had not seen the telescope on a tripod. It was an impressive piece of equipment with a long barrel pointing out to sea. The terrace was otherwise bare except for a wooden table and four chairs.

"Nice view, isn't it? " said Doxat, placing a cup of coffee on the table. "How was your flight?"

She had asked for water, not coffee. She didn't point out his mistake.

"Good, thank you."

"Well, when you've finished your coffee come on through and bring the documents. The study is just on your left."

He was seated at a desk, head down and writing when she entered a long narrow room with windows that gave a view of the ocean. There were two chairs in front of the desk, and she was about to sit at one when he said, "Don't sit down just yet. Here, let me take the documents."

She handed him the briefcase and told him the code to the lock. She watched as he snapped it open and riffled through a sheaf of papers.

"Right," he said, looking up, "let's get down to business. First, I need to take some precautions."

"Precautions?"

"Yeah, I am sorry about this but it's for both our sakes."

"What are you talking about?"

"Miss Tamara Morgan is a scheming bitch who would stoop to anything to damage me, hurt me, implicate me…"

"I don't know what you are talking about…"

"…including wiring you up."

"Wiring me up. What do you mean?"

"I mean you have a recording device hidden about your person to tape our conversation. She's done it before."

"That's simply not true."

"So you say, but I need to be sure. I would like you to take off your clothes before we go any further."

"What?" said Alison. She was sure that she had misheard him.

"Strip. Take your clothes off. Get undressed."

She felt a frisson of panic. Had she been lured into a sex trap? Was she going to be raped?

"What are you talking about? I don't understand," she said.

"My dear Miss Spedding, you are an emissary from a woman who hates me and who has been forced to grovel and pay me a large sum of money to return to her company. I know her ways. She's smart. She will have wired you up."

"Don't be ridiculous. She has done no such thing. I think I had better leave."

"I think not," he said. "You have a hidden recording device on your person. I know that because that's the way she works. I don't blame you – you are doing what you have been told. She hopes to entrap me somehow, because she will do anything to destroy me."

"How can she possibly entrap you by making me wear a recorder? It doesn't make sense."

"You're an attractive woman, Ms Spedding. She might hope I would compromise myself by saying or doing something damaging that she could play back to New York."

"This is nonsense, Mr Doxat. All you have to do is sign those papers."

"I would like to believe you, but it's not that simple, Alison. May I call you Alison? Let me repeat: Miss Morgan thinks, or rather hopes, that I might say or do something in your company that will allow her to discredit me."

"That is absurd."

"I know, but as I said, that's the way she works. Please take your clothes off and let me check. We are both grown-ups. It won't take long and trust me, I have seen it all before."

Alison felt a surge of rage rising within her. She was sure her face had turned bright red. Her cheeks felt hot and clammy. She sat down.

"You think I would let myself be used like that? You think just because you invent some ridiculous pretext I am going to take my clothes off?

Who on earth do you think I am? I have come here to deliver documents and a verbal message. That's what I am going to do. Then, I am going to return to London. Full stop."

"Calm down, dear."

"Don't call me dear."

"Look, I need to know you're not wired."

"I don't give a damn what you need to know. Anyway, I've told you it's not true."

"Prove it. That's all I ask. Then we can get down to business."

At this stage anyone else would have told this creepy bastard to fuck off, thrown the documents in his face and left. That's what Jed would advise. She could hear him telling her to get out and go home. "Stay calm," Alison told herself. That was a fast way to lose her job and the bonus that came with this mad mission. Then there was her mortgage.

"No," said Alison, "I'm not going to."

"All right, if it makes it any easier, I will take my clothes off. Then we can both stand stark-naked and prove that neither of us is recording the conversation that is going to follow."

The thought flashed through her mind that this paranoid man must have a reason for his weird behaviour. His relationship with Tamara Morgan was obviously more vitriolic than company gossip had suggested. There was a whiff of blackmail about the affair.

"I heard you asked for me because you trusted me."

"That's true."

"Then trust me, I am not carrying any recording device."

The remark silenced him.

"OK, let me pat you down to make sure."

Since the airline security woman had been heavy-handed in frisking her that morning, she was not going through the experience again – least of all with a man who seemed mentally unstable.

"No, either you trust me or you don't."

There was another silence. Doxat rose from his desk, paced to the end of the room and returned.

"Let's go out onto the terrace," he said.

They walked through double doors. Doxat gripped the wrought-iron balustrade and gazed out to sea. Without turning around, he said, "If I don't return to London, Foxglove goes down the tubes. You do know that, don't you?"

She told herself to keep calm and try to steer the conversation back to those documents.

"I had heard something like that."

"Taking some 2,000 jobs with it."

"That many?"

"Yes, if you include all the satellite operations. You may not believe this, but I live life to a certain moral standard. My father died fighting for what he thought was a righteous cause. Mine is to save those jobs, keep the kids in school and the mortgage payments going."

The statement seemed so absurd and so grandiose that Alison didn't know what to say. Doxat had assumed the role of a messiah, a godlike saviour of a company that she knew would probably carry on perfectly well without him. Still shocked by the earlier conversation, Alison decided to say nothing and let him speak. He was gripping the railing so hard that his knuckles had turned white. He spoke without turning around.

"You have a verbal message for me from that woman. What is it?"

"I have been told not to tell you until you have signed the documents. Those were my instructions."

He whirled round. The silken features were creased with anger.

"You're just a messenger girl. You mean nothing to anyone in that company. You're a little cog in a big machine. So take a good look at the shining sea, take a deep breath and think carefully. I want to hear what that message is. I will be back in a few minutes."

"I have not come here to be talked to like this," she said furiously. She was going home and forgetting the whole miserable episode. She was being used by two people who hated each other. She moved towards the doors. Doxat got there first.

"I'm not asking much." He was snarling now, a dog with bared teeth. "Think about it." He closed the terrace doors behind him. There was a soft click as the lock turned.

Alison turned. A light breeze was blowing in from the sea. The awning above her flapped and rustled. Along the beach the fringe skirts of the umbrellas danced, throwing shadows on the glistening bodies of sunbathers lying glued to their towels. Jet skis and speedboats towing water-skiers carved foamy trails on the placid surface of the sea. People were walking along the front with babies in buggies, dogs on leashes as the law demanded, while others lounged on the front's stone wall eating ice cream.

The serenity of the scene calmed her. Down there was the real world, in which ordinary people were doing ordinary things, such as eating ice cream and soaking up the sun. She felt suddenly light-hearted, a lightness that lifted her anger. She was going home to forget everything that had happened in this beautiful place. Doxat and Morgan could pursue their poisonous feud without her.

Doxat took his time, made coffee and looked again at the documents on his desk. He felt a pang of remorse. Spedding was only a messenger. It had been a mistake to ask her to undress. It was a power play, designed to show her who was in charge. He always liked to shock corporate clients at the start of every meeting with a surprise. Alison was not corporate. It had been a bad mistake.

Whether she was wired or not hardly mattered. He admitted that to himself. The Morgan woman had been forced to take him back, and he had a good idea why. So, he would play the game and return to give Foxglove what the company so urgently needed: his talents, his energy, his charm and his contacts with the major clients.

As for Spedding, he would make up for his behaviour. He had plucked her from the obscurity of the IT department to make a point to that woman; he trusted no one of executive grade in the company. They were all, and that included Morgan, fat-salaried incompetents. That's why he had insisted on bringing Spedding to Spain and why the poor girl had come all this way with those papers. No wonder she had been so confused and then so angry.

He would take her out to lunch. He would buy a decent bottle of champagne, sign the documents at the table and raise a glass to the girl. He might even persuade her to stay the night, book her into a hotel so he could show her the sights of the city and the secrets that lay behind its elegant façade.

He finished his coffee, turned the key in the lock and stepped onto the terrace. He looked around. Alison Spedding was not there. He looked left and right and then left again. She had vanished. He checked the lock on the terrace doors. Had she managed to somehow open them? Perhaps she had unknown skills as a burglar who could pick locks. He brushed the ridiculous thought away and told himself to keep calm. He sat down on a chair.

A fearful thought made him sit up. He looked over the edge of the terrace. There was no sign of a body, nor the wails of an ambulance or the crowd that would have swiftly gathered around a corpse.

He went to one side of the terrace. A small waste pipe from the roof led to a drain on the ground. So *that* was how she had got down. He gave her credit for such daring. The girl had guts, but had he really driven her to this?

He swung the telescope along the promenade first to the east and then to the west. The long lens moved through the crowds on the front, pausing at a possible familiar face, glimpsing briefly the oil-slicked naked bodies of the naturists and then moving back to search the throng on the seafront.

She had to be there somewhere, unless... Doxat paused and raised his head. Alison Spedding could not have found a taxi and be on the way back to the airport already, could she? No. She wouldn't dare. It wasn't possible. He hadn't signed the papers.

He returned to the telescope. The red dress came into focus quickly; she was standing with her forearms on the wall, looking out to sea. She seemed unharmed and, from what he could judge, quite calm. He grabbed the briefcase and documents and hurried out of the apartment. He took the stairs two at a time, not waiting for the lift. He ran down to the front, zigzagging through crowds of promenaders who turned, frowning, indicating displeasure at this unusual interruption of their unhurried afternoon routine. Alison did not seem in the slightest surprised to see him.

"I am so sorry, are you all right?"

"I am fine," she said.

"But how did you get here? Did you climb down that drainpipe?"

"Maybe. Maybe I had a rope round my waist and shimmied down."

"Don't be silly."

"Don't call me silly. You've already been bloody rude."

"I know. I'm sorry. I should never have spoken to you like that. Never asked you to... ermm..."

"Strip naked?"

He felt embarrassed. What had he been thinking?

"Yes. That was stupid and intrusive."

The words came tumbling out. He looked at her, trying to find some sign of acceptance for his apology. She nodded and gave a thin smile.

"I just can't work out how you got here," he said.

" It doesn't matter."

"But it does. I like to think I understand the world around me. Everyone does. But you just vanished and turned up here. Doesn't make sense. How? "

"I thought you sold dreams. Does that make sense?"

"Are you telling me I'm dreaming now?"

"Maybe."

Doxat stepped sideways to avoid a young couple jogging fast towards them, their faces glazed with sweat, headphones clamped to ears, high-fashion trainers pounding the pavement. They swept past, trailing an aura of irritating righteousness.

Doxat raised his hands in mock surrender.

"I give up," he said. "Let me buy you lunch. There's a good hotel restaurant down the road. I owe you a glass of champagne."

"No thanks," she said. "I want to get the late afternoon plane back. Let's get these documents signed."

She nodded to a café across the road.

"That will do."

They crossed the road to the café, which was full of noisy teenagers playing video games.

Doxat took the documents from the briefcase and laid them carefully on the table. He produced a pen and signed them with a flourish. Alison knew he had not read them properly. Typically, he didn't seem to care. She put the papers in the briefcase and laid it on the table between them.

"Would you like a drink?" he said. "Glass of white wine?"

"I could do with a drink. Red for me."

Doxat waved over a waiter and asked for the wine list. There wasn't a wine list, just the house red or white. He ordered the red.

"You took a risk, coming down that waste pipe. A hell of a risk. I feel terrible that you felt forced to do that."

"I'm glad you feel guilty. You behaved like a bastard."

Doxat blinked in surprise. He had underestimated this woman. First, she escaped from his terrace by climbing down a drainpipe from the second storey – bloody risky, that – and then insulted him. Perhaps he deserved it. The wine was poured, and he raised his glass to hers. She shook her head and sipped her wine, wrinkling her nose in distaste.

"I understand that Ms Morgan asked you to repeat something verbally to me. Is that right?"

Alison had completely forgotten about Morgan's words. She repeated them slowly.

"She said that? That she was looking forward to working with me again?" Doxat had raised his eyebrows in genuine surprise.

"Maybe not those exact words, but that was the sense of it, yes."

"Do you think she meant it?"

"How on earth would I know, Mr Doxat?"

He drank deeply and then laughed, a full-throated laugh accompanied by a thumping drumbeat of his fists on the table that made the glasses jump. Alison pushed her chair back in surprise. He recovered his composure and smiled at her.

This young woman, an office junior, had outwitted him. She had sidestepped every move he had made in the brief hour since they met. She had been the matador, he the bull. Looking at her now, he could see that she was, or could be, very attractive. Maybe it was those grey-green eyes, the way they clouded over when she frowned.

"Let's have a glass of champers before you go. There is a good bar in a hotel down the front."

"No thanks. Let's stay here and finish the drinks. Then I'll go back."

They drank the rough red rioja and ordered coffee. Alison broke the silence.

"Do you mind if I ask you something rather personal?"

"Sure, go ahead."

"What is it between you and our chief executive?"

"What do you mean?"

"There seems a personal animosity which goes way beyond differences in the office."

"What makes you say that?" His tone was sharp. She regretted her question.

"It's just a feeling I got when I talked to her, anyway…"

"Anyway, what?"

"Everyone in the office knows you two argue over strategy, costs and all that stuff."

"And you think there's more to it than that?"

"I don't think she likes you very much."

He laughed again more softly, and she could see his face had paled beneath the tan.

"She hates me. She always will."

"Yet she wants you back?"

"She doesn't want me back. She needs me back. Big difference."

He sat forward now, leaning towards her across the table. His face had lost the silken sheen and looked suddenly older, more lined. It was as if he had suddenly wearied of his role in the executive game that was taking him back to London. For a moment she thought he was going to say something else, but he remained silent.

"I'm going now," she said, and got up, holding the briefcase. He nodded, rose and put out his hand.

"I'm sorry."

"So am I," she said, refusing the handshake.

"I will always look out for you," he said, as if such a banal cliché could make up for what had happened.

She left him sitting with a bottle of rioja at the café table. She felt him staring after her. She thought he was going to follow her. The thought had crossed his mind because he wanted to say more, make her listen to him, make her understand that what had happened was a rash mistake born of misjudgement, not malice.

Then he decided he had made enough of a fool of himself. He paid the bill and made his way back to the apartment. He could see her a long way down the promenade, looking for a taxi.

He paused at the bottom of his building and looked up at his balcony, thirty feet above him. He put his hand around the down pipe and pulled gently. The metal flaked into rusty pieces in his hand, revealing the brown corroded interior. The drainpipe would bear no weight at all. In a few days, the corrosion would bring it crumbling to the ground.

He turned to look for Alison again. She was still standing on the front, clearly visible in her red dress. He saw a taxi stop. She got in and left.

CHAPTER EIGHT

Alison was not surprised to find a summons waiting for her when she got back to the office. She had brought the signed documents in the briefcase.

Please see the CEO at 10.00 am you lucky girl! said the yellow sticker on her screen. It was Jed's scrawl. She looked over to his desk. He had headphones on and was tapping furiously on his keyboard. He looked across, flicked a thumbs-up sign to her and went back to work.

The same two assistants were outside Tamara Morgan's office, both staring at screens and pecking away at keyboards. One looked up and said, "Go straight in."

Morgan was seated as before at the round glass table, tapping a text message into her phone. She looked up briefly and went back to her phone.

"Give me a minute," she said. "Take a seat."

Alison punched the combination into the briefcase lock, took out the documents, placed them on the desk and sat down. Morgan pressed send on her phone, sighed, looked up and smiled. She picked up the documents and looked at them briefly.

"Did he read these before he signed?" she asked.

"I think so."

"You *think* so?"

"It was all a bit of a rush."

Morgan sighed again.

"Well, thank you anyway. Good job well done. Did you tell him what I asked you to say?"

"Yes."

"Any reaction? Did he say anything?"

"No, nothing."

"Was he surprised?"

Alison paused. Should she tell a tactical lie? There was no point upsetting this woman. She clearly wanted to hear that Doxat had reacted warmly to her emollient words. She had said she looked forward to working with him again, hadn't she? The prodigal son may not have been forgiven, but at least he had been welcomed back. The fact that he had laughed out loud would not sit well with this powerful woman.

"He became quite thoughtful," she said.

Morgan frowned.

"Anything else about the meeting?"

"No. I was in and out very quickly."

"And Mr Doxat was his usual polite, charming self?"

The sarcasm was childish, but the inference was accurate enough.

"Yes," she said.

"Well, thank you, Alison. I appreciate that this, erm… job… erm… mission has been above and beyond your normal duties, and I will make sure you are rewarded with a bonus, and that your department head is aware of my gratitude."

Later that day Doxat's return was announced to all staff in the deceitfully ambiguous language loved by big corporations. The email from Ms Morgan said merely that the company had agreed terms with Kennedy Doxat, allowing him to resume his position. She was personally delighted that such a talented colleague had changed his mind and chosen to return to a company he had served so well in the past. She was sure he would continue to do so in the future.

The news added welcome spice to the usual canteen gossip. Even the most ignorant spoke with authority about corporate treachery, blackmail and betrayal. The general surprise sharpened when two leading trade papers headlined the news, calling it a humiliating climb-down for the company. The efforts of the corporate affairs department to sell Doxat's return as a triumph for Morgan failed. Doxat's social media "friends" claimed that she had been forced to crawl on her hands and knees to beg him to come back. The speed of his return seemed to confirm this version of events. Doxat was back at his desk the very next day.

"New York doesn't like it," said Jed. "They are not happy bunnies at all. Take me for a drink and I will tell you all."

"I don't want a drink, thanks," Alison said. "I have lunch with my parents tomorrow."

"I thought you always dodged those."

There was nothing this man didn't know. He was a magpie feathering his nest with shiny gossip, loose tittle-tattle and casual remarks long ago forgotten by those who made them.

"I'm taking a day off. I will be glad to get out of here."

She felt dirty, as if she had been wearing the same clothes for days. The memory of the trip to San Sebastian curdled. She had been used. The miserable experience left her feeling like one of those birds in the foyer – trapped and caged. She pushed the whole episode into the back streets of her mind. Jed suddenly tapped a few words on his screen and got up.

"The great man wants some IT help. I'll take it."

Alison said nothing, but knew what was to follow. Jed returned in a few minutes. It was the first time she had seen him looking really angry.

"Says he wants you, babe."

"I'm not on the rota for the executive team."

"He doesn't care. Said it has to be you."

"Tell him I'm not here. And don't call me babe."

She picked up her shoulder bag and headed for the lift.

*

Her father looked at her and smiled recognition. The saddest thing about senile dementia, thought Alison, was that sufferers could recognise and greet those closest to them with a smile or a hug, yet struggle to put a name to the face or remember anything about the long history of love between them.

"Hallo Alibaba," he said.

He used her childhood nickname. She gave him a kiss and a hug. From the kitchen came the sizzle and smell of frying fish. It was Friday. Her mother always made fish and chips for lunch on that day, claiming that after such a meal a toasted cheese sandwich was all that was needed for supper.

Mrs Fiona Spedding, now in her seventies, had been a World War Two baby and often recalled the spartan wartime diet of tinned spam and cabbage. She claimed that courageous fishermen, who dodged mines and U-boats when they took their boats to sea, allowed her family among many others to enjoy the occasional luxury of fish and chips.

Neither Alison nor her father liked to point out that as a baby she could not have remembered anything about the wartime diet and that, in any case, babies were better fed than anyone else during the war with a privileged diet that included halibut fish oil, orange juice and real rather than powdered milk.

Over lunch, Alison replied to her mother's questions about life in the office, what her friends were up to, her holiday plans and whether she had seen any good films recently. These were the usual preliminaries to the main enquiry as to whether she had found a boyfriend.

"Mum, you always ask me that, and I always say that I have not found a boyfriend for the simple reason that I am not looking for one."

The reply was met with a maternal frown. The meal continued in silence. Suddenly her father looked at her and said, "What do you wish for?"

The question was as surprising as the fact that her father seemed aware of who she was.

"I think you would wish to be happily married with nice children, wouldn't you darling?" said her mother.

"No, Mum," Alison replied. "If I had one wish, it would be that Dad would get better and be his old self again."

Her father looked at her blankly, trying to decode the words. Then he shook his head. It was not the answer he wanted.

"All right, Dad," she said. "Try this. I wish I could go back in time and look at all those birds that are now extinct. I would love to watch them flying, feeding, breeding, whatever."

Before he became ill, she and her father had often talked of the dozens of bird species that had been driven from existence by hunting or man-made changes to habitat. Most were distant and exotic cousins of common species: the Canarian oystercatcher, the Himalayan quail, the New Zealand North Island snipe and, from the same country, the wonderful laughing owl, so named because of its peculiar chuckling sound. These had once been common in their home territories and were now extinct. In Britain, pink-headed ducks and passenger pigeons had joined the list.

"Extinct?" said her father. It was a question. His face had changed. There was meaning in those faded blue eyes.

"Yes, Dad."

"Back in time?"

"Yes, Dad."

He sat back, lowered his head and closed his hands as if in prayer. She knew he was trying to part the curtain of dementia and reach back for some dim memory. The fine mind of Professor David Spedding, who had once taught philosophy to first-year university students, was flickering into life. It was as if someone was blowing on the embers of a dying fire.

"Gödel," he said suddenly and raised his head, smiling.

"What dear?" said Mrs Spedding.

"Gödel and Einstein."

"Oh, that old story," said Mrs Spedding, reaching for the plates.

"Go on, Dad," said Alison, knowing exactly what her father was trying to remember and why he suddenly looked so excited.

"I can't remember it but… but… it's there… and you will see your birds. Extinct."

"Yes, Dad, try and remember more."

He sat back. "I… I… I can't," he said.

Alison's father had become a celebrity to his students, and something of a pariah in the philosophy department, for his lectures on the Austrian mathematician and logician Kurt Gödel. She had attended one of these lectures and could hear him now, addressing his students with the enthusiasm of a conductor bringing an orchestra to life.

He would stand before his class, waving his right arm like a baton. Even if they did not love him – and most did – they would listen because David Spedding knew exactly how to put a hook into his audience. He always spoke quickly at first, anxious to get through the introductory sentences.

"'Kurt Gödel was one of the greatest scientific thinkers of the twentieth century. He forced Einstein to change his theory of relativity and accept that logically and mathematically time travel was possible. Yes, that's what I said. Time travel. You've seen the films and read the stories – well, it's all true – or rather, possible. Through Gödel's theories and the exploration of space, we can now contemplate the reality of travel to our past, if not to our future."

She could see her father standing at the head of the class, rubbing his hands in satisfaction, knowing that he had cut through minds choked by social media and dazzled by a world of takeaway sex, drink and drugs. He had got the attention of the entire class, even that young woman with a braided ponytail of auburn hair at the back who came in late, left early and peered at her smart phone throughout the allotted forty-five minutes. They were sitting rapt with attention. They were listening. He spoke more slowly.

"Gödel was born in Vienna in 1906, with the singular gift of a questioning mind that eventually upended all the assumptions on which the science of mathematics and physics had until then been based. He was a revolutionary; he destroyed an empire of the mind. "'So what?' I hear you say."

At this stage, David Spedding became more of an actor than academic. He had his students in the palm of his hand. He paced back and forth, head down as if lost in thought. He made them wait and was pleased at the resulting ripple of impatience in the room.

They wanted to hear more about this obscure Austrian mathematician. He knew they would hurry from the lecture room and Google his name. The suggestion that time travel was not fantasy but fact had a magical effect on minds struggling with the abstruse thinking to be found in Professor Strawson's incomprehensible *Introduction to Logical Theory*, a standard textbook inflicted upon generations of first-year humanity students as a reminder that they had left school and were now in the world of higher education.

David Spedding raised his head, stopped and turned to face his class.

"Gödel released the genie of time travel from a bottle that had been corked by mathematicians and logicians for centuries. And Gödel knew where this would happen: out there in space, where travellers one day would be able to choose not just their destination, but the time in history at which they wished to return to Earth. How do we know? Well, go out one evening, well away from city lights, and look up at the Andromeda galaxy. It's that fuzzy blob a bit to the left of the moon."

There was always a laugh when he said this. But Alison knew her father hadn't finished yet.

"There are five hundred billion stars in that galaxy – maybe more – and most are circled by their own small planets, like we have the sun and the moon. Gödel said it was a mathematical impossibility that intelligent life did not exist somewhere within the Andromeda galaxy. And that is just one galaxy amid millions, maybe billions, in space. "

"So I think you will see that Gödel was right. We cannot be alone in space. And once you have that fact in your head, time travel follows. Why? Well, you think about that and give me the answer. That is the importance of Kurt Gödel. And I'll bet most of you hadn't heard of him until the start of this term. Any questions?"

There was usually a silence at the end of such a talk. Then came a rush of questions from a forest of raised hands. The central question was always the same: who exactly was this prophet of such inspiring theories? Was Gödel real?

The professor would tell them Gödel was born of wealthy parents in Vienna where, from the age of four, his precocious habit of asking questions earned him the nickname of Herr Warum – Mr Why. He quickly made his name as a mathematician and master of logic at the University in Vienna but had to flee his homeland when the Nazis took over Austria in 1938. He managed to get a post at Princeton University.

"Why is that important?"

Professor Spedding threw out the question and looked at his students, resting his eyes briefly on every one of them. All teaching academics know that the success of a lecture, and thus its value to students, can be gauged from the reaction at the end. If the lecturer has got through to his class, they will compete with questions. If not, he would be best advised to wrap up early and take everyone to the pub. He had done that before, which had made him even less popular with the university authorities than he already was.

"He met Einstein there!" Heads swung round to the back of the class. The accent was American. It was the woman with the ponytail.

"Quite right, well done. But why was that important – anyone?"

"The two men worked together initially as mentor and pupil until Einstein conceded that he could no longer teach the refugee from Vienna anything. He could only learn from him." It was the ponytail woman again.

"Well done again… Ms?"

"Mayweather. Elisabeth Mayweather."

"Can I ask how you know this, Ms Mayweather?"

"My father taught at Princeton in the Sixties. Gödel was famous there, but much more than a campus celebrity. People everywhere really admired the fact that he arrived in America a penniless refugee from the Nazis and made such a huge impression on Albert Einstein."

"Who held a senior position in the philosophy department – right?"

"Much more than that: Einstein was a superstar in the world of mathematics. Gödel came into his orbit as a stranger from outer space and soon outshone him."

Alison knew exactly what her father was thinking. Here was the perfect example of how a student outthinks the teacher.

"Thank you, Elizabeth."

And then, the questions about time travel. A rational mind can concede the presence of intelligent life in space but why, oh why, did that lead to the possibility of time travel?

The class repeated the question in various ways. Infuriatingly, their professor left them to work that out for themselves. That was the whole point of his lecture he told them, to make them think.

There was always a short coda to the lecture, a final firecracker to spur weary minds.

"You have all been to, or are familiar with, the most famous and important of English ancient monuments, Stonehenge. Gödel visited Stonehenge when he gave a series of lectures at Cambridge. He said that in those stones, Neolithic man had given us a clue to the secrets of time. Think about that, work on it and we will discuss it when we meet next week."

Professor Spedding had been rebuked by his department head for using Gödel's "fantastic theories" to challenge Einstein's ground-breaking work and for sowing confusion among his students. He had refused to back down and continued to assert that Gödel was the greater mind. His students, keen to champion revolution and challenge authority, agreed and applauded him for that.

That evening with her father, Alison knew this was what he was trying to tell her: that time travel was possible and that she *could* go back and see those wonderful winged creatures.

She loved the rebel in him and had listened carefully to his constant advice: "Challenge every set of beliefs handed to you by those in authority, and especially distrust the conventional wisdom of fine minds. Treasure the thought that the impossible is always within reach. Ask not why, but *why not*?"

CHAPTER NINE

Alison climbed the hill on a path lined by old oak trees whose branches met to form an arch overhead. The sadness of seeing her father reduced in mind and spirit lifted as she cleared the wood and walked into the surprise of evening sunshine. The crest of the hill gave a view over south London and across the river to the Hampstead heights on the far side of the capital.

She counted herself a north London girl now, but always felt at home in the green and tidy suburb of Sydenham, just south of Dulwich, where her parents had lived for much of their married lives. It was strange to think that Doxat lived in that weird house down the hill. Weird was the right word: gnomes in the garden and rooms inside stripped bare of everything that made a house feel habitable. She pushed him out of her mind and returned to the sanctuary of remembrance.

Her childhood had been spent here. The rituals of a young life had been played out and memories formed in these woods and on this hill. She looked back upon that time in her life with the cinnamon glow of nostalgia. She knew friends who remembered their childhood with anger at what they had missed or been denied. Not her. She had been lucky.

For as long as she could remember, she, an only child, had been cocooned in the safety and warmth of parental love. She wondered if it had all been too much. There was surely a jeopardy in unconditional love because love, like life, was always conditional – wasn't it? It was a Sunday ritual that she and her father would walk this path, she kicking up the leaves in the autumn or picking flowers in spring, he with the dog, while Mum cooked a roast lunch.

Her first kiss had been over on that bench where the path divided, one going over the top and down the far side and the other along the ridge. It had been late on a summer's evening and she could recall everything about Gerry Wadsworth.

He was fifteen like herself, with good looks spoiled by acne, but the kiss could have gone on forever. They sat on the bench watching the sun go down, he kissing her, she fending off his roving hands, until a walker's dog had barked at them and refused to go away. Gerry had got up and kicked out at the dog. It had snapped back and a man had shouted at them.

She stood on the rim of the hill shading her eyes and saw a kestrel hawk hovering close by over the rough grassland. The bird broke away with no perceptible movement from the outstretched wings and hovered again further down the hill. It was a female with dark streaks on its pale breast, holding steady against the slight breeze, eyes fastened on the movement of a mouse or vole below. The sight never lost its wonder.

It was a mystery to Alison how train spotters, plane spotters, collectors of stamps and antiques could find any satisfaction in their lifelong hobbies. How could their strange obsessions compare to the joy of watching living creatures riding the air, climbing the wind, hunting, feeding and often playing with each other in wild aerial displays of wing craft and mischief?

Crows, ravens, gulls and sometimes even hawks had been seen tumbling over each other in flight, only a feather's width apart but never touching as they flew and play-fought in the air. In Scotland, after a snowfall, hooded crows had even been seen sliding down hillsides on their tail feathers, clearly enjoying their brief experience of earthbound movement.

She looked down. The hillside was a steep drop through bush and grassland to the golf course below. Players were still out on the course, the flight of the tiny white balls visible against the darkening sky. The first stars had appeared faintly.

Alison thought back to Kurt Gödel. That genius had gone mad in old age. Convinced that he was being poisoned, he refused to eat and starved himself to death. Even his adored wife could not save him. The mind that unlocked the secret of time travel had collapsed in on itself. That's what happens to stars when their heat and light fade and their inner core grows cold.

She looked up. It was impossible to see the Andromeda galaxy against the glow of London at night. But somewhere out there in the cosmos, whose stars had died many thousands of years ago, Gödel had found the secrets of time. Dead stars lived on as their light travelled through space. Gödel always said that simple fact, undisputed by any scientist, proved the logic of time travel. He had enhanced Einstein's theory of relativity to prove that we could travel out to space and back in time.

Alison shivered. Gödel had gone mad. Her father had lost his mind to dementia. Perhaps those who challenge the hegemony of scientific opinion are cursed.

Only a small group of mathematicians in America gave Gödel any credit for his work. He died impoverished and in obscurity. In a much smaller way, her father had ultimately been driven from his post by university authorities who judged him a recusant. Einstein had paid tribute to Gödel after his death, conceding that he had possessed the greater mind. Who would pay tribute to her father after the death which was now so close?

She looked across London. The lights of the high-rise towers along the Thames were beginning to sparkle. The rim of the sun was sinking in the west, leaving the world to darkness and to her. She could just make out the shape of the kestrel lifting from the ground, a small creature in its talons. In the sky above, an arrowhead of crows flew slowly, seeking sanctuary for the night. She breathed in and closed her eyes.

*

The phone rang on Alison's desk. It was not a mobile number she recognised.

"You've been avoiding me."

It took her a second to place the voice.

"No, Ken. It's just that I am not on the exec rota."

"I'd like to thank you for your help. It can't have been easy."

"Thank you. I was just doing my job."

"That's the whole point, isn't it? It was not your job. Let me take you to lunch at least, and show you how grateful I am."

"It's kind of you, but I'm very busy and I'm going away soon. There is a lot on right now."

She looked over at Jed, who had cocked his head and was listening. He was in the wrong job. He should have been a spy. Maybe he was.

"I'm not taking no for an answer, Alison. Come and see me when you're back. I have got some news for you."

He didn't wait for the reply. The phone went dead.

Jed looked over and grinned.

"I am not sure that was a career-enhancing move," he said.

"Shut up, Jed."

"Take it easy, babe. Stay chilled."

"Jed!"

"Yes?"

"I've told you. Fuck's sake, stop calling me babe."

"OK, what about blossom, maybe cherry blossom even?

She had to get away from Jed, get out of the office, out of the company, out of London and back to somewhere in the sane world where she could be herself again. More than ever she felt shabby, unwashed, tainted.

Crumb-hungry sparrows, the feathered fall of the hawk, the boom of the marshland bittern, swallows sitting on telephone wires like musical notes, chatterbox starlings crowding onto the branches of an oak seeking warmth in winter; such images and sounds released her from the prison of the twenty-four-hour day, the seven-day week, a life conditioned by fear of failure: failure to be normal, to pay the mortgage, to hold a job, to find a boyfriend, to marry and have children – all the little boxes that have to be ticked in pursuit of success in a normal life.

Well, she wasn't normal and did not wish to be. She suddenly hated everything about the office and especially the caged birds in the foyer, captives of the ludicrous idea that such creatures would inspire clients to believe the bullshit they were about to be fed by the marketing genius himself: Kennedy "Call me Ken" Doxat.

But they believed him. Doxat sold dreams and seduced his clients with the fantasy that broadcast advertising, brand enhancement, digital promotion on the ever-increasing number of platforms opened up by the web and eye-catching slogans could add allure and lustre to an exciting new product. Allure and lustre were key words in Doxat's vocabulary of seduction, and so were various formulations of the one word that threaded its way through every sales pitch: *digital*.

He took them into a digital dream world where algorithms could plot the desires of hungry consumers and shape campaigns to feed those desires. All too often such dreams were just a quick fix, a narcotic high before sales fell back and the whole process had to be repeated. There was no doubting Doxat's snake-like ability to mesmerise his clients. He had once given a masterclass in sales techniques in the canteen, open to all staff, and began the talk with a question.

"Name me the greatest advertising slogan of all time," he demanded. He quickly broke into the embarrassed silence that followed. No one wanted to look a fool, especially in front of a man who obviously knew the answer to his own question.

"Guinness is Good for You," he said. "Why? Anyone?"

Again, no one spoke out.

"Here's why. The slogan creates its own truth. The secret is this: tell people what they want to hear, and they will believe you. People want to feel good about themselves. They drink Guinness and feel better because that's what they want to feel. Those five words create a virtuous circle between the consumer, the ad and the product. Say it aloud and it sounds like poetry. There has been nothing like it in marketing history."

It was from this that she wished to escape; the smooth-talking, money-making corporate world of slick presentations, mumbo-jumbo sales techniques and the fake charm of people like Doxat. To escape, to be free, to break the treadmill of an eight-hour working day, a five-day week, two gym sessions a week, fish on Friday, too much wine on Saturday, hangover and roast on Sunday, mortgage payments once a month.

Trying to break the shackles of her humdrum existence was romantic nonsense. She knew that. But the seeds of doubt, or perhaps hope, had been sown early. *Thank you, Dad*, she thought. Perhaps she could decode Gödel's blend of maths and physics and crack the secret of time. If she could turn back the wheel of history, where would she go? Victorian

England would be fine for birds, but not so good for a single woman. She let the fantasy play out as she took the lift down to the foyer.

Elizabethan England, that's where she would go. There was a woman on the throne, Shakespeare at the Globe and love, true love, in the air. No greater love affair has existed than that between the English people and Queen Elizabeth I. A historian had written that. It sounded true and if it wasn't, it sounded as if it should be.

She would ride a horse, wearing a fine woollen cloak with a hooded hawk on her wrist. She would hunt rabbits and hares, removing the hood and releasing the hawk to make the kill. She would find the rare species of oystercatchers, sandpipers and curlews that had fallen to man and become extinct.

The most famous of the lost birds, the dodo and the great auk, would not be found in Tudor England. Sailors from distant seas would bring stories, and maybe even sketches, of such exotic creatures to their home port. She would listen and learn in dockside taverns. She would plot their whereabouts on scrolled parchment maps and plan a long sea voyage.

She left the lift, and Tudor England, to push her way through the usual scrum of people in the foyer picking up passes, going through security, meeting, greeting entering and leaving.

The conveyor belt of people never stopped moving at this time of day, indeed any time of day. No one cast a glance at the caged birds overhead. The birds themselves seemed asleep on their perches. Alison refused to look at them and walked out, head down.

In the street she stopped, bent almost double with her hands on her knees and breathed deeply. She straightened and looked up at the shiny black and silver façade of Foxglove. It was a striking building, well designed to make best use of the natural light by day and the harsh sodium lighting in the surrounding streets by night.

She made a decision. She thought about it for a few moments. It was risky, perhaps too risky. She was an intelligent young woman with a sensible head on her shoulders. That's what they all thought. She did not make life-changing decisions. She was Little Miss Normal from the IT department. So why now? Doubt about what she was about to do clung like paint to a wall.

Then she decided. There would be no going back. She stripped the wall bare. She felt better at once and straightened up. There was a glow of satisfaction in doing something that made no sense at all, meant taking a risk, walking mapless along a path unknown. Yes, that was what she needed. Guinness may be good for you, but what she was about to do was a whole lot better. She tapped a brief message to Jed on her phone.

She would go back to her flat, pick up an overnight bag and take a train to the Kent coast that night. The Romney birdwatching group was due to meet in a couple of days on marshland bordering the Thames estuary. She would find a decent hotel. There she would eat and drink well and meet new people with a shared passion.

She would breathe salty sea air and trudge with mud-clogged boots along the estuary of the greatest river in the world. She would see creatures born aloft by the miracle of flight. Some could even sleep on the wing. Was that not in itself miraculous? Two days alone in a hotel would be the therapy she needed, a decompression chamber to bring her back to sanity.

CHAPTER TEN

There was standing room only on the packed commuter train. She moved into a first-class carriage to get a seat. Others had done the same. The chance of a ticket collector on a crowded train was low. The Faversham Grand hotel was a five-minute walk from the station. She remembered that Kath Ambrose, an old friend from university, lived somewhere near Faversham. She was a birder too and might be in the group tomorrow. That would be nice. They had not met for a while. It was so easy to lose touch with friends.

She had chosen the hotel at random, a decision guided by four stars in an online listing which suggested a reasonable degree of comfort. The hotel had welcomed weary travellers since the Middle Ages in one guise or another, or so it claimed in the short description on its website. It was equally proud of the fact that Faversham could trace its history back to 1,000 years before it was inscribed in the Domesday Book.

"If you looked hard enough and listened carefully, history would take you by the hand in every corner of the country and lead you back into the past." She tried to remember who said that. "The past is not dead, it's not even past," was another favourite saying – and she couldn't remember who said that either.

She checked in and went straight to her room. Here, within these four walls, people had slept, dreamt, made love and probably died, some even committing suicide. That was the past, yet those moments in time, and the people who made them, seemed very real. She looked around the room. Everything; wallpaper, curtains, carpet and a wooden desk carried the faded look of the past. It was small and definitely not four stars, but all she needed was a good bed and a proper working shower. The mattress was firm, and everything seemed to work in the bathroom.

She showered, then towelled herself dry with vigour. "A routine to tone the muscles," she told herself, and considered the decision she had taken. It had been forming like a distant cloud in the back of her mind since she had left the office. In fact, it had been lying on the horizon like one of those black twisters that swirl through the American Midwest.

She was going to resign. There would be a row. Unlike Jed, she was not privy to the inner corporate secrets. But what she did know, and especially that strange mission to carry documents to Doxat, would be regarded as a potential source of embarrassment.

They would set the lawyers on her, enforce her contracted notice period, cite the clauses she had signed about confidentiality – non-compete and all the other legal ties that bind staff to a big company. They would threaten to sue her. Doxat especially would do everything to make her stay. She knew too much about him.

Her mobile rang before she had dressed. The dawn chorus ringtone made her jump. She rattled around in her handbag looking for it. It was an unfamiliar number, but she knew who it would be. He had many mobile phones. She clicked the answer button.

"I hear you've taken leave," he said.

"Just a few days, yes."

"Have you seen the *Evening Standard* tonight?"

"No. I'm out of town."

"May I ask where?

"I'm not on company business, Mr Doxat."

"Well, take a look at the *Standard* when you get a chance."

"I have to go. I can't talk now."

She felt embarrassed talking to him while naked. It felt indecent, as if his eyes were riding into the hotel room on the phone signal. She jammed the phone to her cheek, bent down, picked up the towel and wound it around herself. She wanted to end the call. He did it for her.

"Come and see me when you are back. Executive order," he said and rang off. Doxat always liked to end his calls first.

*

The birdwatching group met early the next morning in the car park outside the hotel. There were six of them, three men and three women, identically dressed in camouflage clothing and hiking boots, and all carrying rucksacks. Alison felt slightly out of place with her blue jeans, leather jacket and trainers. That was what she usually wore on such trips, except in wet weather.

She had a sandwich lunch in a rucksack and the usual 10x42 wide angle German binoculars around her neck. The others looked at them approvingly. There were handshakes all round as she was introduced, and then they climbed into a small bus.

Twenty minutes later they parked on the side of a narrow gravel lane. To the right, a sheet of water broken by reed beds and clumps of fern and grass stretched to the earth embankment of a flood wall. Beyond the wall, just visible from the road, chocolate-coloured mudflats lay as far as the eye could see in either direction along the estuary of the River Swale.

On the other side of the road, fields of rough grass split by deep dykes rolled into a line of woods rising to the crest of a low hill. Weathered telegraph poles, some tilting against their connecting wires, were strung out across the fields, a modern addition that seemed out of place in a landscape that could hardly have changed since Roman times. A herd of Jersey cows munched grass on the far side of the fields. Otherwise, there was no sign of life, at least not to the naked eye.

A bicycle was coming down the road, the rider pedalling fast and waving. It was a woman with a rucksack and a long tube slung over her back. There was something familiar about the figure. Alison shielded her eyes with a hand. It was Kath Ambrose.

"Ali! How good to see you, I didn't know you were coming."

Kath Ambrose walked over, arms outstretched for a hug.

"I decided at the last minute," said Alison. "I didn't know you belonged to this group. How long have you been a member?"

The two women embraced warmly. Kath did something important in a City bank but had never told Alison exactly what it was. They saw each other occasionally for coffee or an early evening drink, but always at Kath's request. She never had time for anything else. Her life was her work, she always said. Alison remembered that Kath had admitted to being lonely. Both women agreed it had been far too long since their last meeting.

Around them the group were setting up telescopic lenses on tripods and unpacking cameras and binoculars. Flasks of coffee and tea were produced and poured into plastic cups. The aroma of coffee mingled pleasantly with the salt tang of the air.

Alison poured coffee and handed Kath a cardboard cup without asking. She remembered how much her friend had enjoyed the drink, strong and black. They had been good friends at university, where they were regarded as oddballs, preferring to vanish together at weekends rather than join in the beery nights in local pubs where too much drink led to furtive and unsatisfactory drug-taking and casual but equally unrewarding sexual encounters in damp bedsits with mouldy wallpaper.

The whispers among their fellow students was that they were lesbians. The women ignored the gossip and remained discreet about the reasons for their weekends away together. To be thought of as lovers added a glamorous sheen to their student lives, while the fact that they spent their spare time watching birds would be regarded as evidence of despised bourgeois behaviour suitable only for parents and other dull, middle-aged bores.

Both had kept in touch while they made their separate careers, Alison in London and Kath in Manchester at the northern headquarters of a big bank. When Kath was transferred to the London office, Alison was the first person she called.

"Let's get moving," a voice said. The group threw the remnants of their drinks into the bushes, shouldered their equipment and walked down the road. Feeling very much an outsider among this group of strangers, Alison followed. Kath walked beside her. They stopped where there was a clear line of sight across the marshes.

"Let's set up here," said a voice.

For a few minutes telescopic lenses were focused, telescopes trained and binocular lenses polished and raised. With military precision the team leader, a short wiry man named Mike, gave clipped descriptions and locations of sightings.

"Grey plover, female, on the edge of the reed bed on the left."

Telescopes, cameras and binoculars swung as one. The plover was not as rare as some who flighted through these marshes, but it was a good way to start the day.

"Can't get him!" Alison spoke first, echoing the general frustration.

"See the three moorhens just left of that branch sticking out of the water? Bear left and she's just on the fringe of the reeds, feeding now. Young bird, maybe this year's brood."

The young plover came into sharp relief as Alison found the bird and adjusted her focus. The precise pattern of silver and black crescents on the upper body had such delicacy of colour that the bird might have stepped from an artist's painting. The colouring rose to the neck, melting into a broad white stripe which ran from the head down each side of the neck.

The young bird, much larger than its cousin the golden plover, had been born and reared somewhere in the Arctic that spring. The first flight would have been when it was only two or three weeks old. At some point, by a mysterious message from the heavens or a signal from deep within in her genetic make-up, the bird had taken flight and headed south.

At four months old or so here she was, a thousand miles away on a stopover to feed and build up strength for an even longer fight across Europe to southern Africa, there to winter among palm trees on the coastlines of Kenya, Tanzania and Mozambique and feast on a rich diet of airborne insects and worms.

Alison wondered why such birds bothered to make the long journey back in the spring, beating tiny wings against the perils of predators, storms, thirst and hunger.

"Got it!" called a voice. "Spotted redshank!"

"Where?" whispered everyone almost as one.

"Take a line on that old mill, drop down and she's there on the water's edge."

There was the redshank, the size of a small seagull, black plumage mottled with white spots, jabbing a long bill into the muddy bottom of the pond, seeking worms. Alison had seen redshanks before in the reedy marshlands of the Norfolk Broads, but never as close or as visible.

Beside her, Kath had produced a long-lens camera, which she laid on the wooden fencing to focus. The redshank raised its head, showing the long bill with a red marking at the base. The whirr and click of shutters were the only sound in the soft, salty air.

"Alison, come and look." Mike was bending over a long-mounted telescope. She walked over. The powerful magnification drew the bird from its surroundings to within touching distance, showing every feather and the black line threaded through the glistening orb of the eye. The bird began swimming, occasionally stabbing into the water. It had almost reached the fronded bank when a large ripple behind signalled the appearance of a water rat; a possible predator but not the only one on the marshes to threaten such a bird.

The red shank lifted off with one beat of wings that seemed outsized for the body. Red legs trailed behind as it flew fast and low, finally gliding in to land among reeds and ferns a few hundred yards away.

There was an audible intake of breath among the watchers. No one spoke. The fierce concentration demanded silence. The spotted redshank was not the rarest bird to be seen in these marshes, but it was unusual to see one so close in flight. On occasions like this Alison wished she had a camera with a telescopic lens. Kath was now hunched over hers. The birds around showed no sign of unease as the redshank splashed down beside them and began to feed.

"Nice one," someone said, and everyone relaxed. Notebooks were opened and details of the date and time of the sighting, and an exact description of the redshank, were taken down to be posted online that evening.

"Fancy another coffee?" asked Kath, holding up the thermos flask.

"Sure," said Alison, "but show me what you've got."

Kath handed her the digital camera. The video swept over the watery marshland, zooming in on birds; some feeding, others waiting, watchful, the sentries posted to give early warning of the only predator that really threatened them: a hawk – any hawk, kestrel, osprey even the smaller sparrow hawk. A water rat was hardly a threat to feeding birds, but a hawk would take one off the water in a single swoop.

"Is that a ruff?" asked Alison, stepping back.

"Right on," said Kath, "female juvenile. You can tell by the marking on the front that she's probably bound for Africa, but some birds winter here – if they are sensible. You should see the grown male in summer, absolutely gorgeous with a ring of dark mottled feathers around its neck. Beautiful to watch in flight."

"I've got a whimbrel," said a voice, "just below the sea wall, left of the old lighthouse."

Once again the cameras, telescopes and field glasses swung almost as one.

"Brilliant. Never seen one before," said Kath.

Alison was grateful for the opportunity to show her superior knowledge.

"You're looking at a champion migrant," she said. "You can't see it now, but the wingspan is bigger than most and takes that little chap all the way down to South Africa for the winter. Returns in May. An African winter is usually not much colder than our summers."

The morning passed quickly. Sandwiches and coffee flasks were produced for a roadside lunch. The men slipped off behind a patch of gorse on one side of the road and the women on the other, by unspoken agreement. Then the party trekked up the road, awkwardly carrying their expensive equipment, and set up again to focus inland. Passing cars nosed past the group, paying no attention to a familiar weekend sight on the marshes.

A young cuckoo provided the first excitement. The bird was perched only a hundred feet away in what looked like an old henhouse. This outlaw of the avian world, ill-famed for occupying other birds' nests and pushing out their eggs to make room for itself, was also bound for Africa.

This was the beauty of watching, Kath said later as they shared the last cup of coffee. A day like this cleaned out the insides of the mind. It detoxified the soul.

Alison laughed. "I like the idea about the soul being detoxified by all those birds out here on the marshes. I'm not sure a good Christian would agree with that."

They often laughed when they recalled how they had first met. Very early on a late summer morning, as sunrise lightened the sky, Alison had walked to a long-abandoned fishing harbour with a crumbling stone jetty a mile down the coast from her Scottish university. In previous years at just this time, the great skua had been seen resting here on the migration south to the warmer climes of West Africa. The bird looked like a gull but with different colouring. It had recovered from extinction in the last century, only to face falling numbers once again.

Alison had used a tumbledown cottage as a hide, and for an hour had swept her binoculars over the rocky forelands that enclosed the harbour on either side and the choppy waters beyond for sight of the bird. It was then that she had seen a hooded figure crouching at the end of the jetty.

Alison focused on a young woman, who turned and peered through binoculars at her. That is how they had first seen each other – through the magnifying lenses of their own binoculars. Kath turned out to be the same age and also in the second year at the university, although studying in a different department. She too had come to this lonely spot seeking sight of the rare skua.

Their friendship was forged over a thermos flask of black coffee that morning, and mutual commiseration that their quest for the skua had been a failure. Walking back over the headland, the two women probed each other to find out what exactly had taken them out of bed so early.

"I mean, here we are, two reasonably attractive young women – well, I'm not sure about me, but you're very attractive, Alison – getting up with the dawn to see, if we are very lucky, the distant image of a small creature with wings. I mean, people would think us mad if they knew."

"Maybe we are," said Alison.

"So why do we do it?"

"Difficult to explain," said Alison. "These creatures are beautiful; they lift those tiny bodies with a handful of feathers and wing their way halfway round the world to the sunshine of Africa. Then they come back every year. That's just amazing. To see one of these creatures before they set off, to watch them feeding to build up strength for the marathon ahead, to take photos, make notes and somehow make oneself part of their lives – it's pure magic."

"It's not magic when you get up in the dark, tramp for hours across moor and hill, finally get to a damp shack of a hide and then see nothing at all," said Kath.

"It makes it all the more exciting when you *do* see something special, a bird you have dreamed of and only ever seen in the pages of a book."

"I suppose so, like winning a prize at school," said Kath.

"Yes. Pure pleasure. Hard to describe, really," said Alison.

"You mean like sex?"

"Better than that," said Alison – and wished she had kept her mouth shut. Kath laughed. "Sex is for the birds. Let's leave men out of this, shall we?"

From their occasional meetings over a glass of wine, Alison knew her friend remained bitterly unreconciled to the failure of an early marriage.

Everyone had told Kath she was too young to marry at twenty-three. What they really meant was that she was too kind, intelligent and attractive to waste herself on a man who had never really left school. She divorced eighteen months after the wedding. The disastrous union had, thankfully, been childless.

Kath hugged Alison goodbye, a long clinging hug that seemed to go on rather too long. Kath just didn't want to let go. "Let's do cocktails soon," she said. "I've missed you."

Alison watched her cycle off to the railway station. The rest of the birdwatching group went home after cheery handshakes and repeated requests to Alison to join them for the next field trip.

She returned to the hotel, had a quick shower, changed and went down to the bar. It was early Saturday evening. A solitary drinker sat before a pint of beer doing a crossword. Alison remarked to the elderly barman how nice and peaceful it was. The rush would come later, he said.

She bought a gin and tonic, took it to a corner table, opened her laptop and looked up the *Standard* story. There was a blurred photo on the front page of what looked like a large model aircraft about a hundred feet in the air, approaching the Thames from the south. The story said the object had been seen by dozens of people in south London. Theories ranged from an alien craft visiting from outer space to a large kite being towed by a vehicle.

The most popular explanation was that it was a drone, kitted out to look like a large bird. Then again the "dozens of people" mentioned by the newspaper were probably no more than a couple of old age pensioners with poor eyesight and vivid imaginations, thought Alison. The press loved bizarre animal stories, especially of the escaped panthers-prowling-the-suburbs variety. The animal always turned out to be a large black cat. That didn't stop readers being ever anxious to supply the press with such blatant fantasies.

She sipped her gin and looked at the front page again. The image was vague enough to allow for any wild interpretation, giving the newspapers the opportunity to float theories about flying saucers, half tongue in cheek and half because readers loved such stories. The police took the sightings more seriously, and issued a warning about the danger of drones being flown near any airport, in this case Battersea heliport, a mile west along the river.

A couple had come into the bar. She signalled the barman for another gin and tonic, making a gesture to indicate a large measure. She thought back to Sydenham Hill.

Memory had left her in that wooded upland, and returned as she was making tea in her flat. That was some four miles across London. She could have made the journey easily by train and tube or taxi. But she simply could not recall how she had got home. It was the same in San Sebastian; she had no idea how she had moved from the balcony of Doxat's flat to the seafront.

She pushed the questions away. She had not interrogated herself closely on such matters because she didn't want to. In both cases, she seemed to have suffered a temporary blackout. She would see a doctor about that next week.

The questions continued. It was as if she had closed her front door on a stranger and he kept knocking. There was the fall from the mountain and the shadows on the floor of the valley. The sea eagle was a huge bird, with a seven-foot wingspan. Surely that could have cast such shadows. But how had she seen such shadows *beneath* her and, in any case, what was she doing in the air above the valley floor? It made no sense.

The answer came with the second gin. She normally only drank red wine, but somehow tonight the quick hit of a large gin seemed essential. It was obvious, really. She must have dreamed of herself floating down the valley casting those shadows on the ground, a dream that had emerged from a sudden fainting fit.

As for the fall down a mountainside clad in bushes, young birch and studded with rocks, well, she had been lucky. Skydivers whose parachutes don't open sometimes land in trees and survive, don't they? What about survivors of earthquakes who emerge weeks after being buried by the collapse of their homes? They were just lucky. Like her.

She finished her gin and ordered a third.

"Another large one, please."

The barman gave her a quick look. He could see she was going to get drunk, and that meant trouble. He knew she had booked into the hotel. She would be better off taking one of the several remaining trains back to London. She wouldn't, of course. She looked as if she had settled in for the night.

Alison poured a little tonic into the glass and drank the gin in one, head back, the ice bumping against the tip of her nose. The quick hit of straight, hard alcohol acted like balm on a wound. She was tired. She wanted to drown out a small but insistent voice inside her. It was as if the stranger had opened the door, sat down beside her and begun talking. His voice was calm but insistent, asking questions and suggesting answers, answers she did not want to hear.

She pulled out her mobile and paused, feeling a pang of hunger. She waved to catch the attention of the barman. He raised his eyebrows and looked at her over his spectacles as if inspecting an errant schoolgirl. She asked for a packet of nuts. She spoke loudly. The bar was beginning to fill up, and a few heads turned. The barman came over with the nuts.

126

"You are staying the night with us?" he asked.

"Yes, I have a room."

"Can I have the number?"

No, you can't, thought Alison. *You're checking up on me because I'm a woman drinking on my own, and you think I'm going to get drunk and leave without paying.*

"Fourteen. Top floor," she said.

"Right, I'll charge the drinks to the room. Can I have the name?"

"Spedding." Suspicious bastard.

"What about dinner? It's Saturday and we get very busy."

"Can you book me a table? And another gin, please."

"A large one?"

It was less a question than a statement. She nodded.

The alcohol slipped down easily, sliding into her bones, easing into the marrow, glowing inside her head. She felt happy, sleepy and wide awake all at the same time. It had been a long day, and they had walked almost ten miles. Her feet were sore. She bent down to unlace her boots. The barman returned with the gin. He put the drink on the table and gave her one of those looks men give a woman alone in a bar: part predatory, part pity.

The questions wouldn't stop. The stranger had moved closer, taking the chair beside her. He was asking one question now, the same question but cunningly phrased in different ways. She drank more slowly than before, savouring the hint of juniper and the tang of tonic. The gin tasted good, but it brought her no answers. She felt light-headed. A few drinks and the stranger would leave her alone and take his boring questions with him.

Then she could fly like a bird on the wings of time. She could transport herself back to the Elizabethan age. She frowned and swirled the ice in her glass. The barman had been mean with the cubes. She raised her glass and caught his eye.

"More ice, please."

The barman gave an exaggerated shrug of the shoulders. He was busy with a queue of drinkers. He slid an ice bucket down the bar towards her. She walked over and took the bucket back to her table. She wondered if Queen Elizabeth I had ice in her drinks. Perhaps there was no ice in those days. There certainly wouldn't have been any gin. What did they all drink back then? Beer? Or didn't Shakespeare mention sack? What was that?

She decided to call Jed. He'd be at home now, fiddling around with his computer. It was all he ever did.

Jed answered on the second ring.

"Hi," she said.

"Hi babe, sorry, blossom, where are you?"

"I want you to do me a favour."

"It's Saturday night, blossom, where are you?"

"Never mind. I want you to do something for me."

She was speaking slowly and quietly, careful not to slur her words. People on tables around her were trying to listen. She was a woman alone in a bar. That made her interesting. The fact that she was drinking large gins made her even more so. There was even a chance that this woman would get drunk and make a scene.

"Almost anything for you, blossom, but are you OK?"

"Yes, why?"

"You sound… erm… sleepy."

"I'm getting drunk if you must know, because I'm tired, fed up and fucked over."

"Take it easy. I thought you had been out birdwatching all day."

She hadn't told him where she was going but he knew, of course. Maybe he also knew that her days spent birdwatching were part of another life, one that only made her feel worse about her real life.

She wanted to shout down the phone that she was weary of the office and everything in that shiny black and silver building: screens glowing with emails, memos, yellow Post-it notes stuck on her desk, pointless meetings, meetings about meetings, meetings to discuss the last meeting, meetings to plan the next meeting, meetings to decide whether to cut down on meetings, stupid executives, boring canteen food, bad coffee in cardboard cups and birds in cages. But she didn't. He had heard it all before. Instead, she told him what she wanted him to do for her. She heard his intake of breath. There was a silence.

"Jed?"

"Yes."

"Well?"

"You're mad. There'd be big trouble."

"But can you do it?"

"Maybe. But why? They'd find out, probably get us both fired."

"You can fix that. I know you can."

"No, blossom, not this time. Go to sleep. Come in on Monday, and let's see that bright, shining face looking all eager and ready for the week ahead."

"You're not helping, Jed."

"I am. You're drunk, blossom. Go to bed".

*

She woke up the next morning, throat sore, head throbbing. She never got drunk – well, very rarely. She felt ashamed. She had no idea what she had eaten for dinner, maybe the sea bream, maybe the rabbit. Certainly she had ordered a bottle of red wine, so it must have been rabbit. She vaguely remembered a long climb up steep stairs to her room. She had tripped on the stairs and clung tightly to the banister. Then she had been sick, head down in the lavatory.

Stupid maybe, but worth it. Somewhere last night, in the fog of gin and wine, she had stumbled across a truth. Running away to the Kent coast to watch red shanks and plovers was not the answer. Dear sweet Kath was not the answer, either. She knew what Kath wanted, but that would remain a secret between the two of them. Maybe she would, maybe she wouldn't. But that was definitely for later. Now she needed answers, and the stranger in the bar had given them to her. Every question he asked, everything he said, pointed in one direction.

He told her to ignore fantasy stories about winged creatures flying across London. Ignore that bastard Doxat who is trying to provoke you. He hated what you did to him in San Sebastian. He wants revenge. If you want to find the truth and nail the lie that squirms like a worm in your mind, this is what you do and that's where you go.

The stranger had calmed her doubts and fears. As the song said, she could see clearly now. The sea eagle drifting like a ghost just clear of the sheer mountainside, the white fantail at full stretch, the finger feathers spread taut from the wingtips, then without a beat, riding a thermal to crest the top and gliding down to the valley on the far side. The image was as clear in her head as if she was seeing it.

That's how she knew. And that's where she would go.

CHAPTER ELEVEN

"Alison, where are you? Everyone is asking for you. It's midday."

The dawn chorus woke her up and she fumbled for the phone. She had been expecting the call. The train had just passed Manchester. She would be in Glasgow in two hours. The carriage windows were smeared with rain, but she could see the dim outline of the Pennines to the east. Breakfast had been a stale croissant and a plastic cup of dishwasher coffee at the station. She had fallen asleep the moment the train left.

"Everyone?" she said.

"Well, you know who," said Jed.

"Tell him he's got better things to do. I'm just an IT girl, remember?"

"That's not the point. Why aren't you here?"

"Because I'm taking a few days off."

"You can't do that. You haven't logged any leave."

"Tell them I'm ill, then."

"Stop being silly, Alison. You're needed back here."

She felt a sudden affection for this man. He really seemed to care about her. He was charming in his own strange way. He broke all the rules and got away with it. People were wary of him. He was an outsider, a little like her father perhaps. Maybe that's why she liked him.

"Jed, do me a favour, just cover for me. I'll be back in a few days."

"OK, blossom. I don't know what's going on in that head of yours, but for God's sake take care."

"I'm fine. But please do what I asked – and be careful."

*

There was no lock on the door to the hostel, on the basis that any climber or hiker who had come to grief on the mountains could come in at any time of day or night. Alison opened the door and dumped her rucksack on the floor. It was evening and almost dark outside. Mrs MacLeod was sitting behind the kitchen counter with a cup of tea in her hand. Not much surprised Mrs M, but this young English girl did so all the time.

"Well! look what's blown in with the wind," she said. "What are you doing here, lass?"

Alison held up her phone.

"Sorry, I meant to call. Battery's dead. Have you got a bed for the night?"

Mrs M made a great pretence of riffling through a large engagement book on the counter. Alison knew there was no one else staying. It was the wrong time of year.

"I can give you the back room," said Mrs M. "Looks like you could do with something to eat."

Mrs M watched as her guest ate the standard hostel supper of fried eggs, black pudding and slices of home-baked bread.

"Nasty fall, that. You've recovered, have you?"

Alison nodded, mouth full.

"That was quite a bump, wasn't it?"

Alison swallowed her food and nodded again. Mrs M was watching her, wanting to talk. *Running a hostel like this must be a lonely business in the off season*, Alison thought.

"You've had a busy summer, have you?" she asked.

"Och yes, tailing off now though. We had a fellow killed last month. On Ben Bruda. Got lost. Came back too late, almost dark, missed his footing. Fell 200 feet. Stone dead he was. Only thirty-two. Married with three kids. Shame."

Alison left early the next morning with Mrs M's protestations trailing behind her. She had consumed only an apple and a cup of tea for breakfast, which Mrs M considered akin to starvation rations. She had slept well and felt clear-headed. The rucksack felt comfortable on her back. The binoculars in their leather case swung from a shoulder strap. The sky was a misty blue patched with fluffy clouds. Ahead lay the mountain.

Far down the valley, Ben Bruda rose to a grey-green crest, moss, heather and lichen giving way to hard granite; a tough place to climb but a great view from the top over the sea to the mainland. Men had died for that view. The man with three children had been one of them. He had no reason to climb the mountain except that it was there, a 3,000-foot challenge rising to a crown of granite. A dangerous climb unless you knew the right ascent.

Someone should have told him. The east flank of the mountain was treacherous, very steep and lined with a sheer rockface in parts. Only professional climbers took that route, not weekenders with three children back home in a semi-detached house in suburbia. They take the relatively easy way up the west side and then work their way round and up to the summit. Except this man didn't. She hoped no one told his widow what a fool he had been.

She reached the foot of the mountain and checked her watch: it was 8.30 am. The climb would take maybe three hours if she took it slowly. She would pause, drink from the canteen in her rucksack and eat a few biscuits. She would admire an ever-changing view. Rain, hail, sometimes snow or just shifting patterns created by passing clouds and shafts of sunlight reshaped the mountains with fresh colours and new dimensions. Whenever she heard the song *Take My Breath Away*, Alison thought of these mountains. They brought the old cliché to life.

Once atop the west flank, she would need a further half-hour to work her way across to the far side, the side where the nest lay. There would be no chicks at this time of year. They would be seven months old now, and flighting on their own over these mountains and lakes, seeking prey wherever a young fish or small mammal caught their eye.

No one taught these young eagles how to hunt and kill. Hunger was a great teacher, but an instinct buried deep in the birds' DNA was the true guide to survival. The ancestral urge to feed and fly would take a young eagle, barely grown from a fledgling, and send the newly feathered bird across the mountains to rip a vole from the heather or out to sea to claw a herring from the waves.

It was almost 11.30 am when she reached the ledge just below the nest. The granite rock was still patchy with moss. There had been no recent rain, and her boots firmly gripped the rock beneath her. She could see the spot where she had fallen. She stared, felt a surge of panic and began to breathe heavily, inhaling and expelling lungfuls of air. This is where it had happened. It was easy to see how. The ledge was narrow. It had been slippery from overnight rain.

She should never have led her group that close to the nest. The sheer excitement of what they were about to witness had blinded her to the risk. She did not need to go any further along the ledge to realise what she had done that morning. She had put her own life in danger and those of Xanthe, Douglas and Nick.

She shuffled towards the edge, taking care to keep her feet planted firmly on the rock. Below, the valley was sere and russet brown after long rainless weeks. She looked over the edge as far as she dared, trying to judge how far she had fallen and what had stopped her descent. The stranger's question in the hotel bar came back to her: *how* had she survived such a death fall?

A tangle of small bushes lay thickly two or three hundred feet below her, spreading down to the base. Before that, there were outcrops of rock and rough grass. She must have been in freefall until the undergrowth broke her descent. A climber's helmet, boots and thick clothing had saved her from injury as she tumbled head over heels down the mountain. *That* is how she had survived.

She climbed away from the ledge. She could just see the remnants of the nest below, nothing more now than a few small branches and dried bracken. Four young people had come all the way from London to see a white-tailed eagle feeding her young on that nest. They had taken an absurd risk to do so. No, it wasn't them. It was her. She had misjudged the danger. They trusted her, and they could as easily have slipped over the edge as she had done.

She climbed further, still breathing heavily to calm herself. Feelings of guilt and panic spun around like a Catherine wheel in her head. She paused on a small plateau below the craggy peak. The ground was dry and covered in moss and lichen.

She sat down, opened her rucksack, pulled out a flask of coffee and drank. The kick of caffeine calmed her. She had no reason to feel guilty. She had made a genuine mistake. It was natural for anyone to panic when seeing how close to death they had come. She had survived, that was the point. She half expected the stranger to appear beside her with more boring questions: *OK, you survived the fall – but how did you get back to the hostel?*

But there were no questions. She had found the answers, or rather she persuaded herself that everything that had happened that morning fell within the realm of logic. After all, if a philosopher could use mathematics to prove that time travel was possible, why could she not satisfy the doubters that her fall and swift arrival at the hostel had a perfectly reasonable explanation? It wasn't the doubters that worried her, of course. Nick, Xanthe and Douglas could think what they liked. It was the stranger that had to be satisfied.

A shadow down the valley caught her eye. Floating without a wing-beat on a windless day, the sea eagle wafted on a current of warm air, casting a clear shadow on the ground, moving silently in her direction. This was an old bird with a wingspan close to eight feet, wings that had carried it from mountain to lake and sea for twenty years of its short life. The head was held straight ahead, the curved beak visible, but the eyes would be scanning the ground below.

This was the image that had floated into her head on that hungover morning in Kent. Now the eagle was before her, its eyes scanning the small burn that threaded through the valley. Fat young trout, the favoured food of all eagles, would not be found in such a meagre stream, but there would be water voles, rats and maybe even a water hen to feed on.

The shadow moved faster than its creator, or so it seemed. It was difficult to measure the speed of the bird in the air, but the shadow was certainly gliding across the valley floor faster than anyone could run. The eagle banked, lifted on the warmth of a rising air current and swung towards her.

It was a female, larger and with darker plumage than the male. The feathers on each wing fanned out into long fingers, a puzzling characteristic until some ornithologist worked out that it created the airflow that allowed such a large bird to manoeuvre so skilfully, changing height and direction without losing speed.

The eagle did just that now. The bird had seen her and banked to the right, clearly showing the white tail feathers fanned out in striking contrast to the burnt umber colour of the body.

The sight of Alison would not have alarmed the bird. The sea eagle was a sociable creature, undisturbed by the presence of man except when on the nest with young. She had probably seen a lake on the far side of the mountain and maybe, even at this distance, the ripple of a fish in the water. Alison would have been no more to that eagle than a splash of white on the mountainside, but the bird would have known exactly what that meant.

Alison watched the eagle out of sight and lay back, her head resting on the rucksack. She would spend the day here on the mountain, watching, dreaming, letting mind and body drift. She still had coffee in the flask, a sandwich and a few biscuits. That would do until Mrs MacLeod's heart attack evening fry-up.

She fell asleep and woke to the distant thrum of a helicopter. She sat up and saw the insect shape in the distance coming across the sea from the mainland. It was heading for the landing pad behind the hostel. Another climber or hiker had fallen to death or serious injury. It was hard to see how such an accident could happen on a day like this. The weather was good, and the clarity of the northern light allowed better visibility than anywhere else in the country.

Alison lay back again. The problem was always the same. Amateurs coming up from the big cities to trek the mountains in search of eagles and God knows what else, perhaps a beautiful view that could be translated into digital files on mobile phones and sent around the world.

Falling off a mountain in those conditions was stupid and selfish. It was not necessary to take any risks. A bad fall imperilled not only the climbers involved but those sent to rescue them.

Then, she laughed out loud, a strange sound on a mountain top: that is exactly what she had done – although there had been no helicopter to rescue her. She hadn't needed one. She had saved herself or rather, she had been saved by good fortune. She had beaten the long odds on her survival.

She walked the mountain ridge, hoping for another sight of the eagle. There might be a honey buzzard up here, easily spotted with its grey-brown underparts barred in black. It was a rare creature and rarer still to be seen in September, when most of its brethren would have migrated to winter in the Mediterranean or further south to Africa.

There might also be ospreys down by the lake if she got that far. But there would be nothing compared to the sea eagle. Sighting such a bird for the first time was the start of an addiction. You had to do it again and again. Even a blurred sighting seen through binoculars at a great distance provided a joyous sense of discovery.

Compared to such satisfaction, wherein lay the magic of dead butterflies in glass cases or musty old stamps yellowing in albums that no one else would ever see? Books she could understand. Open an old book and history, romance and comedy take wing in words on every yellowing page.

But books lived for a lifetime or more. Birds had only a short season alive. A bird aged twenty-five years would be counted very old in the avian world. You had to see them while in their prime, because each was different. The markings, the flight patterns, feeding and breeding behaviour might look the same, but they weren't.

It was afternoon now, and she should be thinking of the climb down. A whirring thump and thrum broke the stillness again. She shaded her eyes, looking over the valley to the ridge beyond. The helicopter lifted off, just visible against the afternoon sun. It would head for the mainland, taking one or two dead or injured climbers on a journey that would end at the hospital or mortuary.

It was an essential and admirable service but, as with the weekend trekkers, the solitary grandeur of the mountains was diminished by such intrusions. She picked her way slowly back down the mountain regretting the need to leave and thinking, as she always did, that a small part of her would remain there along with the buzzards, the eagles and the silence.

Her thoughts swung like a compass needle back to the office. It was the pull of magnetic north and she hated it. Jed would be there. He probably hadn't done what she had asked. Maybe he was right about that. She knew he was fond of her, perhaps more, but he masked his feelings with sarcastic quips.

Doxat would be there too, asking to see her. She could hardly refuse again. In a distant way, she worked for the man. Besides, his popularity with the staff spoke kindly of him. He took their side in pay claims and made sure the women were treated equally with the men in terms of salaries and benefits. He positioned himself as the staff champion, a counterfeit posture designed to irritate his executive colleagues and especially Tamara Morgan. Helping the staff was a secondary consideration.

It was no surprise that they adored him. But Doxat's game-playing revealed a wider truth about the man. Behind the designer stubble, the suspiciously blond hair, the rumpled linen suits and the silk shirts lay a faint odour like body sweat, a whiff of deception, the greasepaint of an actor playing a role in which he did not believe.

She had every reason to think this. He had behaved dishonourably in San Sebastian. She checked herself. That was not quite right. Dishonourable implied honour lost. She doubted Doxat had ever been honourable. There was something psychopathic about a man consumed by ego and twisted by ambition.

Then again, looking back on that bizarre day on the Spanish coast, maybe he had been right to be so suspicious. Maybe his relationship with that woman had reached the point of such conflict that both sides feared hidden tape recorders and cameras. And then there was the strange thing he said at the end. The words came out of the blue without any prompting or obvious reason. He had promised to look out for her. But what did that mean? *Don't worry*, he had said, *if this goes wrong, I will look out for you.* Patronising bastard.

She reached the valley floor and lengthened her stride along the track back to the hostel. She occasionally turned, looking for a final glimpse of the eagle, but the sky was empty. The bird would have settled on a branch or a sheltered crevice on the face of the mountain.

It was dark when she pushed open the hostel door and bent to undo her bootlaces. Mrs MacLeod did not take kindly to mud being tramped into her domain. Alison straightened. The frowning face of Mrs M looked at her from behind the counter. Her lips were pursed and the lines on her face were etched even deeper.

She nodded to the far end of the room. A table had been laid with a white cloth and a tall red candle placed on a saucer. Two places had been set, each with silver cutlery and crystal glasses that certainly didn't come from Mrs M's kitchen. There was a bottle of wine on the table. The bottle had been opened. It was red wine. The label showed an ancient chateau. Alison began to pull off her jacket. She was confused.

"What's all that for, Mrs M?"

Mrs M jerked her head towards the door to the staircase. There was a clatter of steps growing louder as someone descended. The door opened.

Kennedy Doxat stepped into the room.

CHAPTER TWELVE

Alison stood silent for a moment. Shock turned to surprise, and then to anger.

"What are you doing here?" she demanded.

"You know each other?" asked Mrs M.

"We do indeed," said Doxat, smiling at her. The barometer of Mrs M's face had swung to stormy. Doxat turned to Alison.

"I was on business in Glasgow and thought I would drop in and see what you are up to."

"That doesn't answer my question. You know very well what I am doing here. I want to know why *you* are here," Alison said.

"Come on, don't get ratty with me," he said. "It's almost your birthday, isn't it? As a good colleague, I thought I would give you a nice surprise."

He waved to the table. Mrs M emitted a sound halfway between a snort and a cough.

"He's brought with him some fillet steak and a birthday cake," she said. "Said he would pay me well to cook them for you. I said I would only if you agreed."

Alison shook her head. "Don't think me rude, Mr Doxat..."

"Ken, please."

Alison sighed. "Mr Doxat," she said firmly. "I like being on my own up here. That's why I come. I don't know how you knew I was here, but I regard this as an intrusion and a very unwelcome one at that."

"He came by a helicopter," said Mrs M, as if that would explain Doxat's reason for being there.

"That's crazy," said Alison. "I mean, the cost of that, just for this…"

She waved at the table. There were candles on the cake. It was indeed a week short of her birthday. She would be thirty-three. Getting old. Another way of looking at this weird scene was that Doxat was acting, as he always did, on impulse. He had done something that was both generous and perhaps well meant. He was mad, of course. She had already decided that. But how the hell did he know where she was?

"How did you know I was here?" she asked.

"Does that matter? If my presence troubles you, I will call the pilot and have him pick me up."

"They won't come across from the mainland at this hour – it gets dark soon," said Mrs M grimly.

Doxat looked at his watch.

"My pilot said he could get here and back up to 6.00 pm. It's now 5.30. So, what about it?"

Alison suddenly felt exhausted. She wanted to go upstairs, have a bath in the old stained tub in an open annexe to her room. Mrs M would have turned the water heater on. She needed a good soak. Then she could come down and Doxat would have vanished back into the strange dream from which he had emerged. Except this was no dream. He was very much here, still smiling at her, waiting and watching. He seemed very calm. He had done what he always did, used surprise to take control.

"All right, Ken. Let's have this nice dinner you have brought, and let me say thank you for the kind gesture," she said. "I will be down in a few minutes. Mrs M will give you a drink and fix you up with a bed."

"He can sleep on the sofa over there," said Mr M. "All the rooms are taken. Shall I light the candles on the cake?"

The non sequitur did not disguise the obvious untruth. The were no other guests in the hostel, leaving two empty bedrooms. Alison went upstairs.

Doxat was at the table fiddling with his mobile phone when she returned. He didn't seem to realise that there was little chance of a signal. She said nothing and sat down. A circular mound of potted shrimps lay on a plate in front of her, holding the shape of the container from which they had been decanted. A large slice of lemon lay beside the shrimps, with bread on the side. A glass of red wine had been poured. The sizzle and smell of cooking wafted in from the kitchen. Doxat put the phone down and raised a glass.

"Here's to you," he said, "mountaineer, birdwatcher and birthday girl."

"It's not my birthday for another week, but thank you."

If nothing else she felt she had to humour this strange man who had appeared quite literally from out of the blue with an entire dinner, an extravagant bottle of wine and even the cutlery and crystal glasses.

"It would have been champagne but you told me you only drink red."

"Excuse me if I sound ungrateful, but can we clear something up?" she said.

"Of course." He was smiling at her with one of those smiles that meant rather more than a friendly greeting.

"Why have you come all this way? I don't understand."

"A reasonable question," he said, "and I will give you a reasonable answer – but later, if you don't mind. We're both tired. Let's allow the wine to revive us and enjoy the meal that the delightful Mrs M is preparing for us."

Mrs M heard the remark and gave him the kind of look that a rhinoceros might bestow upon a white hunter before charging. They ate the potted shrimps, drank the wine and said nothing beyond the occasional comment about the food and the weather.

"How do you like the wine?"

"It's a bit difficult to say," she said, putting down her fork. "When I haven't the faintest idea what you are doing here."

"Would you mind if I asked you the same question?"

"I would actually, because it's none of your business. But if you must know, I come occasionally to watch the eagles and to rest and to empty my mind. I find peace here – if I am left alone."

"Well, I am sorry to have disturbed your peace. Let's try the steak – fillets of the finest scotch beef, I was told. Have some more wine, then we can talk."

Mrs M put the plates on the table none too gently and walked off. Alison was half-tempted to push her plate away. But she was hungry, and the steak was very good. Between mouthfuls, Doxat began to talk.

He told her of the pending acquisition of a smaller company, of a new scheme for a six month staff exchange with the New York office, of the commercial perils of a radical new Labour government. Alison listened with growing incredulity. Had he come all this way to give her a business update? Did he really expect her to listen to this nonsense?

Doxat famously came straight to the point in business meetings. In his "meet the staff" canteen sessions he liked to bestow business wisdom on his listeners. "If you're dealing with clients, begin any meeting with a question you know they can't answer," he would tell them. "When the client is fumbling around for a reply, get straight to the point and make them understand exactly what it is you want."

Sound advice, no doubt, yet here he was, wittering on about staff exchanges as if she would be remotely interested. Just what was the reason for an expensive helicopter flight and a lavish dinner to be followed, no doubt, by a cake that would have thirty-three candles and a birthday greeting picked out in black caviar? The whole thing was ludicrous. The man was a charlatan.

"Forgive me, Ken, but I am as confused now as I was when I first saw you here. I am going to bed shortly because I am tired, but before I do, I would like to know what this is all about."

"Please wait for the cake," he said, "and let me explain. I think you are an extraordinary person. You have talent and a very strong character."

"Thank you, but…"

"And more than that, I don't think you realise quite what qualities you have."

"Which are?"

"Difficult to say in a few words."

"Try. Then I am going to bed."

"Supernatural."

"I beg your pardon?"

"I said, *supernatural*."

"I heard you. Meaning what exactly?"

"Have you ever wondered how you survived that mountain fall? How you suddenly vanished from my balcony and reappeared on the seafront? I thought you had climbed down the drainpipe. You could not have done. It was nothing but rust. And then…"

He paused. Alison got up. She felt faint. The blood had drained from her face. She must have looked sheet white.

"And then *what*?" she said.

Doxat fiddled with his glass, pushed his plate away and avoided looking at her. The silver tongue was lost for words.

"Oh, I see," she said, "and then there was that strange creature flying over London?"

Doxat looked at her and nodded.

"This is simply outrageous. Who the hell do you think you are? Do you ever listen to yourself?"

"OK," he said, "I'm being stupid. Forget all that – my imagination gets the better of me sometimes. Fact is, you fascinate me, there's something about you that is so different, compelling, mysterious. What I mean to say is, you're just…"

"…Fascinating?"

"It's the wrong word, but yes."

"So I fascinate you?"

"Well, yes. Surely you can see why?"

"Are you trying to tell me you've come all this way to try and sleep with me? Is that what this is all about?"

"No, no, of course not."

Alison banged the table with her fist. She had him now. The fabled charmer who could smooth talk clients into spending their riches on dreams spun out of thin air looked like a little boy lost.

"Then what the hell *are* you doing here?" She was going to use the word fuck but caught herself at the last second. Mrs M would probably have thrown her out.

"I've told you."

"No, you haven't told me anything. All I have heard is bullshit. I've had enough," she said. "I'm going to bed. I suggest you call your pilot."

"Please don't. I have a question for you."

"I have had enough of questions and enough of your weird behaviour. Have you got that? Weird. Goodnight, and have a safe flight back."

"Too late for that," said Mrs M helpfully from the far end of the room. She had heard every word.

*

The next morning, Alison woke to the whirr of the helicopter as it warmed up and then the roar of the engine as it took off. She looked at her watch. It was 7.15 am. She got up, washed her face in cold water and dressed. Doxat would be back in the office by midday. It would be evening before she arrived home. She would be at her desk early the next morning.

She wondered if Jed had done what she had asked. There would be a huge row. Good. As for that weirdo, fuck him. Mrs M would agree with the sentiment, if not the language.

CHAPTER THIRTEEN

The birdcage over the lobby entrance was empty when she arrived at the office the next morning. She looked up. There were feathers scattered around the floor of the cage and entwined in the mesh sides. She walked over to the reception desk. The two women on duty didn't seem able to take their eyes off the empty cage. Alison asked what had happened.

Both receptionists started talking at once, then paused and began again. They had come on the early shift at 6.00 am and found the cage door open. There were birds everywhere, flying around, bumping into windows, fluttering up to the ceiling, all seeking escape. Some had even flown into the lifts and been taken to higher floors. The women said they had been told to open the front door and let them out.

"The cage door was open when you arrived?"

"Yes."

"Do we know who did this?"

"No. There's been a terrible hoo-hah about it upstairs."

"Surely the CCTV cameras will have seen who did it?"

"No. The cameras were switched off. They are not working anywhere in the building."

Jed was at his desk when she arrived at her office.

"Morning, blossom. Fall off any mountains?"

"Jed, the cage…"

"I know. Not a bird to be seen down there. There's one in the canteen, though. Came up in the executive lift apparently. Yellow canary. Going to be given a job, I think."

"This isn't a joke, Jed. What's happening?"

"There is a huge inquest going on. That's what's happening. Miss Morgan is on the rampage. Expect a call."

"Why me?"

Jed leant over and whispered: "You know bloody well why you. You've been banging on about that cage ever since you got here. Number one suspect."

"I was in Scotland when this happened."

"What's more, you can prove it, can't you?" he said with more smirk than smile.

The phone rang on Alison's desk. A voice asked her to report to the chief executive. *Immediately*, said the voice.

"And so it begins," said Jed.

"You'll back me up, won't you, I wasn't here, was I?"

"Sure."

She blew him a kiss and mouthed, "thank you".

As a young girl, Alison had been taken by her father to the National Gallery in London for an exhibition of Victorian paintings. The purpose was to expose her young mind and eyes to great art.

She was fourteen years old, and the dreary procession of faces and landscapes painted against unvarying backgrounds of large country houses bored her. Her father tried to explain that if she stopped yawning and fidgeting and looked at the paintings properly, she might learn something about great art. There were important lessons in life to be learnt from such works of genius, he said. He was always saying things like that.

Alison continued to yawn, always a good way to signal her boredom without being rude enough to say so. Her father ploughed on, saying the big question was why the impressionist movement that had revolutionised art in France had never crossed the Channel and attracted English painters.

Recognising that he had lost his daughter with a question that had long been debated in the art world, he gave her a small kiss on the cheek and said that if she paid attention to the paintings he would take her to the gallery café afterwards. There, bored little girls would find tea and a biscuit. She walked patiently around with him, wondering whether there might also be cake in the café. At one painting she stopped and stared.

The picture showed a small boy dressed in blue standing on a stool, facing a group of grim-looking men. The boy's arms were clasped behind his back as if they had been bound. The men were dressed in olden-day costumes, all ruffs and pointed hats. In the background stood a guard in armour. A few figures, who she took to be a nanny and relatives, were looking on with terror in their eyes.

The caption to the scene read: *When did you last see your father?*

Her father explained that the painting portrayed a scene from the English civil war in the seventeenth century when republicans, led by a man called Oliver Cromwell, fought a war with the king.

As Alison later discovered, this was a crude and not entirely accurate rendering of history, but that did not matter. The painting captured her imagination. A little boy faced by hostile interrogators was being asked a simple but dangerous question; the wrong answer might give his father away and condemn him to death. She wanted to reach into the painting, take the boy by the hand and lead him to safety.

She was reminded of the scene the moment she entered Morgan's office. Seated behind the glass table, the chief executive was flanked by David Shortfield and Kennedy Doxat. Nobody was smiling. Everyone looked quite as grim as the little boy's interrogators in the painting.

"Please take a seat," said Morgan, gesturing to a chair.

"I would rather stand," said Alison.

"As you wish," said Shortfield, looking more than ever like his popular nickname, the bald boiled egg.

"You are aware that visitors here have long commented favourably on the display of caged birds in the foyer?"

This was from Ms Morgan. The approach suggested that this was not going to be an easy or a short meeting. Alison sat down in the proffered chair.

"Of course."

"That was a living work of art, which conveyed the message that this is an innovative company prepared to fly high in the service of those clients. It was widely admired and reported on in the press."

"I am aware of that, but I don't know what this has got to do with me or why I am here."

"You are also aware that someone broke into that cage and released the birds?"

"I saw that when I came in this morning," said Alison.

There was a silence. Alison waited for the inevitable accusation and wondered how they would frame it. They would have to be careful. She could call for the HR department and demand legal representation at any time.

Doxat knew perfectly well that she had been away at the time of the incident. As Jed said, she had a perfect alibi. How he knew that Doxat had followed her to Scotland was a matter she would deal with later.

"We were then forced to release the entire flock and let them fly away," said the boiled egg.

Alison waited. There was a rustle of papers as the three executives fiddled with various documents in front of them. *They don't know how to do this*, thought Alison.

The two men glanced at Morgan, who said, "You have long and openly campaigned against the presence of those birds in our lobby. I must ask whether you had anything to do with this."

"No. I was away at the time, as Mr Doxat can tell you."

Morgan and Shortfield turned their heads to look at their colleague. Doxat shrugged. He obviously had not told them of his Scottish trip. There would be an almighty row over an expenses claim for the helicopter.

"That is true. We bumped into each other when I was on a business trip in Scotland. Same day as the bird break-in," said Doxat, looking uncomfortable.

His colleagues stared at him for a few moments then turned back to Alison.

"We want you to help us, Alison," said Morgan. "This was a sophisticated crime that not only involved destruction of an important installation but also the disabling of our CCTV security cameras.

"We have not called in the police, because this is an embarrassment to the company, and we wish to avoid publicity. But we are taking this seriously. Our in-house security team is carrying out a thorough investigation. Do you have any idea who organised or carried out this crime?"

"All I can tell you is that I am glad they did, because I think it an outrage to cage birds such as those in conditions that amount to cruelty."

The outburst surprised Alison as much her interrogators. She waited for an angry response. At least she would not have to write a letter of resignation now.

"Well said." Doxat smiled at her.

"I appreciate you speaking to us with such honesty," said Morgan.

"But you didn't answer the question," said the boiled egg. "Are you sure you have not even an idea who might have done this?"

"I think if we go any further I would need an HR representative as my witness at this meeting."

"That will not be necessary," said Morgan. "Thank you for your help."

Shortfield threw his pen onto the papers. Doxat smiled. Morgan looked out of the window.

Jed was not at his desk when she returned.

"He's around somewhere," said a colleague.

Alison looked across the room. Jed never stood still. He could move through the office without disturbing the air. He seemed ethereal, a wraith who could materialise as if by magic. Unkinder colleagues likened him to a rat swimming across water with only the tip of its nose visible, leaving hardly a ripple in its wake.

Alison saw something floating towards her. Others looked up. A paper dart sailed over several workstations and landed gently on her desk. It had been cleverly put together with a paperclip fastened to the nose and small squares of paper raised on the edge of the wings to give lift. It could easily have flown over the entire department. She looked towards the door. There was no indication of where the dart had come from, but she knew who had thrown it. She unfolded the paper.

Same place at 6.00 pm was written in purple ink.

CHAPTER FOURTEEN

Alison slid onto a bar stool in the Dark Side without looking at the figure hunched up beside her with a hoodie pulled down over his face and a bottle of beer in front of him. An unfamiliar figure was behind the bar. Seamus must be having a night off.

"What can I get you?" asked the barmaid, all bosom, bling and scarlet lipstick.

"Gin, Tanqueray for preference, ice, lemon and a splash of angostura bitters if you've got it."

The barmaid raised her eyebrows and turned to the shelves behind her.

"Where did you learn to make proper paper darts?" Alison said.

"You learn a lot at a sinkhole secondary school, but not necessarily what they try and teach you."

"Like how to turn off CCTV cameras?"

"Anyone could do that."

"But anyone didn't, did they?"

"Look," Jed swung towards her. "I did it for you – aren't you pleased?"

"I didn't ask you to, Jed."

"Yes, you did."

"Well, not the CCTV."

"Don't be naïve, blossom. I had to fix those cameras."

"I'm afraid they'll find out and fire you."

"No, they won't. Anyway, I know too much about them all. How was Scotland?"

"You know how it was."

"And your unexpected visitor?"

"How the hell did you know *that*?"

"Mr Doxat leaves a digital trail a mile wide. Clear as the silver slither of a snail. Maybe that's what he was, in his last life."

"Too slow. He was a weasel back then."

"I'll bet he's going to put that chopper on expenses."

"There's nothing they can do about it if he does."

Alison's gin appeared. They drank in silence. Jed ordered another round.

"I am going to—"

"I want to—"

Their words collided over the bar top. Both laughed.

"You go first," said Jed.

"I'm going to resign."

"Whoah! Wait till they fire you. Get some money."

"They're not going to fire me. They can't. They haven't got a reason."

"You mean because Doxat would stop it? You're right. He's got a thing for you."

"I don't know what thing that would be. He's just weird."

"Simple. He fancies you. Did he try to get his leg over, up there in the mountains?"

"You're a crude bastard, Jed, but no."

"Well, he wants to. I can tell you that. I'd let him. You've got a big mortgage."

"Do shut up. What was your question?"

Jed tipped up the bottle of beer, drained it and put it down with a bang on the zinc counter top.

"I want to come with you. Watching birds."

Alison was about to laugh, but then she saw the look on his face.

"Don't be ridiculous. Why on earth do you want to do that? You'd hate it. It's not your thing. You would have to spend hours stuck in the same place with complete strangers who would probably think you were a weirdo."

"Why would they think that?"

"Well, you are, aren't you?" she said and laughed.

"Who's calling who weird?" he said. "Anyway, I really, really want to come on the next trip."

"I doubt there will be another one soon. Dad's very ill. That's why I am going to resign. Mum wants me at home to help look after him."

"Oh, I'm sorry to hear that."

"Thanks. It's a nightmare. He is just fading away. Every time I go there it's worse. He hardly knows who I am."

"That's terrible. No more birding then?"

"I'm never giving that up – just for now, while Dad is so ill. Anyway, what brought all this on?"

Jed ordered more beer and another large gin. He took a deep breath. For the first time, Alison saw he was unsure of himself. He spoke haltingly, reaching for words. Then he talked in a rush, the words tumbling out in a stream of breathless sentences.

He told her that when he saw the birds fluttering around the lobby, flying into the windows, trying to escape, some even falling to the floor with sheer exhaustion, they reminded him of his first days in the care home. The birds had panicked, not knowing where they were, where to go or what was happening to them.

He had felt like that among strangers, with strange new rules and sleeping in a strange bed in a strange house run by the council. He had panicked and tried to throw himself out of a window. Life in his new surroundings had improved quickly, but he never forgot the feeling of so suddenly being alone, estranged and cast adrift.

"Those birds felt like that," he said. "I could tell."

"Good lord. There's a beating romantic heart beneath that fuck-you exterior."

"Don't laugh at me," he said. "I just have this wish to see them as they really are, in the wild, flying free instead of locked up in the entrance to some fucking office."

"I hate that word."

"You've just used it."

"That was an exclamation, not an adjective."

"Spot the difference. Anyway, that's why I want to come with you," he said.

"I don't think it's for you. If I go out on the next trip, I will let you know. But the others have to agree as well."

"Others?"

"Yes. I'm in a group of four."

"Are these the people who saw you fall?"

"They didn't *see* anything. I had a blackout, that's all."

Her mobile rang.

"I've got to go," she said. "Doesn't look too good."

He slipped off the stool, held her in a brief hug and kissed her, a soft kiss on the cheek. She didn't mind.

"Good luck," he said.

*

Her father was in bed, the sheets drawn tightly up to his chin. His face was the faded yellow of parchment, and he seemed to be asleep. When Alison took his hand, he rolled over towards her with a deep sigh.

"The nurse has been," said her mother. "She says there is nothing we can do. She gave him some pills."

"What for?"

"To help him sleep, I think."

She squeezed her father's hand.

"Dad, can you hear me? It's Alibaba."

Her father rolled onto his back again and opened his eyes. His face had shrunk into itself, the yellowing skin loosely laid over forehead and cheekbones. It was hard to reconcile the figure in the bed with the vibrant, intelligent man who loved her, made her laugh, cupped Arthur in his hands and brought the bird back to life; the man who inspired his students to believe Kurt Gödel might, just might, be right and that time travel was possible. Perhaps that is what he was doing now, travelling back in time.

"Is he in pain?" she asked her mother.

Her mother shook her head. "I don't think so. He's calm."

"Who's that?" said her father, raising his head.

"Alibaba, Dad. Your daughter."

Her father shook his head slightly and closed his eyes.

"Good," he said quite clearly.

She bent over him, kissed his shrivelled cheek and said, "Can you hear me, Dad?"

"Good," he said again, but this time as a mumble, the word struggling through the fast closing doors of his mind.

"What are you giving him to eat?"

"Just what the nurse gave us," her mum said, nodding towards the jars on the side. Alison picked one up. It was baby food, suitable for infants from three to eighteen months.

So, it's true, thought Alison. *This is how we end up, in bed being spoon-fed slop while waiting to re-enter the womb of eternal night. Like a film played backwards.*

"I hate seeing him like this," she said. "I would rather he died now, peacefully."

They were sitting in front of the fire in the living room. Her mother nodded.

"I know," she said. "My head says let him die now, my heart says no, don't let him go. And I won't."

Alison put her arms around her mother and held her tight.

"The nurse says that if he becomes restless or distressed, she will give him a little morphine and that would do it. But I couldn't bear it." Her mother began crying.

Alison sat by the bed, holding her father's hand. She talked to him in a whisper, bending close to his ear. "It's Alibaba," she said. "I'm here, Dad. Alibaba."

Occasionally, the eyes fluttered open and his hand tightened in hers. She was sure he was listening.

"Do you remember saying you wanted to go back to Neolithic times, Dad? Be one of those men drawing cave paintings of wild animals and raising huge stone circles? No greater engineering feat had ever been carried out in the history of mankind, you said – remember? Men with ropes and axes chiselled those stones into shape and pulled them on rollers a hundred miles or more to that great plain. But why? You kept asking that, didn't you? It wasn't just the sun, you said. There had to be more to it. And thousands of years later, we still don't know."

She waited, looking at the face that had almost become a death mask.

Then the chest rose imperceptibly, and the lips parted, venting a long sigh like air escaping a balloon.

There was not much time. She leant down again, whispering more urgently.

"How you loved those people, loved the way they left us a mystery we are never going to solve. Neolithic man's great joke. Gödel visited Stonehenge when he came here to give a talk on Einstein at Oxford. You wrote about that in the *Times Literary Supplement* – remember?

"He said the stones were a portal to another world and you believed him, didn't you? You really thought that time travel was possible, and that Gödel was right. Well, maybe that is where you are now, going now back in time, taking Gödel with you to visit those stones."

He murmured something and she leant forward to catch the words.

"What is it? Say it again, Dad."

"Good," he said and turned his head away. She held his hand and felt the pulse flicker and stop.

"He's gone, Mum," she said, although her mother was in another room and could not hear.

She laid his hand upon his chest and kissed the still warm forehead.

Then she cried long, warm, salty tears. She fished in her bag for a handkerchief and dabbed her eyes. Her mother came in, looked at the figure lying quite still in the bed and pulled the sheets over him.

"Let's have a cup of tea," she said.

*

The funeral was held two weeks later, in a small chapel that raised its cross amid a field of graves. It was a raw November day drained of colour. Bunches of flowers, some fresh, some plastic, lay at the foot of many burial headstones. Each grave carried the name and life dates of the occupant carved on the headstone with various euphemisms for what had befallen them: *gone to rest, fallen asleep, risen a to new life* and *gone to meet his* or *her maker* were the most popular.

Alison and her mother had arrived early. There was a queue of services that morning, and they had an hour to wait before the time for theirs. A black-clad attendant with a top hat stepped from the chapel every thirty minutes and called out the name of the next family.

"It's a bit like being in an airport, waiting to be called to the departure gate, isn't it?" said Alison. Her mother frowned, shook her head and said nothing. They walked along the tarmac lanes between lines of graves.

"Well, I'm glad he's not going to end up here," said her mother.

In his will, David Spedding had asked to be cremated but had either forgotten or deliberately overlooked the need to state where he wished his ashes to be scattered. It was normally in a place that the deceased was known to have loved. Alison wondered vaguely where that would be.

Perhaps the ashes could be attached to a rocket and fired at night towards the stars. At least that would be in the right direction. Space holds the key to time. Look up at the stars and ask yourself whether you are seeing an illusion; light travelling towards you in space, or the star itself. How many times had he told her that?

Stonehenge was an obvious place to scatter the ashes, but she felt there must be a bye-law against that. The sacred circle would be a foot deep in ash, if that was allowed. A burial in the garden seemed the most obvious. Her mother would object, though.

There was not enough room for the mourners in the small chapel, and a loudspeaker had been set up outside to relay the service. Many of Professor Spedding's students, past and present, came. He had issued instructions about the service, asking everyone to wear not black but their most colourful clothes: for men, bright ties and those garish shirts that the middle-aged bought, thinking to look young again. He asked the women to wear summer straw hats, broad brimmed with sashes and other finery twirled around the top.

"I will probably die in a dark, cold month, so try and turn the service into a summer's day. Serve Pimm's in the local pub," he had said in his will.

Alison and her mother shook hands with a steady flow of arrivals, most wearing the requested colourful outfits. Women added gaiety to the sombre surroundings by wearing bright summer dresses beneath their overcoats and beribboned straw hats. They seemed happy to do so, but the men just looked embarrassed by their gaudy ties and shirts and a range of corduroy trousers, mostly red and yellow.

Alison could put only a few names to the faces that shook her hand and murmured words of regret. She had left her long Puffa coat unbuttoned to show a short white summer dress patterned with a butterfly motif. Her mother, standing beside her, was dressed in black with a veil over her face.

"I loved your father, but I am not looking as if I am off to the races on a day like this," she had said.

The last of the mourners had gathered around the loudspeaker, and Alison and her mother were about to go into the chapel when she saw him. Kennedy Doxat was striding towards them, wearing a black overcoat over a dark suit with white shirt and dark red tie. There was a red carnation pinned to his coat lapel.

She watched him with disbelief. He walked over to her.

"What are you doing here?"

"I came to pay my respects."

"But you didn't know my father!"

She almost shouted the words.

"I had a father too, Alison. I know what it's like."

She remembered his annual lunches and how he talked to an empty place at the table. Everyone in the office knew that. He would be doing that again in a few days' time. It was that time of year.

"Of course," she said. "I'm afraid all the seats are taken inside."

"That's OK. I'll join the others out here," he said and turned away.

The service was brief with only one speaker, a colleague from university. He talked of her father's fascination with great events and ideas that challenged convention and broke with accepted nostrums of the day. The building of Stonehenge was a prime example, he said, because we still do not know what it was for and how they erected those huge stones.

"But our departed friend and colleague David Spedding always believed that Stonehenge carried the secrets of time in its circle. In theory at least, those masters of the universe of the mind, Einstein and his protégé Kurt Gödel, proved mathematically that we can travel back, but not forwards in time."

"There is no question where our friend and colleague lying here before us in that cold coffin would have chosen to go in our long past history. Even now, he may be among the ancients he so admired."

After the customary prayers and a hymn, the woven-wicker coffin was carried out by pallbearers. The vicar told everyone they would be welcome to join the Spedding family at a local pub for what he called *refreshments*. What most people wanted was a large gin and tonic or something similar to lift the gloom. They did not wish to refresh themselves, but rather to allow the afternoon to slip away in a wash of memories, retold stories and a lot of alcohol.

Alison came out and looked for Doxat. A crowd was trooping towards the main gate beyond which a pub sign swung gently in the wind, proclaiming the Two Dolphins. She couldn't see him. She regretted her harsh tone when he had arrived. She wanted him to join them. She would get him a drink and apologise for being less than welcoming. He had come as a colleague and a son who still mourned his father. That meant something.

She briefly thought he might already be in the pub. No, that wasn't Doxat. He was never one for the crowd. She looked over the rows of crosses and headstones. Then she saw him walking along a small path to a side entrance. She wanted to shout, but the vicar and her mother were nearby, deep in conversation, no doubt about the ashes. He stopped and leant forward over a grave, examining the inscription. She waved to attract his attention. Whether through intuition or chance he straightened up, turned and waved back. She waved again and smiled.

"Come on, dear," said her mother, taking her arm. "We have to go to the crematorium."

*

In any large company human resources, an inelegant retitling of what was formerly known as the personnel department, occupied neutral ground between management and staff and thus was distrusted by both. HR, as the department was commonly called, did management's bidding in firing people, but also defended staff against common workplace misdemeanours, such as bullying and unfair dismissals.

Alison was not surprised to be summoned to meet the HR director the day after the funeral. She had chosen to return to work immediately in order to discuss the date of her departure. The director was a kindly man in his late fifties, whom rumour had it was only in the job because of a distant family relationship with the bald boiled egg.

"Come in and sit down, Alison," he said. "Tea?"

"No, thank you," she said and sat down.

"I am sorry about your father."

"Yes, it's been a great sadness. But also a relief. He was…"

She stopped. She was going to cry. All the emotion that had been locked away during the final weeks of her father's illness: the funeral preparation; the fake balm of the short ceremony with that hideous hymn and those prayers; the savage sight in the crematorium of the coffin sliding away on silent rollers through a curtain of dark plastic strips, all this had burst a dam somewhere in her mind. She felt the tears on her cheeks and reached for a handkerchief.

"I'm sorry," she said and blew her nose.

"Please, take your time," he said, looking embarrassed. "There is no need to be sorry."

He told her gently that she had come back too early and that the meeting could be rearranged. She said she would like to continue. In which case, and not so gently, he said her offer of resignation had not been accepted. Certain legal obligations would have to be met first. He looked even more embarrassed.

"What obligations? What are you talking about?"

"Well, you can't just resign and walk away from the company. To start with, you had high security clearance that gave access to confidential information. You signed a confidentiality agreement. We need to make sure you honour that undertaking."

She was tempted to walk out on this cardboard cut-out of a corporate executive, slamming the door of the office behind her. Why not leave now and say goodbye to the lot of them? She would meet Jed for one last drink at the Dark Side. Then she would disappear and fly like a bird to warm southern climes. Jed would understand.

As if reading her mind, the HR director said, "You have to work out your notice period, I am afraid. Three months. And there are documents to sign."

"Work out my notice period?"

"You'll be on gardening leave at home."

"Meaning what?"

"Meaning we can call on you at any time to sort out problems on any of the work you have been involved with."

"And if I refuse?"

"Please don't think about that. They will sue you."

"You mean *you* will sue me."

"Yes, I am afraid so. The law is on our side."

She didn't take the lift the two floors to the executive level. She was too angry to share space with strangers or worse still, someone she knew. She ran up the stairs, taking them two at a time, instead. She had left the HR director, pale and mouth agape after venting her fury with ill-chosen words that she now regretted.

She had not sworn. She had merely called him a disgrace to his profession and the pathetic cat's-paw of a vicious management. Halfway up the stairs she bent over to catch her breath. What she said had been unfair, the man was only doing his job. But threatening to sue her just because she wanted to make a clean break with the company? Why? What skills or secrets did she have that mattered so much to them?

She walked past important-looking executives in the glass-walled offices, all bent over laptops, their secretaries sitting outside with Monday morning faces that looked like the stone lions in Trafalgar Square. She turned, swept past Doxat's secretary and walked into his office.

Behind her a raised voice: "You can't go in there, he's in conference!"

She pushed hard against the door and walked in. Doxat was seated at his desk on the phone. There was no one else in the room. He put the phone down. She opened her mouth to speak, but Doxat got up, raised a hand towards her like a policeman signalling the traffic to halt and said, "My car is outside. Go and fix your face and join me. I've got something to tell you."

With that he walked past her, picked up his coat from the rack and, nodding to his secretary, headed for the lifts. Alison was so surprised she watched him go without a word. She touched her cheeks. She'd been crying, warm tears of anger. She hadn't even noticed. She pulled a handkerchief from her bag and dabbed her face. It was stained with black streaks of mascara. He had known she would do this. He had waited for her. There wasn't a conference call. He had been on the phone to his driver.

Everyone stared at her as she walked back. Even the executives in their shiny offices swung their heads towards her. She must have been quite a sight. A pale, blotchy face looked back at her in the ladies' loo. There were black streaks down her cheeks. She wondered what to do. Join Doxat in his car? Find Jed? Walk away from the whole mess and let them sue her? But Jed wouldn't be there. He would have floated off as usual. And she didn't want to be sued. She had the mortgage to think about. She loved her flat. She didn't want to lose it. She walked to the lifts.

The car door swung open as she approached. Doxat shuffled over as she got in. She leant back and closed her eyes. The car moved off. Neither of them spoke. She should not be here. She had fallen for a typical Doxat coup de théâtre, a surprise twist in the story of the day that delighted his clients and so irritated everyone else. She should have known better. Don't get in a car with a stranger. The old advice. And Doxat was a stranger, well he was very strange, which was the same thing. But like most people she was never going to be old enough to know better.

"Where are we going?" she said.

"You'll know soon enough."

"I'd like to know now."

"Somewhere I like, and I think you will, too."

Alison slumped back in her seat and looked at her watch. It was just past noon. She hadn't noticed the time, just as she hadn't noticed her tears. The morning had slipped away. She felt stranded, a piece of driftwood left on a beach at high tide. She had lost control; life was happening to her and not the other way around.

The car drove through backstreets to Marble Arch and headed south along the park towards the Thames. She knew where they were going now: the heliport further up the river. He was going to take her up in a helicopter and push her over the side, to see if she could fly. That was what this was all about. It was all he wanted to know.

He had called her supernatural, because he thought she could fly. He thought she had wings that would lift her into the cloudy skies over the city or the calm blue skies of Scotland. That's what he thought. A maniac lurked behind the linen suits, the silk shirts and the polished smile.

The car turned left at Hyde Park Corner and drove towards the West End. They stopped at traffic lights. She reached for the door handle and pulled. It was locked. Doxat did not look at her. He was staring ahead. The car turned suddenly, throwing her against him. They righted themselves. They drove down one broad street, up another and finally stopped in a small street barely the width of the vehicle.

The driver got out and opened her door. She stepped out and looked around. The shops that lined both sides of the street sold luxury goods for men: shirts, suits, shoes, ties, shooting accessories and shaving equipment. The mullioned windows of a restaurant broke the sequence of luxury male accoutrements. Doxat came around and opened the door.

"After you," he said, gesturing towards the restaurant.

They sat at a corner table. There was a mirror on the wall behind them, allowing her to see the back of Doxat's head. His hair was neatly combed but longer than usual, falling well over the collar of a white shirt. Without being asked, a waiter brought them both a glass of champagne.

"Cheers," he said, raising his glass. Alison did not raise hers.

"What am I doing here?" she asked.

"I may well ask why you stormed into my office just now. You wished to complain, I assume, that you have been asked to abide by your contract of employment and serve out your notice before leaving the company. That is normal practice."

"You mean you have taken me here just to recite some HR nonsense?"

He ignored the remark.

"I understand you wish to leave immediately without regard to your contract. In which case, you would face legal action. To answer your question: you are here, as am I, to have a civilised lunch in a decent restaurant and sort this matter out. That's not HR nonsense, it's an act of collegiate kindness."

She looked at the menu. It was a stiff cardboard rectangle with the dishes printed in elegant handwriting. The name Wiltons was embossed in gold at the top. The name was familiar. She looked down the list of starters and main courses. Her menu did not have prices, but she guessed from the variations of caviar and lobster listed and the tastefully luxurious décor that the restaurant was one of the more expensive in the West End.

"There was absolutely no need to bring me here to discuss that."

"There was no need for you to get into my car and come with me, Alison."

"I hardly had a choice did I? I was threatened with legal action on the one hand and lunch on the other."

He laughed at that, and she felt faintly pleased with her joke.

"I never offered lunch, actually, but let's stop playing games. Have some champagne."

169

He raised his glass again and held it towards her. She raised hers, but did not clink glasses. She sipped her drink and then drank fully. It was classic champagne, velvet smooth without the acid aftertaste of the cheap stuff.

"Let's order, shall we?" he said.

She chose a quinoa salad followed by the catch of the day. She didn't ask what the catch was, it didn't seem to matter. He ordered venison pâté and roast duck. The wine waiter appeared and looked enquiringly at Doxat. He nodded, the waiter refilled his glass and paused before her. She nodded. The champagne was poured. The head waiter appeared and took their order. Doxat called them by their Christian names.

He leant forward. "I have an apology to make to you."

"So this is why we are having lunch? So you can say sorry?"

She was not going to give an inch to this man. She had been wrong to get into the car. She had been upset, almost hysterical, and it seemed the only way out.

"It's one reason," he said. "There is also the question of your resignation. We really need to get that sorted."

She put her glass down sharply on the tablecloth, spilling champagne.

"I am going to leave the company. I am not going to spend another day there, let alone three months."

"Keep calm," he said.

They both leant back as the first courses arrived.

"I don't understand. What has made you so upset?"

She was astonished by the question. The man was so deeply in love with himself that he seemed impervious to the feelings of others.

"Oh, not much really, just little things. The chief executive asks me, an unknown from the IT department, to go on a secret mission to Spain. There, a senior executive asks me to take my clothes off.

Then I come back, mission accomplished, and am given a bonus. Soon after that I am accused by the bastard finance officer, among others, of a criminal act.

"Finally, the aforesaid senior executive, who asked me to strip naked, turns up out of the blue in a bloody helicopter, thank you very much, when I am on a break alone seeking some peace in Scotland. He tells me I am supernatural. I find little things like that quite upsetting – but then maybe I am being oversensitive."

She forced a smile as she said this. Doxat swallowed the sarcasm and smiled back.

They drank more champagne in silence. She wondered what this extraordinary man was going to come out with next. He raised his glass to the light and stared at it as if seeking something to say from the gently rising bubbles.

"I really am very sorry. For everything," he said finally. "Asking you to strip was stupid, pure paranoia. But you have no idea of the lengths that woman will go to."

"You think I would allow myself to become a party to blackmail?"

"I didn't know you very well."

"You still don't."

Doxat cut a piece of toast in half, spread some pâté evenly on it and raised it to his mouth. It reminded her of the scene in his kitchen, when he had given her carefully prepared pâté on thin biscuits accompanied by chilled rosé. With such finicky personal habits, he must spend a long time in the bathroom every morning.

"And I should never have dropped in on you at Scotland like that," he said. "It was rude, uncalled for and I can see that it must have been an unwelcome shock."

"This is turning into a quite a confession, isn't it?"

"I have told you I'm sorry. I misjudged you."

"Really?"

"Yes, really," he said. "Glass of wine?"

"Yes please. Red."

"Your main course is fish."

"I'll stick to red, thank you."

"Good. I'll join you."

Doxat nodded to a waiter, picked up the wine list and ordered. The sleek good looks were still there beneath the stubble, but his face was a blank, giving no hint of expression or emotion. It must have been difficult, she thought, for such a man to apologise so fulsomely to someone like her. For the first time in the last mad few hours Alison felt calm, confident even. The lunch had turned her way. She was going to enjoy it. And get drunk.

"So you accept my apology?"

"Apologies plural, I think. Yes, if they have been given in good faith."

"They have. I'm glad. Let's drink to that."

The wine had arrived, and they raised and touched their glasses.

"I said there is another reason we are having lunch."

"If you think you can persuade me to go back, you're wrong."

"I'm not going to try. What I will do is try and get the notice period waived, so that we don't have a fight about it."

"Tell me, who is behind this? Who is insisting I work out my notice?"

He rolled his eyes and pointed to the ceiling with a single finger.

"But why?"

"She blames you for the birdcage affair. She was furious. That was her baby."

"Oh, I see. I thought you could deal with her."

"No one can. Don't worry. We will sort something out."

They finished the first course. Doxat ordered two more glasses of wine.

"Might as well get a bottle," she said.

He laughed and nodded to the wine waiter. Doxat addressed him by his Christian name. She suddenly realised why he knew them all so well. This is where he came every Remembrance Day, 11 November, to salute his fallen father. She looked around. The waiters were paying close attention to them.

"You come here every year, don't you?"

"Yes."

"To remember your father?"

"Yes."

"Can I ask why here?"

"He took me here for my twenty-firstst birthday. A special treat. It was the last time I saw him."

He spoke with emotion and looked away across the room. For a second she thought she caught a glimpse of a tear. He was undeniably handsome, perhaps more so at a vulnerable moment like this. She felt a sexual frisson, a bat squeak of desire. She wondered how many women he had slept with. He had been out with other women in the office, or so everyone said, but nobody knew whom.

"I'm sorry," she said.

"I loved him, just as you loved your dad. We are suckled at birth by our mothers and given the gift of unconditional love ever after, but fathers are different: they teach us, defend us, guide us through the rough gates of life. Sometimes they save our lives."

"He saved your life?"

"Yes."

She wanted to ask how and when, but the face across the table told her it was not the right time. The main course arrived and they ate for

173

a few minutes in silence. He laid his knife and fork on the table and dabbed at his lips with a linen napkin.

"I didn't bring you here just to apologise," he said.

"So you said."

"I think you are an extraordinary woman."

"I have never enjoyed flattery, Mr Doxat."

"Ken, please."

He paused.

"I mean it. I think you have powers that you don't really understand."

"And you do, I suppose?"

At your father's funeral, the speaker talked of his passion for an Austrian philosopher; Gödel I believe his name was."

"Yes. He was a mathematician, actually."

"And Gödel, if I have got this right, persuaded Einstein that time travel was possible – in theory at least."

"That's true. Einstein said so himself."

"So your father believed that. In fact, he taught his students that time travel is an example of how what science holds to be logically impossible can be proved otherwise. Gödel proved that the impossible can become possible. Have I got that right?"

She felt suddenly tearful again at the memory of the crematorium, and her father's coffin vanishing through the curtains to some council furnace. Doxat was right. Fathers do guide their children through the rough gates of life. Her father had shown her the path ahead and guided her for so much of the way.

He had been there for everything she had done; like all good dads, he had passed on his passions and prejudices. And her father had persuaded himself, if not his students, that time travel was theoretically possible.

"You've lost me," she said. "Have you got what right?"

"If you believe in time travel, you must believe in the supernatural."

She banged her glass hard on the table. Doxat blinked and sat up straight. A waiter moved closer, looking anxious. She put both hands palm down on the table and leant across.

"I know what you're trying to say. You said it in Scotland. Remember? You said I was supernatural. It was fucking gibberish then, and it's fucking gibberish now."

She spoke the words low and slow, stretching out the esses in what she hoped was a hiss.

Doxat put both hands on hers.

"Please don't be angry with me. I am only saying that this is what your father believed."

She pulled her hands away from his and sat back. She drank some more wine. The waiter looked relieved and turned away.

"So what? I never said I believed that stuff."

"But your father did. He was something of a rebel I gather, a contrarian challenging the cosy consensus of those above him. I rather admire that. I wish I had met him. I think we would have got on."

You have to admire this man, thought Alison. *One minute you want to throw the salt cellar at him and the next he disarms you with admiring talk of your much-loved father.* She thought of a meeting between the two. It wouldn't have worked.

"Well, my father believed in the abstract theory of time travel because it overturned an established truth that no one had ever dared question. That's not supernatural. It's just good science."

"Did you ever wonder if he was right?"

"This is beginning to sound like *Question Time*."

"Let me put it another way. Surely you must wonder how you survived that fall from the mountain, how you suddenly left my balcony in Spain and magically, so it seemed, appeared on the seafront."

"There you are again, going back to Scotland. As it happens, I don't wonder about that at all."

"And then there was that strange flight across south London."

"What are you trying to say?"

"If your father believed in time travel and, who knows he may be right, then why should his daughter not…"

"Not what?"

"Overturn another cherished scientific principle."

"Which is?"

"You know what I am trying to say."

"Do I? Do I really?"

She spat the words out, then leant back in her chair and laughed out loud. The waiter looked worried and approached the table again. Doxat waved him away. He poured more wine and placed a glass in front of her. There were tears of laughter on her face. Damn, she thought, the mascara has gone again. She caught herself in the far mirror, a wild woman with an open mouth. She stopped laughing, took a gulp of wine and coughed.

"Sorry, went down the wrong way."

Doxat waited until she recovered herself. She had taken out her compact and was dabbing at her face. He spoke fast, as if he feared she might leave before he finished.

"I sell dreams. Make clients believe in the impossible. Your father was the same. He dreamt that Gödel was right."

"I'm sorry, I've got go," she said and rose from the table.

"There's one more thing," he said.

"No there isn't."

"Sit down. Please."

"I know this has been a difficult day for you, so what I am going to say may come as another shock. But take your time and think it over."

She felt a quiver of alarm, a faint sound in her head like the distant siren of a police car.

"I don't want another shock, thank you. I am going if you don't mind."

She dabbed her mouth with the napkin and picked up her bag.

"Thank you for lunch."

Doxat said nothing. He followed her to the door, which was swung open by a uniformed attendant. They stepped into the street. A light rain pattered onto umbrellas and awnings. She looked left and right for a taxi. The doorman stepped out behind them with a large umbrella. Doxat took her gently by the arm.

"Let me get you a taxi," he said and waved at a welcoming orange light coming down the street. The cab driver turned off his "for hire" light as he pulled in to the kerb. She turned to say goodbye. He stepped closer and took her gently by the arm. She realised he was going to try and kiss her, out here on the street in the rain, in front of everyone. She didn't turn her head offering a cheek, she didn't step back. He kissed her on the mouth, a soft kiss, lips brushing lips. She accepted the kiss and stepped closer to him.

She would look back at the moment and wonder what on earth she was thinking of. Too much wine was one answer. That wasn't the only one. They had kissed again, arms around each other in a tight embrace. People walked past, pretending not to notice. The doorman unfurled the umbrella, stepped forward and raised it over them as if this was a normal part of his duties. The cab driver shrugged, turned his "for hire" sign back on and drove off.

*

Jed was at his desk working on software support for yet another algorithm designed to increase ad sales, but which seemed to have done the opposite, when his phone pinged with an incoming text.

Meet me NOW. You know where.

*

She was sitting on a bar stool, rather unsteadily, Jed thought. He slid onto the next stool.

"Are you all right?"

"Don't ask stupid questions. Of course I am not all right. It's half past three in the afternoon and I'm drinking a large gin and tonic. Have one yourself and get me another."

"Looks like you have already had a skinful."

"Just get the drink in…"

"And shut up?"

"I didn't say that."

They drank gin and tonic. Alison taking long gulps, Jed sluicing the ice round in his glass, watching her.

"So, tell."

"What?"

"He booked the table yesterday. Very swish. Wiltons. What was all that about?"

She might as well tell him, she thought. He'll find out anyway. He always does.

"He apologised. Twice, in fact. Then he fixed my departure from the company so that I won't be sued. Then he said he thought I had wings."

"What?"

"Well, that's what he implied."

"Wings? Is that a new word for boobs?"

"Wings are on your back, you idiot."

Jed ran his hands over her back.

"Definitely no wings. Exactly what did he say?"

"He said he thought I was supernatural, had special powers. Then he kissed me."

"You're joking?"

She nodded into her gin.

"And what did you do?"

"That's what's so weird. I kissed him back."

"What! Like tongues and all?"

"Yes, if you must know."

"Jesus! What got into you? I thought you hated the bastard."

"I do. I mean, I did. No, I do. He said that if my dad believed in time travel, then maybe…"

"Maybe what?"

"Maybe I could fly."

"Maybe you can."

"Not you as well!"

"Just a joke, take it easy!"

"It's not a joke. I am going to see a doctor. Either I have gone mad or everyone else has."

"What on earth do you want a doctor for?"

"Because certain things have happened to me that I can't remember. I have had blackouts. Memory loss, amnesia, whatever."

"Look, let's get you home and I'll make some tea."

He put an arm around her and gave her a hug. Minutes later they were swerving through backstreets, the bike tilting at an impossible angle on the corners, before turning onto the traffic-heavy highway of

Tottenham Court Road. She clung on with her arms tight around his waist; rear lights, brake lights, indicator lights, headlights, street lights all merged into a kaleidoscope of colours with a soundtrack of car horns and curses as they wove through the traffic.

Jed was hunched over a motorbike that was going too fast. Life was out of control. She had been threatened with legal action, lured into an expensive lunch, seduced by too much wine into a long kiss with a stranger in the rain and now this. Definitely out of control. Again.

*

He had never been to her flat before. Jed looked around. Nice prints on the walls, mostly of birds; sparrows and eagles seemed the favourites. The small kitchen was equipped with an array of gadgets: microwave, juicer, toaster, sandwich grill and a smart-looking kettle bathed in a red light. He filled it and turned it on. The kettle changed to green. There was a big American-style fridge and a split-level oven.

"Jesus, blossom, you could start World War Three with what you've got in there."

"It's a normal modern kitchen, Jed. Come and sit down."

He sat down. "All I've got in my kitchen is a kettle and a jar of teabags."

"Just make the tea, Jed."

She was sitting hunched up on the sofa, head down almost between her knees. He gave her a mug of tea and watched her cup it tightly in both hands as if it were going to fly away.

"What am I going to do, Jed?" Her voice was low, broken. She breathed in deeply, trying not to cry.

He took the mug of untouched tea away and sat down beside her. He said nothing. Silence settled on the room like falling snow. Everything suddenly seemed cold. He reached out a tentative arm, held her briefly and pulled back. She was as rigid as a stone sculpture, staring at the floor, lost in a reverie.

"Listen to me," he said, his voice a whisper.

She shook her head slightly.

"First, go and see the doctor. That woman in the office. She's a GP with her own practice. She'll refer you if she thinks you need help."

"I don't need help. I just need to get out of that place."

"I know. So, after the doctor go and see Doxat. He's promised to help you, and he will stand by his word."

"The man's mad. He kissed me on the street in the pouring rain, for God's sake."

"And you kissed him back, so who's mad?"

"I was drunk."

"So was he, by the sound of it! It doesn't matter. You have to talk to him."

Then she cried and made no effort to wipe away the tears. She sobbed, whimpering like a small animal in distress. Jed watched the tears falling silently onto the carpet. He put his arms around her. She softened, allowing him to draw her close so that her head rested on his chest. She pulled away suddenly and put a hand on his shirt.

"Your shirt is getting all wet," she said.

"So's your carpet." They both laughed.

"Let's have some more tea," said Jed.

"Bugger tea. Give me a drink. There's gin in the kitchen. Second shelf. Tonic and ice in the fridge."

*

"Just keep still," said Dr Sampson, pumping up the blood pressure pad around her arm. "121 over 70. That's very good, better than a Masai warrior."

"What?" said Alison.

"Masai. They drink a lot of blood and eat nothing but raw meat."

"Yuk," said Alison.

"So, you are feeling depressed."

"Frankly, I think it's more than that. I feel as if, as if…"

Dr Sampson folded her arms.

"Take your time, Alison."

"…As if I'm going mad."

"Hmmm," said the doctor, "you're leaving the company, I gather."

"Yes."

"And your father died recently?"

"Yes. Dementia."

"You were very close to him, weren't you?"

"Yes, I was."

"These feelings of yours are a common form of grief after a shock – the loss of a loved one or a close friend or a cherished job. It's an expression of inner anger."

"I know," said Alison, "but that's not it. I lose memory sometimes, and when I try and look back it's a blank. I don't know what I have been doing or where I have been."

"How long are these episodes?"

"Maximum fifteen minutes, sometimes just five."

"Periods of amnesia are not uncommon and can be caused by stress. Transient global amnesia, it's called."

"Transient what?"

"Global amnesia. It's not as rare as you might think, but often misdiagnosed. When an episode occurs, a person doesn't know where they are and cannot remember where they have been. But throughout the episode the patient retains the mental and physical powers to walk, talk, use a phone, even drive a car. The memory has gone, but not the mind."

"And does one dream during these episodes?"

"If you did, you wouldn't remember it."

Alison sat back and relaxed, feeling the warmth and comfort of someone lowering themselves into a hot bath. For the first time, someone was making sense of what had been happening to her. She wasn't going mad. Dr Sampson explained that the episodes of amnesia fell into two types: epileptic and transient. Drugs would alleviate the symptoms of either, although epileptic amnesia, caused by what Dr Sampson called minor electrical storms in the brain, was the more difficult.

"Otherwise, it's just a case of taking the stress out of your life," she said, "and doing something different, something not too strenuous, something that gives you pleasure and takes you out of yourself."

Alison was about to say that birdwatching did exactly that for her when Dr Sampson's mobile phone rang. She looked at the number on the screen, frowned, apologised and took the call.

"Yes, she's here, but I am in the middle of a consultation. Yes, I will tell her."

She went to her desk, scribbled something on a piece of paper and handed it to Alison.

"Twice a day, morning and night. My advice is that you change your lifestyle. Learn to live with yourself, find the real you and work out what makes that person happy."

"Thank you, doctor. Was that someone on the phone for me?"

"Yes. Mr Doxat. He wants to see you when we have finished. He says it's important that you do. He has news that he says will be helpful."

She noted Alison's expression.

"Look, Alison. This is a big company. It has sharp corners and steep stairs. I see all sorts of people, senior, junior, new and old, who have bumped into those corners and tripped on the stairs. The company does its best, but it can't look after everyone all the time. But when they do try and help you – take my advice – just say yes. You are a special case and they will do their best for you."

"A special case, doctor?"

"Epileptic amnesia is not that common and, as I said, often misdiagnosed."

"Thank you."

She knows, thought Alison. Everyone seems to know what's happening in my life. Except me. She got up, grabbed her handbag and headed towards the door.

"May I ask where you are going?" asked Dr Sampson.

"I was going home to rest."

"That's a good idea. But first I suggest you see Kennedy Doxat."

Alison nodded. The doctor was right. Doctors always are.

She climbed the fire staircase towards the executive floor. So she was suffering from episodes of transient or epileptic amnesia. Great. Her life was now divided up into episodes. Perhaps they might turn them into a medical drama on TV. She would star in the series.

Episode One: You fall down a mountain.

Episode Two. No one, including yourself, can work out how you survived.

Episode Three: You escape from a predatory executive by somehow leaving his third-floor balcony and find yourself safe but several hundred yards away on the seafront of a lovely Spanish city.

Episode Four: To make up for his appalling behaviour, the executive takes you to a wildly expensive lunch and suddenly kisses you, not because you are beautiful, sexy or a rich heiress but because he thinks you have supernatural powers.

He dare not say this, because it is well beyond what is rational, sane and credible. But the fact is, he thinks you are some kind of witch with the power of flight. And you kiss him back right out there in the street. Tongues and all. In the pouring rain. Terrific.

Episode Five: You go stark staring mad and throw yourself into the Thames.

Episode Six: Three people turn up at your funeral. Mum, who cries a lot; Kath, who throws flowers on your grave with the label "We never found our love" and Jed, who chews gum and says in a loud voice as your coffin follows your father's into the fiery furnace: "Have a good trip, blossom, and don't forget to call."

Doxat was standing by the window when Alison walked in. He didn't try the usual trick of making his visitor wait while he stared into the void. Alison had heard that sometimes he waited for several minutes before swinging around to begin the conversation.

"I hear you've been ill," he said.

"You hear wrong."

"As you wish," he said. "I'm glad you came to see me because I have been able to sort out your departure. If you sign these papers, you are free to walk out of here once you've cleared your desk. I hope, however, you will stay to say goodbye to your colleagues and join them for a farewell drink."

Alison did not wish to accept anything from this man. She wanted to fling the offer of farewell drinks back in his face. The trouble was that she liked the idea. It would mark a suitable end point to her three years at Foxglove and give her the chance to say goodbye to her few friends. She never went to such occasions, not least because she couldn't stand the endless promises to keep in touch which nobody honoured. Then there were the silly speeches. These were especially gruesome when made by an executive who had fired the departing person and then praised their work, character and commitment to the company.

"All right," she said, "I will do that."

"In the wine bar across the road?"

"The Dark Side. Yes."

"Good. We will pay for that."

"I would rather you didn't."

Doxat shrugged and shook his head.

"Well, let's compromise. You pay for the drink, and we will cover the food."

Typical, she thought. There was always a deal to be done, a compromise to be found, a middle way to navigate between yes and no. Cutting a deal, that's what business was about and especially this business.

"There will also be a financial settlement."

"I won't accept it."

He looked at her this time with real surprise.

"Are you sure? It's a lot of money."

"How much?"

"About £9,000."

He was right. It was a lot of money. It would make a small but much needed dent in her mortgage.

"Very well, I will accept that."

"Good. One of life's great lessons is not to make hasty decisions."

Coming from Doxat that was a bit rich, she thought. He turned his back, walked to the desk and looked at the framed photo of his father.

"Alison, I am sorry about what happened after lunch," he said. He appeared to be talking to the photograph.

"Let me explain."

He heard the swish of a moving door and turned. Alison had gone.

CHAPTER FIFTEEN

Alison saw Kath pushing through the crowd in the Dark Side wine bar. She was pleased. She didn't know half the people who had turned up at her farewell, and most of them didn't know her. They had come from various departments, pecked her on the cheek and said how sorry they were that she was leaving.

Then they went straight to the bar, where Seamus was pouring free drinks. A friendly face was what she needed now. Jed was at the bar, handing glasses of wine to the throng behind him. She smiled, remembering his kindness and how she cried into his damp shirt. It was so unlike Jed. He reverted to type the next day. They had a row in the office, an unnecessary corridor shouting match. Stupid, stupid, stupid – but then Jed could be a real bastard at times. She waved to Kath, who came over and gave her a long hug and a kiss on the cheek.

"I am sure you are doing the right thing," she said.

Jed materialised as usual without seeming to part the crowd. He handed a glass of white wine to Kath and a red to Alison.

"How are you feeling?" he asked.

She shook her head and shrugged off the question. People were always asking that. What was she supposed to say? I snogged the mighty Doxat in the pouring rain in the middle of a street and got a £9,000 payoff?

"This is my friend Kath," Alison said.

"Alison has told me all about you," said Jed.

"Liar," Alison said and kicked him in the shin rather too hard.

"Fuck," said Jed, hopping around in a small circle.

Kath changed the subject. "Are you making a speech, Ali?" she asked.

"No speeches. I plan to have a few drinks, and then Jed here is going to buy me supper. Aren't you, Jed?"

Jed's face registered one of those expressions her mother had warned her about. "Don't look like that or the wind might change and you'll be stuck with that face for the rest of your life" had been a frequent reprimand at home.

"And I hope you will join us," Alison said to Kath.

Alison looked around. It was a Thursday night, allowing everyone to get drunk in the knowledge that they would probably finish after midnight when it would be Friday and thus almost the weekend. This, and the mistaken belief that the company was paying, was giving Seamus a busy time.

Little paper twists of fish and chips were handed around by professional waitresses. Through the window, Alison could see a large van marked *Fiona's Mobile Catering*.

"He doesn't do anything by half," murmured Jed.

"They're delicious," said Kath, eating one after another. The trio had not moved as the crowd ebbed and flowed around them. Occasionally, heads and hands emerged to peck Alison's cheek or shake her hand and wish her well. She had no idea who these people were.

"Let's go," she said.

She, Kath and Jed began to squeeze through the crowd towards the door when a loud clink of glasses stopped them. Every head turned to the far end of the bar where Doxat now stood on a chair.

"Colleagues and friends," he shouted. The crowd fell silent. "We are here tonight to say farewell to a remarkable colleague. Alison Spedding has given the company great service in her three short years with us, and I want to say both professionally and personally how sorry we are to see her go."

"Hear, hear," said someone.

"Oh, God," said Alison.

"We can't go now," said Kath.

"Yes, we can," said Alison.

Doxat continued with a few pleasantries. Alison had almost reached the door when he then said, rather louder than before, "I now call on Alison, who I see over there, to say a few words."

"Bugger," said Alison.

"Do your best, blossom," said Jed.

Kath gave her an encouraging hug. "Go on, gorgeous," she said.

Alison threaded her way through the crowd and mounted the chair, trying hard to give Doxat a smile.

"My father, God rest his soul, told me the only way to go in life was my own way. That's what I am doing, and I hope you'll do it, too. Goodbye and good luck."

There was a moment's silence while people tried to work out what had been said. Was it criticism of the company or a sly dig at Doxat? It didn't matter. The speech had been much shorter than the usual rambling and embarrassingly emotional farewells. There was loud applause and then people turned back to the wine. The hum of conversation resumed and then stopped. Everyone looked at the door.

Alison saw a large black car outside with a chauffeur standing by the front door. The crowd at the door parted as Tamara Morgan entered the bar. People stepped back as she cleaved her way towards Alison, trailed by one of her assistants.

Alison stood still. A hand pushed her gently forward. Tamara kissed her lightly on both cheeks and said, "I'm sorry. I wasn't told of your party. We're going to miss you. Remember, you can always come back."

Someone handed her a drink. Tamara clinked glasses with Alison, turned to raise her glass to those around her, sipped her drink and left. There was a momentary silence in the bar. Alison watched through the window as she got into the car. It was beginning to rain. A babble of talk broke the silence. Alison looked across to Doxat, who was standing at the bar. He was smiling at nobody in particular.

*

They were all drunk and swayed into one other as they walked down the street, heads bowed against the rain. Kath linked arms with Alison, while Jed strode ahead, peering into cafés and restaurants. Nobody had an umbrella. Alison had told them she wanted one last glass of red wine – a large one – a big bowl of linguine and a long sleep.

They ate in an Italian restaurant in a side street. The wine arrived in a bottle encased in straw. Jed ordered linguine for three. Kath objected and chose tagliatelle. Alison poured wine for everyone.

"Thank God that's over," she said.

"This wine is rubbish," said Jed, raising an arm and signalling a waiter.

"I think it's fine," said Kath. "So that was Tamara Morgan – pretty, isn't she?"

Kath and Jed talked over each other, vying for attention with their accounts of the evening. Kath liked the way Doxat had spoken and said it was good that so many people had turned up.

"You couldn't just walk out of there without saying goodbye," she said.

Jed thought the whole occasion an exercise in corporate hypocrisy. Alison wasn't listening. She drank the wine and they ordered another and better bottle. The food arrived, but she pushed her plate away, drained her wine and said, "I'm done here. You two stay on."

She got up unsteadily. They both wanted to take her home, but she refused. She sat in the back of an Uber feeling nauseous and miserable. The car drove slowly as the rain-slicked streets unreeled on either side. She wished he would drive faster. The driver kept flicking eyes at her in the rear mirror. She dimly thought he was either afraid she was going to vomit all over his back seat or was weighing the chance of a sexual assault.

She managed a small smile. *At least projectile vomiting might deter his advances*, she thought. That was what she felt like, spewing out the whole evening and everything she had ever known at Foxglove, a long, putrid, sea-green purge of wasted years.

She felt her stomach heave and the nausea rise. There was an acidic taste in her throat. She was going to be sick all over the back seat. The driver glanced in his mirror and registered the discomfort of his passenger's pale face. He began driving fast, desperate to be rid of her. Alison fumbled for her handbag. She was going to need tissues. The bag wasn't there. She reached around the seat. Definitely no handbag.

The car braked sharply. She hadn't been wearing a seatbelt and was flung against the seat in front. She looked up. She was outside her flat. She groped for the door handle. Before she could reach it, the door opened. Jed was standing there. With her handbag in his hand. She glimpsed his shiny motorbike parked up the street.

"Let me give you a hand," he said. She got out, doubled up and was sick, splattering vomit over his smart trainers. He jumped back too late.

He helped her into her flat and into the bathroom. He closed the door on the sound of long, painful retching and went to the kitchen to find some wine. He uncorked a bottle and looked down at his trainers. They had been his best pair, gold lamé stripes on black. He unlaced them and began to wash them in the sink. Alison appeared looking paler than the white dressing gown she wore. She sank onto the sofa and turned sideways. Jed held up a bottle of wine.

"Nightcap?" he asked.

"That's not funny."

"Mind if I do?"

"No, just don't bring it anywhere near me."

She rolled onto her back and closed her eyes. Her dressing gown spilled open at the top, revealing a black lace bra. She began to snore softly. Jed lent forward to open her gown, stopped and stepped back. He waved away the waft of vomit rising from the sleeping woman. "Alison Spedding," he whispered. "You're mad, bad and beautiful." He got a blanket from the bedroom, covered her and left.

CHAPTER SIXTEEN

The plane bumped and twisted on the final approach through cloud and rain. Passengers were jerked upwards and sideways, straining against their seatbelts. Jed hated flying and looked out of the window, hoping for sight of land. Beyond the smeared window there was nothing but grey swirling cloud.

A voice said, "Cabin crew, take your seats for landing." The lights of the cabin darkened. The crew sat in their seats, looking unconcerned. The cloud broke, and Jed could see an unending expanse of slate-grey water, wind chopped into white waves.

They were over the North Sea or a loch, it didn't really matter. The plane was descending fast. The water rose to meet them. They were never going to make the airport. Jed gripped the arms of his seat tightly, wishing he had bought an extra small bottle of wine from the steward.

He would have drunk it in one long gulp to dull the panic that rose and fell with every lurch of the plane. Then he felt sick and pulled a vomit bag from the seat in front. He put it back again. That would be too embarrassing. He fought the nausea down and prayed for a quick landing.

He looked at Alison beside him. She was asleep, or at least had her eyes closed. Her hands were folded loosely in her lap. She was impervious to their impending doom.

Two days ago she had been a junior member of a technical support team, and now she was free to go her own way and find a place in a new world to be herself again. That's what she had told him. She said she was going as far away from London, the office, Doxat, Morgan and you, Jed, as is possible in a few hours' flight.

He told her he was coming, too. "Just like that?" she had said. "You try and barge into my life just like that? You think I am a door that can be kicked open whenever you want? Do you?"

The harsh words flashed between them in the corridor outside their office. Staff hurried past, embarrassed, faces averted.

"I'm coming," he said, "because you need me and because I want to."

"So you always get what you want – is that right? Well hear this. I don't need you, any of you," she said.

"I'm coming," he repeated.

"You work here. You can't just walk out. Stay and slime your way into people's secrets like you always do. Ratface."

"Ratface?" he said. "Coming from a spoilt, up herself little madam, who loves nothing better than to take a cold bath in her own misery every morning, that's quite something."

She raised her hand. For a moment he thought she was going to hit him. But the gesture was more of anger than intent. They were both surprised. She dropped her hand and stepped back. The air hung heavily between them, an invisible cloud waiting to burst. He also stepped back, a small signal of regret for what he had said, waiting for her reaction: she would burst into tears, turn and walk away.

She did none of these things. She just looked at him with those cold grey-green eyes. Everything went quiet. If a spider had descended on a single gossamer thread and hung there between them, it would not have moved in the still silence.

"I'm sorry," he said, "I shouldn't have said that."

"You're not coming. That's final – get it?" she snapped and left.

Her farewell party, the nauseous cab ride home and Jed's vomit-splattered shoes had forced a change of heart.

They landed with a thump. Alison was awake. Jed had his eyes closed, white knuckles gripping the armrests. The pilot welcomed passengers to Inverness.

"We're here," she said, nudging him. Outside, a large sign read: *Inverness: Gateway to the Highlands of Scotland.*

This was as far from London as Jed had ever been. He was proud of being a Londoner. Wales was his heartland, but London was his homeland. He never had the slightest desire to live anywhere else or even travel outside the city. The very thought of green fields, cows, wooded hills and lakes bored him. On occasions when he had to travel to other cities by car or train, he worked on his laptop, read a book or closed his eyes without once looking out of the window. What others called the beautiful vistas of rural England, he termed "obscenery".

Jed's love of Wales did not include admiration for its mountains and valleys. The secret of his heartland lay hidden beneath those valleys, deep in the tunnels and galleries of the coal mines. Jed held that the heart and soul of his country could be found in those mines, not on the mountains.

Long before coal, there had been tin. The mines made men of the Welsh and had sent them into battle over centuries. The poetry, music and songs of the Welsh lay in the dark heart of the country, down in the fold of the valleys where streams ran black with the coal below.

As in Wales, so in London. Jed found beauty in the traffic-choked streets, the dark side-alleys, the uncollected rubbish piled in plastic sacks on pavements and the air thick with diesel fumes. The humming anthill of the capital, crammed with all that was best and worst in humanity appealed to some anarchic instinct within him.

These eccentric views did not endear Jed to his countrymen and found little favour with anyone else. It merely reinforced the opinion at Foxglove that Jed, or John Edwards to give him his full name, was a stranger in their midst and best avoided. Jed was content with the feelings he aroused in his colleagues. He enjoyed his status as an outsider.

Alison drove the hire car fast, while Jed slept beside her slumped back in his seat. She was pleased to see that he looked pale and ill, suffering the after-effects of plane sickness. She was going to open the eyes of this city boy with his weird views about "obscenery" to the glories of the Highlands. She jabbed him in the ribs.

"Put on your seatbelt and open your eyes."

They were passing a large loch that stretched through mountains until the ruffled water disappeared into the horizon. Pine forests climbed the hillsides. Beyond the tree line, the small brown shapes of antlered deer stood out from the purple heather. Sheep were scattered like confetti across the terrain.

"Where are we?" said Jed, looking around.

"Beautiful, isn't it?" she said.

"Erm... sure. Where are we going?"

"I told you, before you funked out on the plane."

Jed ran his hands over his unshaven face and fastened his seatbelt.

"Skye?"

"You got it."

"Why Skye? You got a boyfriend up there?"

"Shut up and look out of the window."

Jed wound the window down as if to see better.

"Don't even think of being sick," she said.

"I'm enjoying the fresh air. What are we going to do in Skye?"

"You're going to climb a mountain."

"Really?"

"Really. All the way up to the clouds."

"Supposing I don't want to climb a mountain?"

"You said you wanted to come. Remember?"

"I said I wanted to do birdwatching with you, not climb bloody mountains."

"Shut the fuck up, Jed, and do as you're told for once."

It was lunchtime when they checked into a hotel in the town of Portree, the capital of Skye. The weather was mild for October, but it would be cold on the mountain. The climb would take four hours both ways. It was not a high peak, in fact more hill than mountain, but it suited her purpose. They would be back before nightfall.

Alison made Jed buy mountain boots, a wool cap and a weatherproof jacket. He grumbled about the cost, saying he was only going to climb a mountain once in his life, so what was the point?

She packed a rucksack with sandwiches, bottles of water and her mobile phone. She gave the rucksack to Jed.

"Do I have to carry this?"

"Yes."

"But it's heavy…"

"… and the mountain is high, I know. I didn't ask you to come with me."

They walked around the bay of the sea loch that lapped the harbour of Portree and struck inland.

197

"Just follow me and don't look back," she said. "Never look back when you're on a climb."

An hour later they paused, well up the mountain. Jed sat down on the heather, breathless and sweating.

"Now you can. Look at that view," she said.

It wasn't the molten copper of the loch struck by morning sun, or the shapes of the seven mountains that reared around them that struck Jed. It was the colours of the wilderness that challenged his long-held view that scenic beauty could only be found in the mean streets of north London.

Shades of green, grey, blue, purple and orange glowed and dimmed as the clouds filtered the sunlight. He suddenly knew why people wanted to paint. To be able to translate the beauty of these mountains onto canvas with a few brilliant brushstrokes must make an artist feel magical.

"I could paint this," he said, without turning around. There was no answer. Alison had continued the climb.

They stopped on a patch of heather an hour later and ate their sandwiches. Jed was exhausted.

"Can I ask why we are doing this?"

"No, you can't. I've told you; I didn't ask you to come."

"So how much further are we going?" asked Jed, looking up. The mountain rose above them, the summit just visible through mist. He knew he wasn't going to make it to the top. "I think I will stay here and rest up," he said.

"OK. Give me a bottle of water."

He watched as she set off, apparently untired by the morning climb. He lay back against the rucksack and looked at his watch. Just after 2.00 pm. He closed his eyes. When he woke it was almost an hour later. He felt chilled. There was no sign of Alison. He focused his binoculars on the summit.

Shreds of mist obscured the view. It began to feel colder. The colours had vanished with the sun. Grey clouds, fat with the promise of rain, chugged across the sky. Below, the waters of the loch had turned to steel. He swept the mountain with the binoculars. There was no sign of anyone above or below. Most of the sheep had sought shelter down the mountain. Even a city boy realised there was a storm coming.

He got up, shouldered the rucksack and began carefully to walk down. She must have passed him while he was asleep and left him there. He smiled. Alison's little joke, a suitable punishment for his insistence on coming with her to this strange place where the mountains met the sky and the water flowed to an infinite sea beyond the horizon.

He had taken only a few steps when he stopped for one last look. He took his binoculars from the rucksack and swept them to and fro over the mountain, moving towards the summit. He did this without thinking and without any obvious reason. Perhaps a final look at the mountain would reassure him that she wasn't somewhere up there still, that she had not fallen again.

He was worried about her, which surprised him. It was strange that she chose to come back to this place. It obviously wasn't to watch birds. She had survived a terrible fall somewhere near here, a miracle, her friends had said. So why come back? This wasn't a birdwatching expedition, it was something else.

Had she come all this way to exorcise the nightmare of what had happened here? That didn't make sense. She should celebrate life, not obsess about near-death in the past. *There you have it*, thought Jed. The woman was obsessed, blindfolded in a dark room searching for the door. That gave him the answer to another question that he had been batting away like a persistent fly. He now knew what he was doing on this godforsaken mountain. He had come to look after this woman, rescue her from herself. She needed him.

The binoculars brought nothing into view except barren moorland, rock and gorse. He almost missed her when the huddled figure flashed briefly through the lenses. He tracked back slowly, adjusting the focus. There she was: right at the top, squatting on a gentle slope in front of a craggy rockface that led to the summit.

Mist briefly obscured the view then parted, showing Alison staring intently at the horizon. He shouted her name, but his voice was lost long before it reached her. He turned, slipped on the damp heather and fell, bouncing down the hillside with the rucksack beneath him acting as a sledge.

He slithered to a stop, breathless, cursing the mountain and his own stupidity. He wiped clean the binoculars and scanned the approach to the summit. She wasn't there. Alison knew these mountains well. She would find her own way back.

He put down the rucksack, thinking that she might need the biscuits and water on her descent. She had said there was only one way up and down. She would be thirsty and hungry by the time she reached this point in her descent.

It was 6.00 pm and getting dark by the time he got back to the hotel. He was tired, sweat-soaked and in need of a long hot bath and a large drink, although not necessarily in that order. He considered telling them that Alison was missing on the mountain but decided against it. She wasn't missing. She had come here for a reason. She was determined, resourceful and was doing exactly what she wanted to do. Jed had no idea what that was, but at least he knew why he had come with her.

They had small but comfortable adjoining rooms at the end of a first-floor corridor. Jed unlocked his door, went in and flung himself onto the bed. He wished he had picked up a large malt at the bar. He was too tired to go and get one. He doubted they had room service. He thought about Alison. It would take her a good hour or more to get back.

He sat up. Through the thin partition walls, he could hear the sound of sluicing water in full flow. Someone was having a shower next door, someone in Alison's room. He got off the bed, opened the door, stepped down the corridor and knocked on her door. She appeared in the doorway, wrapped in a towel with wet, stringy hair.

"What are you doing here?" he asked, realising at once what a stupid question it was.

"What does it look like? I was having a shower. How do you feel? You got back in one piece, I see."

"Yes, but how the hell did *you* get here?" he asked.

"I'll see you for a drink before supper downstairs. I won't be long. I'm famished." She closed the door.

Jed stripped, briefly dipped into the tepid water of an old clawfoot bath and changed into the only other clothes he had brought with him: black jeans, T-shirt and an old jersey. He wanted a drink, badly. His brain had stopped working.

She was sitting on a bar stool, studying the menu when he came down. She had one hand around a glass of amber liquid.

"Mussels," she said, "straight from the cleanest waters in the world."

"What are you drinking?" he asked.

"Large malt: Highland Park. Half and half with water. Better than most – none of that smoky taste."

Jed nodded to the barman.

"Same again – twice, please."

He drank the whisky neat in one long gulp and doubled up, coughing. The barman, from Poland as it turned out, was impressed. "Same again?" he asked.

"You are supposed to dilute it with water and sip it," she said.

"Thanks," he said, "now can I ask you a simple question?"

"No," she said, tossing the menu at him. "Order now. The restaurant's fully booked, and we have to give the table back in an hour."

For a small hotel, the food was surprisingly good with variations on steamed, fried or baked scallops, mussels, prawns and white fish, all fresh from the sea.

Jed ordered a bottle of red wine for both of them and waited. He thought the idea that you had to drink white wine with fish was just another middle-class, metropolitan, we-know-best fairy tale. Alison raised her glass to him and talked of the old myths that clung to the bleak hillsides and the many enjoyable if dubious stories about Bonnie Prince Charlie's escape to the island after the disaster of the '45 rebellion.

"'45?" said Jed.

"1745."

"Oh, I see, " he said, seeing nothing at all except the huge question looming over the meal. He expressed polite interest, but said little as Alison moved on to the problems of tourism on Skye where the local population resented everything about "furriners" except their money. Finally, as plates of aromatically tempting mussels arrived, Jed put down his wineglass and said, "How the hell did you get here before me?"

She looked at him and smiled.

"I left you on the mountain and you said there was only one way up and down," he said.

"Real mountaineers might take a different route, but you're right, there's only one way up and down for people like us," she said.

"So how did you get here so quickly?"

"Why do you want to know? I'm here, aren't I?"

"Come on, Alison. Help me out. Either I'm missing something or the whisky has addled my brains."

"Probably both," she said, prising open a mussel with her fingers and sucking it into her mouth with soft, slurping sounds. "These are great."

"Alison, what are we doing here? I don't understand."

She dropped a shell in the bowl and lifted herself in the chair, stretched back, then straightened up. She picked up another mussel and pointed it at him.

"Exactly. You don't understand. But I do. I know what I am doing here. You don't know, and you don't need to know. I got what I came for. That's all you need to know."

"None of this makes sense. You're holding out on me."

"For the third time, I didn't ask you to come. I came for a reason. You insisted on joining me. Why? What's your reason for being here?"

"Good bloody question."

They glared at each other. Alison remembered their corridor argument.

"Eat your mussels," she snapped.

They ate in silence. Jed poured more wine and looked around. The restaurant was filling up with a group of Chinese tourists. He marvelled at how these people flew across the world to a remote island off the Scottish coasts – to see what, exactly?

"What are they all doing here?" he said. "I mean, all the way from China just to say they've been to a Scottish island called Skye?"

Alison looked across the room at the crowd.

"The Chinese love legends. Their history is full of myth and magic. They believe, or perhaps they just want to believe, the stories around these mountains and lochs: the myth of a dragon-like monster deep in a Scottish loch; the myth of Bonnie Prince Charlie. Actually, that's not a myth because he certainly fled the English to take refuge here – over the sea to Skye, as the song says."

"Song?

"Sure. A ballad to celebrate a great escape from the hated English."

"You know the words?"

"Sure. Everyone does."

"Sing them then, the words, the song."

"Don't be silly."

"Go on, please."

She laughed and looked at him. What an odd couple they were. Jed, unwashed, unloved, a thief of the company's digital secrets. And she, a refugee on Skye like Bonne Prince Charlie. They both had buried secrets here. Prince Charlie's money, all gold coins, was said to be hidden somewhere in the mountains. Her secret lay in the mountains, too. There is magic in these mountains, the local people say, dark secrets of gods and fairies, giants and ghosts; that is what lures people from all over the world, to the mystery and magic of the Highlands and Islands.

"Please!" He was looking at her, his misshapen face arranged into a pleading expression. His nose looked more adrift than ever, as if it was about to break away from his face like a chunk of ice sliding off the Arctic shelf. A person you see every day in everyday clothes with an everyday smile, scowl or simpering grin can became someone else entirely in unfamiliar surroundings. That was Jed now, a lost soul in the Highlands, a stranger who happened to be sitting opposite her.

She suddenly felt sorry for him. He probably didn't realise how pathetic he was, living the lonely life of a London bachelor, eating takeaway food, occasionally taking rancid-smelling clothes to a laundrette, sitting at home most nights drinking beer, tapping away on the laptop and listening to his vinyl collection. He would have his song. She remained seated and sang, a clear soprano voice that cut through the babble of conversation and the clink of glasses.

Speed, bonnie boat, like a bird on the wing
Onward, the sailors cry;
Carry the lad that's born to be King
Over the sea to Skye.

The group of tourists were staring at her. They raised their cameras as one and began taking pictures. Jed stood up and bowed low to them. A battery of cameras flashed.

"They think we're part of some act laid on by the tourist board," he said. "Keep singing."

Alison sang, enjoying the hypnotic effect she was having on her audience.

Loud the winds howl, loud the waves roar,
Thunderclaps rend the air,
Baffled our foes stand by the shore,
Follow they will not dare.
Speed, bonnie boat, like a bird on the wing
Onward, the sailors cry;
Carry the lad that's born to be King
Over the sea to Skye.

The visiting Chinese clapped enthusiastically. An elderly woman from the group came over with a camera on a selfie stick, an accessory as essential for tourists as a guidebook. Alison posed obligingly and Jed followed suit. The Chinese tourists took more photographs. They were taking pictures of a member of their group taking a photo of herself with a complete stranger.

"This is weird," said Jed. "I bet they've been to Loch Ness and believe all that stuff."

"Many people believe in the Loch Ness monster," said Alison, "not just Chinese tourists."

"You might as well believe there's a man on the moon and fairies at the bottom of the garden."

"You don't think there's another world out there, that tells us we will one day be able to escape this planet?" Alison said.

She's serious, she believes this stuff, thought Jed. For the first time he noticed what she was wearing: a roll neck jersey with the collar of a white shirt peeping over the top; no jewellery except a bracelet of thin gold links. Her auburn hair, sleek and damp from the shower, was combed straight back. She had put on eyeshadow that highlighted her grey-green eyes.

Otherwise, her face was bare of make-up, the skin glowing from the climb and shower. Jed realised that the woman he had worked with for almost two years was very pretty. No. Pretty was the wrong word. The woman across the table eating her mussels with small sucking noises wasn't pretty. She was desirable. He remembered her lying asleep before him, dressing gown opened to reveal a pale body clad only in wispy underwear. The image flashed back with a quiver of lust. That was the word, he thought. Lust. The sexual attraction of this woman lay not just in that pale body but in the distance she put between herself and the world around her. Alison was desirable but distant, a mystery to him and probably to herself.

"How's work?" she asked.

"Something is going to happen in the office this week."

"I've left, remember?" she said.

"I thought you might be interested. New York's involved."

She was interested. When New York remembered that it owned a high-rolling ad agency in London which, given the extent of its other global operations, was not often, things tended to happen. But Jed was bargaining with her.

"You thought wrong," she said.

"OK, take it easy. What are we doing tomorrow?"

"We're going home."

"What, all this way just to climb a mountain?"

"Yup," she said, "and you didn't climb the mountain, I did."

CHAPTER SEVENTEEN

Kennedy Doxat looked at the framed photo of his father on the desk and wondered if he would approve. The old man loved his Shakespeare and had taken his son as a young boy to many performances at the National Theatre.

The boredom of listening to the archaic language of men and women dressed in ancient costumes for three hours never changed. If he had not been forced to watch hours of *King Lear*, *Hamlet*, *Macbeth* and all the other tragedies in the Shakespearean canon, it might have been different. As it was, like generations of schoolboys before him, he squirmed and fidgeted through hours of the school productions and the grand stagings at the National.

The one break in the tedium was when the knives and swords were drawn, screams and shouts echoed around the stage and groaning bodies stained with fake blood fell to the floor. Shakespeare well knew that a splash of gore on stage appealed to squirming schoolboys and illiterate groundlings alike.

Of all such scenes, the one in Julius Caesar where Brutus leads the assassins and is the first to plunge the knife into Caesar appealed most to the young Doxat. It wasn't the gush of blood as the knife went in, although that was a welcome relief after all the speech-making. It was the suspense of a well-planned conspiracy leading to the surprise of assassination.

Doxat liked to reflect on that moment. Power had blinded Caesar to the conspiracy. He had become a prisoner of his own vanity. He could not see old friends closing in on him. The traitors had planned carefully. The circle of power was tightening on the supreme leader at the centre. Caesar had forgotten the oldest rule in the game of power: fear those closest to you; it is always they who will wield the knife.

He looked at his watch. It was lunchtime in London. New York would be awake and at their desks in half an hour. One phone call from the Great Man would do it. It had been difficult to organise the meeting on his trip to New York. Indeed, it had not been easy to explain to Tamara Morgan and the boiled egg why he was going to America in the first place.

There were clients to meet, new business to explore, fresh contacts to be made, he said. Morgan had looked at him suspiciously. The Atlantic could be crossed in seconds on Skype, why the need for an expensive plane ticket and all the hotel, bar and restaurant bills that would follow?

Nothing beats personal contact, he had said. You can't pitch to a face on a screen, you can't look a prospective client in the eye on Skype and use charm to steer them towards a big contract.

"Especially if the client is a woman and a few cocktails are involved," said Morgan.

Touché, thought Doxat, adding the satisfying afterthought that this would be the last crack she would make at his expense. Realising that she had little choice, Morgan sanctioned the trip with the caveat that first-class travel was forbidden.

In New York, it turned out that the Great Man was busy and his staff were unwilling to make space in his diary. Perhaps he could see another executive in the pyramid of power at headquarters? Doxat was grateful for the offer, praised by name every other New York executive that he could think of, but politely said that the confidential nature of the business could only be discussed with the Great Man.

And what *was* the nature of the business? The question was posed by a woman with the title of chief strategy officer, a role in which, among many other duties, Doxat assumed she acted as the guardian of the Great Man's diary. As became clear, the woman had no desire to help Doxat, perhaps remembering his outlandish speech at that corporate conference on the West Coast.

Doxat refused to see anyone else, pressing his case for a personal interview. The strategy officer suggested none too kindly that he return to London and request an interview with the Great Man on one of his infrequent visits to Foxglove. He took a risk. From a chauffeur, he learned the approximate time the Great Man departed in the evening most days of the week. A carefully arranged chance meeting outside the office allowed him to talk his way into an appointment the following afternoon. The Great Man had looked at him, waved away his bodyguard, listened and nodded. He was given ten minutes and told he had better have something important to say.

In fact, the interview lasted fifteen minutes. The Great Man had shaken his hand politely and asked: "What's on your mind?" He had listened carefully as Doxat explained that behind good trading numbers from Foxglove lay a disaster waiting to happen. The foundations of the market were shifting. Foxglove and its CEO did not see the avalanche about to fall on them. Doxat had tried to warn of the impending disaster, but no one wanted to listen.

Clients were panicking. Traditional media companies, print and broadcast, were watching their advertising revenues drain away. Big high-street retail companies were cutting budgets and dithering over how to attract the huge youth market lost to social media and online shopping.

Doxat had been careful not to suggest any criticism of Tamara Morgan. He merely made it clear that he alone was aware of the dangers confronting the company.

It was the first time Doxat had met the Great Man alone, or virtually so since there was a lawyer present. It had been an unnerving experience. The Great Man had never taken his eyes off him. Occasionally, he turned to nod at the lawyer. At the end he asked no questions and dismissed Doxat saying, "You have done a fine job in London. I appreciate that. Thank you for your information. You are quite right. We need to look into this. It was good of you to come all this way. I will call London tomorrow."

Doxat returned, upgrading his ticket to first class and drinking champagne most of the way across the Atlantic. The following day, despite jetlag and a slight hangover, he spent the morning pacing back and forth across his office.

He measured the distance in footsteps. No question. Tamara Morgan's office was almost twice the size. His assistant brought in successive cups of coffee, asking every time with a worried look whether he was all right. He smiled at her. A nice woman, but middle-aged, blowsy and suburban. It would never do to have her sitting outside the CEO's office. He would need someone smarter, sharper, younger.

A third cup of coffee was cooling on his desk. He could hear his assistant taking calls at her station outside the office. For the first time in years he wanted a cigarette. The buzzer rang on his desk. Tamara Morgan would like to see him urgently.

He breathed a long, deep sigh, sat down for the first time and leant back. Now it would begin. Tamara Morgan had no doubt been thanked by the Great Man, complimented and promised lavish compensation. There would be an all-staff email and an announcement to the trade press. Staff would be invited to the main conference room for her tearful speech of farewell.

She would be out of the building within the hour. The legal negotiations would be long, bitter and expensive. Her successor would be announced before nightfall. There was only one candidate.

Doxat walked down the corridor to Morgan's office, reminding himself to show surprise and give no hint of triumphalism. Hubris would be a big mistake at this point. It would be an unpleasant meeting. She would be incandescent and seek to blame someone. But he was not in the firing line. His meeting in New York had been confidential. There were no fingerprints on the knife.

She would, of course, blame him, seeking somehow to entangle him in the mess. There would be a long harangue about his lack of team spirit, his constant indiscretions about the company and its trading figures. She would try and drag him down with her. Other executives would get the same treatment, but he would bear the brunt of the storm.

He would listen and make consoling noises. At the end of it all, she would have to explain that she was leaving the company. She would pretend it was her own decision. The fiction would be believed by no one, but it was a face-saving gesture. That would be very difficult for a woman who had fought for every step up the ladder of success. At least he would never have to endure another such meeting.

Morgan's personal assistant looked up with her usual stony expression and nodded him in. She would be gone by the morning. It was a pleasing thought. He didn't plan a bloodbath of his colleagues but small acts of vengeance for past slights would be highly satisfying. One or two faces would not be at their desks next week.

He didn't go into Morgan's office immediately but turned down the corridor to the executive washroom. He could feel the frown following him. He grimaced at his reflection in the mirror over the basin. The teeth were white and even, with a hint of gold in the back fillings. He ran his fingers through his hair to give it a ruffed look and pulled his shirt collar up over his jacket lapels. The white shirt looked good with the blue linen suit. The tan had faded, but he still had a good colour, that set off the strong features of his face nicely.

He splashed water on his face and dried off with a paper towel. He was ready for Morgan's storm-force tantrums. He walked back, nodded to the frowning stony face and entered the chief executive's office. She was sitting at her desk, looking pale but surprisingly calm.

She looked up. "Please sit down."

Doxat sat down. "Thank you. How are you?" he said.

"I am fine, thank you. But I have just had some bad news from New York."

"I'm sorry to hear that," he said. "When will the bastards learn to leave us alone?"

Morgan look at him sharply.

"We will have to handle this carefully with the staff."

"I will do everything I can to help."

There was a pause as Morgan toyed with her pen.

"I appreciate that. And I want you to know that, although our personal relations in the past have been…"

She paused.

"…complicated, I do not regard this as personal matter between us. I am acting purely as New York wishes."

Get on with it, thought Doxat. *The woman can't bring herself to say it out loud.*

"I quite understand," he said, "and I will do everything to ensure the smooth transition."

"Transition?" she said.

"Yes."

"So you know?"

Doxat kicked himself. He should have kept his mouth shut.

"There have been rumours of staff changes at the top. That's what I was referring to," he said.

"The rumours are right, for once."

She looked at him with a smile which could have been one of farewell or triumph. He wasn't sure. She certainly didn't look unhappy. A terrible doubt seeped into Doxat's mind.

She cleared her throat, sipped from a glass of water and said, "You have been relieved of your duties and dismissed with immediate effect. The HR director will see you after this meeting. You are then to clear your desk. You are to be out of the building by the end of the day. I know this is a shock, but equally I know that you have the character and talent to forge a new career elsewhere."

Doxat stared at her in disbelief, his brain befuddled by the enormity of what had been said. He had been fired. By this woman. Tamara Morgan. The Great Man must have called her last night. He had been betrayed. He rose from his chair.

"You can't do this!" he said, almost shouting.

"I just have done. The HR director is waiting."

"You can't fire me twice in six months. You'll be a laughing stock. How's it going to look to everyone out there?"

Doxat waved an arm at the window beyond which, he had no doubt, his many admirers, colleagues and clients would be waiting to express their outrage at his treatment.

"This was not my decision. It came straight from New York. How *was* your trip, by the way?"

There was no mistaking her smile now.

CHAPTER EIGHTEEN

They say that contemplation of infinity can drive a person mad. A logical mind cannot accept the rationale of time without end, because science holds that beginnings must have endings. "Forever" is not a concept known to science. "Nothing lasts forever" is a self-evident scientific truth.

Alison looked up the winged vertebrate hanging in the Natural History Museum in London. It was suspended from the high ceiling by almost invisible wires that lent the impression of flight to the skeleton of a pterodactyl, a creature that had once been a prehistoric bird.

She had come to the museum to discover approximately when and how birds had emerged from primaeval swamps to take wing. It was natural for anyone interested in birds to do this. That's what she told herself. Flight allowed these creatures to escape the many predators that roamed the planet at the time. To fly was to survive. Somehow, in the prehistoric swamp a small dinosaur had climbed a tree to find food or more probably to escape enemies.

Many millions of years later that creature developed the ability to fly. Dinosaurs grew feathers, became smaller and smaller as the old giants of their kind died out. The new branch of the family became winged creatures and learnt to fly. Dinosaurs became birds. They survived.

It was all there in in the museum guidebook. In other words, birds are the living relics of dinosaurs. That fact – not a possibility or a theory but an established, proven fact – left Alison in an electric trance. She shivered at the thought that a lumbering monster such as tyrannosaurus rex, a creature that haunted the nightmares of children and terrified cinemagoers, could be related to, indeed one day became, a hawk or a sparrow. It was just not believable. It was like infinity, an impossible thought that could drive one mad.

Mr Bonzo the school magician had opened his hands to reveal not a beaky little budgerigar but the descendant of a dinosaur. It was absurd. Yet there was the evidence in photos of dinosaur fossils, all clearly showing the winged structures of the beasts.

She looked up at the skeleton again. That crucial ability to fly enabled dinosaurs of the Jurassic period to embark on a steady evolution over 100 million years to become the birds that continue to amaze mankind.

The collection of bones hanging motionless above the craned necks of visitors, mostly groups of schoolchildren, contained the DNA of a dinosaur. What is more, those bones had flown as a bird many millions of years before man put in an appearance on Earth – at least that is what it said on the information sheet below the skeleton.

Alison examined laminated graphs on the walls tracing the development of winged creatures in simple timelines. Around her, chattering schoolchildren sucked sweets and lamented the temporary confiscation of their mobile phones. Teachers shushed them and bid them look up. Before their uncomprehending eyes lay the answer to one of the great secrets of world history, the secret of flight, a secret that had allowed the creatures of primaeval swamps to develop into both friend and enemy of man in their long journey through history.

She decided on lunch at a small café in South Kensington, where she ordered pumpkin soup and falafel cakes. The café was full yet quiet, except for the tapping of computer keyboards. People were staring at screens on every table. Some were forking food, or even spooning soup, clumsily into their mouths with one hand while thumbing text messages into their phones with the other.

She opened the phone, tapped in the code and watched as a series of text messages scrolled down. They were from Jed.

Your friend Doxat fired.

All over social media

Foxglove no comment to trade press

Where are you FFS?!

Jed and his little jokes. He really should stop behaving like a schoolboy. She flipped to the weather app and saw that it would rain later. She thought of her father and imagined his delight at her journey to the Jurassic age that morning. He would have clapped his hands and laughed in delight as she talked of the thrill of her discoveries.

"If you're that excited about the history of birds, think what Gödel must have felt when he proved the theory of time travel was mathematically possible. He must have felt he had been struck by lightning."

She could hear his voice. He would urge her to learn more, go further, investigate the geometry of flight and find out how birds lifted into the air with such ease. How did wings work? The mystery was evident every day in the skies over London. What kept those noisy metal tubes in the air? That's what he would say, but he wouldn't stop there.

Remember what all those experts said when Orville and Wilbur Wright claimed to have invented a machine that could fly? Her father would pose the question and then answer it. The experts laughed out loud. Man could never fly. Man could never stand on the moon. Man could never descend to the depths of the ocean and film the ghostly remains of the Titanic.

"Everyone who mattered, the great scientists and thinkers of their day, said these things were impossible," her father had told her. "They were the experts. Yet Orville and his brother Wilbur took to the skies in the first powered flight back in 1903. Nothing is impossible. Gödel knew that and you should too, my darling daughter."

She could hear him as clearly as if he was sitting beside her, looking askance at her healthy vegetarian lunch. She took a deep breath. Suddenly it all began to make sense, as if the pieces of a three-dimensional jigsaw puzzle were being assembled in front of her by unknown hands. Maybe, after all, there *was* an explanation for what had been happening to her since that fall from the mountain. The thought was clear, terrifying and yet joyous.

She steadied herself. She wanted a glass of wine, but the café did not serve alcohol. She raised her hand to attract a waitress and ordered a large Americano. "No milk, no sugar, as strong as you can make it," she said. She pushed the plates of food away.

If dinosaurs learnt to fly hundreds of millions of years ago was is not possible that sometime in the future man would learn to develop wings and fly as well? And if that was the case and if Gödel was right, surely man could return from the future blessed or cursed with the ability to fly? Or a woman. A woman with wings.

She drank her coffee. She wanted to talk to someone, someone sane, in the real world not the world of her wild thoughts and scary imagination. Not Jed. He would ridicule her and buy drinks and, in his charmingly clumsy way, then offer supper with the same old motive in mind. She would call Kath. Later. First she would go back to the museum.

Another text pinged in from Jed.

FFS call me everything kicking off here.

Her afternoon in the museum delivered the technical facts of flight in a way that was not easy for her to understand. Alison noticed that the school parties of children seemed to understand the graphs, audio talks and films which explained in scientific detail how large airplanes took off and remained airborne. There were also films of heavy waterfowl, especially geese, taking off from water, their webbed feet skittering across the surface until they lifted clear. The schoolchildren watched, bright-eyed with interest. They had all been in planes on long flights for holidays abroad. They, too, wanted to know how flight worked.

She left and called Kath. More than ever, she needed someone to talk to. It was early evening. The clocks had gone back the previous weekend and it was already dark outside. Kath agreed immediately, almost too eagerly, and suggested meeting in an hour's time at her club, a well-known haunt of artists, media folk and celebrity poseurs in Soho.

Alison was relieved. She needed a fix of the real world. Good red wine, a smart media bar and the seedy surrounds of Soho with its restaurants and cafés all jostling for space amid massage parlours and strip clubs. That should take her mind off feathered dinosaurs.

*

They sat on a sofa and ordered drinks. Kath watched as Alison took in the scene around her. A few famous faces were pretending not to notice they were being noticed, pretty young women wearing short cocktail dresses carried trays of drinks confidently through the crowd and a small man in a gold lamé jacket and flared jeans, with psychedelic earrings and a long ponytail that fell to his waist, leapt about randomly hugging and kissing men and women. No one seemed to mind.

"That's Bernie," said Kath. "He's the club manager."

"I am going to get drunk," said Alison. Her drinking was now out of hand – rather like her life. She was becoming an alcoholic, or perhaps she was one already. One drink was never enough and two led to four. *That's what stress does to you*, she said to herself. It was a great excuse.

"Good," said Kath. "You look as if you need to."

She leant over, gave Alison a tight hug and moved closer on the sofa. They drank more wine and nibbled nuts. The crowd around them thickened. Bernie swooped over them like an exotic bird, bent low to kiss their hands and vanished without a word.

"What's the most surprising thing that's ever happened to you?" asked Alison.

"Falling in love with another woman," said Kath.

"That wasn't a surprise, was it? I mean, you knew that…?"

"…that I was gay? Not really. I was young. My husband was as surprised as I was."

"But you were leaving him anyway."

"Yeah, it was mutual. He wanted out as much as I did."

"So?"

"The woman I fell in love with was, well…"

"Who?"

"His sister."

"You fell in love with your husband's sister? God, Kath! What drama – and tabloid hell if they ever found out."

"It was rather a surprise for all of us."

"You're telling me. What happened?"

"He called us a pair of dirty dykes and swore he wouldn't talk to either of us again. That was a bloody relief."

"Did it work out?"

221

"For a while. We were together for two years. She left me for an older woman."

A shadow passed over Kath's face and then she brightened.

"Why am I telling you all this? What about you?"

For a butterfly moment Alison was tempted to let it all out, to tell Kath the whole story, expose her fears and doubts to someone who she did not know that well but who might, for that very reason, offer unprejudiced advice and persuade her she was not going mad. She was certainly drunk enough to be that indiscreet. And Kath was drunk enough to understand.

"I found out today that dinosaurs grew feathers and learnt to fly," she said.

Kath leant back and laughed so loudly, an unattractive high-pitched cackle, that Bernie reappeared, the crowd parting like the Red Sea to let him through.

"Everything all right, my lovely ones?" he asked.

"Bernie, be a darling and get us some more wine."

Bernie sashayed off, swinging his hips and blowing kisses left and right.

Kath was still laughing. She leant over and gave Alison a long kiss on the cheek.

"You're hysterical" she said. "One minute you are up a mountain looking for eagles, and next it's dinosaurs."

Alison got up to leave. The atmosphere was claustrophobic and as usual she had drunk too much. Kath put a hand on her arm.

"I wasn't laughing *at* you. It was funny, that's all. Stay here. We will get something to eat. You need cheering up."

Bernie reappeared with the drinks.

"I heard that," he said. "We all need cheering up. What a bloody world."

He darted off again into the crowd. Alison put on her coat. Kath rose and gave her a long hug.

"There's something inside of you that needs to come out," she said. "You can't lock yourself away in a birdcage for ever. It's not a substitute for life or love. When did you last have a boyfriend?"

"I have enjoyed this evening, but I really must be going," said Alison, wondering how to work her way through the crush of bodies around her.

"For God's sake, Alison, live a little! You're so up yourself. Snort some coke, fuck a nice-looking stranger, lie on a beach in Barbados and read Proust while the sun goes down. Do something different!"

Kath was exasperated. Alison was flattered. This woman seemed to care for her. She bent down and gave Kath a quick peck on the cheek.

"Thanks, Kath. I'll do my best."

Kath caught her by the wrist and put a hand on the side of her head, drawing her closer.

"You could always start with me," she said.

Alison made to kiss her again on the cheek. Kath turned her head. Their lips touched lightly. Again, that bat squeak of desire. Alison straightened up.

"Remember, I'm always here," said Kath.

*

The bus back to north London was crowded but quiet. Electric whispers of rock and pop filtered through from cheap headphones. She felt hungry. Why hadn't she stayed and had supper with Kath? She would make an omelette when she got home. And have another glass of red wine.

She would talk to her father. He was just as real now as in life. She would not have to tell him anything, because he knew. He would tell her to stop worrying and go to sleep. "Get that pretty head down, Alibaba," he would say. She would dream drunken dreams of dinosaurs with wings.

Her phone rang, a musical jangle that pulled her from the reverie and went unnoticed on the bus. It was Jed. He never normally called, always texted.

"Why aren't you replying to my texts? Doxat's been fired."

"Oh, it's true is it? I'm not surprised."

"Is that all you can say?"

"What do you want me to say? Hip, hip, hurray? How's everyone taking it?"

"It's been rock and roll all day," Jed said. "He's gone. Out of sight. They fired his PA as well. Everyone's across the road getting plastered."

"I'm tired, it's late and I'm on a bus," she said. "Let's talk tomorrow."

"OK, blossom, but I think you're going to hear from him."

*

The kitchen the next morning was a disgrace. Eggshells, filthy plates and the remains of a bowl of muesli. She must have been hungry. She took two aspirin with a glass of apple juice well past its sell by date and sat down with a coffee. What to do next? She had no job, a large mortgage and very few friends she could call on. The payoff money Doxat had arranged would last for six months.

He was going to try and get in touch. That's what Jed had said. She might see him, if only out of vulgar curiosity. In human affairs there is no sight so pleasurable as the downfall of those in power, especially if you happen to have been a person in thrall to such power. There was another reason, but she did not like to admit it to herself.

She thought of going to see Dr Sampson again at her private practice. She at least knew something of her background. Sampson had diagnosed epileptic amnesia. But was that true, or even likely? Epilepsy isn't something that appears suddenly in adults. It can arise after a major operation. The long hours under anaesthetic can cause minor damage to the brain. She had found that out on the web. But she hadn't had an operation. The doctor would probably say she was suffering from depression. Maybe that was true. Trapped between two certainties, the possible and the impossible, wouldn't anyone be a little depressed?

She sipped her coffee and looked out at the small communal garden through rain-streaked windows. At least, they gave that impression even though it wasn't raining, their panes blurred by the filthy London air. She would organise a window cleaner and a cleaning lady. That would be a start to getting her life in order.

House sparrows were playing in the branches of a bay tree. They were a sight to lift the heart. Here were the great survivors of the avian world, tiny birds smaller than a man's fist who had spread from their native Europe all over the world. By the mid-nineteenth century, the size of the sparrow population in Europe forced the birds to migrate. They moved easily through the Middle East and across the land bridge into Asia and then on to China, flying overland all the way. The bird was too small to cross oceans, but somehow the sparrow established colonies in all the towns and cities of Australia and New Zealand, probably by hitching lifts on cargo boats.

Only one continent defeated the sparrow: America. The long distance over salt water, storms and headwinds, and the lack of any food made the flight over the Atlantic impossible – until man intervened.

That's why, when people asked her what bird she would choose to be, Alison always said a sparrow. It wasn't quite true, because her preference changed depending on mood and who she was talking to, but the answer was useful because she could explain it easily. The tiny sparrow had the courage of a lion.

The phone rang. It was Jed. She cut the call off. A second later a text pinged in.

You're running out of road, blossom. Put your head back on your shoulders.

He thought she was going to run away again. She had fled to the marshes of the Kent coast and then to the mountains of Skye, not once but twice. She had been running away for ever. And Jed was right. She would go on running. Like the sparrows who found themselves homeless in their own homeland, she needed space and time to settle somewhere else.

The sparrows finally made it to America. Trapped in baited cages in London, they were shipped to New York to fight a plague of moths. Then they themselves became the plague and a bounty was paid for every beak. Life's vicious circle.

Jed was wrong. She couldn't stop running. Kath had been right. She should escape, break out of a life that had become no more than an existence. The attraction of a long birdwatching trip maybe up to the Northumberland coast, there to seek sanctuary and, who knows, peace of mind, was obvious. It would be easy to arrange and guaranteed to place her among friendly, like-minded people with a shared passion.

But she couldn't. She had two lives to live, and there was no way to reconcile one with the other. There was herself in a milk-white skin that she soaped and rinsed in the shower every morning, clothed and fed throughout the day and lay wearily and sometimes drunkenly between the sheets at night. In that skin, she was just another of the billions on the planet breeding to extinction. That might take centuries, but it would come. Then the birds would be on their own again.

The other Alison Spedding was not a fictional character in a psyche-delic novel, not a Halloween phantom or even, as she had long hoped, a figment in a dream from which she would one day awaken. She was not dreaming. She had proved that on the Isle of Skye. Although he did not know it, Jed had been the witness. He could not understand how she had got from the mountain top to the hotel so quickly.

Alison knew perfectly well how that had happened. She had the ability to see round corners, as her school teacher had said. Jed would work it out, too. He had the slippery mathematical mind that could slither into cyberspace, unlock codes and passwords and steal secrets that could start world wars. During World War Two, a cataclysm that Hollywood often revisited to attract new generations to the cinema, Jed would have been a codebreaker at Bletchley Park, working alongside the genius of Alan Turing.

Turing suspected what Gödel later proved. There was a space in human existence where knowledge stopped and the impossible became real. That's how Turing had cracked the unbreakable code of the Enigma machine. That's how Gödel and Einstein had long ago solved another enigma that has puzzled man since he first struck fire from a flint: was he alone in the universe?

She had to tell someone. As Kath had said, she needed to let go, step out of the birdcage and reveal her secret to the wider world. Bonzo the magician had thrown the budgerigar into the air and watched it flutter away. She would do the same. She would tell Jed and do so quietly and convincingly. He would declare her to be in need of psychiatric care and would mutter abut witchcraft and madness.

If some of the greatest minds of the twentieth century believed in alien life and time travel, why could not Jed accept that she, Alison Spedding, had supernatural powers? Wasn't that what Doxat had called her – supernatural?

She would persuade him. He would believe her. He would shield her, help her find a new way. They would go somewhere by the sea – a small hotel. They would drink wine and talk. They would eat lobster and drink more wine. Jed would not believe her at first. His mind would wrap itself around her story like an octopus and squeeze out the real meaning.

In his endearingly clumsy way, he would flirt with her and then make the usual proposal. Unusually, and unlike previous occasions, the idea had a certain appeal. Maybe she would, maybe not. What had Kath said – live a little! But Kath wanted her, too. That had appeal. Maybe that's what she needed, unconditional carnal satisfaction or, as Kath would put it, great fucking. She would see how she felt at the time.

She made another coffee and tapped out a text to Jed.

Come to the coast with me. Couple of days. Straighten everything out, clear everything up.

The reply came within seconds.

No can do. Too much on at the office.

Liar, she thought.

Take time off. You can do easily. Brighton good.

Best you sort yourself out blossom. Just too much on here.

He was lying. He just didn't want to be with her. Scotland must have upset him. So much for friendship. She sent back one word.

Bollocks.

Seconds later, her mobile rang.

"Stop feeling sorry for yourself. You've become self-obsessed, self-pitying and a bloody bore. Get back into the real world."

"Self-pitying? How dare you! Look at yourself for a change. You're just a low-life eavesdropper getting off on other people's secrets." She was shouting at him now, screaming down the phone. "Get it? Now fuck off and leave me alone."

She began to clear the kitchen, hands shaking with anger. She wasn't feeling sorry for herself, quite the reverse. But Jed was her only real friend. He would not forgive her for talking to him like that. She looked at the garden. The sparrows had gone. She turned, hearing the rustle of an envelope being pushed through the letterbox. This was not the normal delivery time. The letter lay on the doormat addressed in swirly handwriting unknown to Alison.

She opened and read:

I helped you once. Please meet me.
Doxat

His mobile number was written below.

CHAPTER NINETEEN

They met in a small Chinese restaurant near Victoria station. It was Saturday on Halloween weekend and, in a meagre effort to adjust to the seasonal madness, candlelit pumpkins with cut-out teeth had been placed in the windows.

Doxat had changed. His usual linen suit hung more loosely on him. His face looked thinner and more lined. The stubble on his face was turning to grey. The year-round tan had faded. He smiled as he got to his feet.

"Thank you for coming."

She wasn't sure why she had. It was a step back into a world she had left behind. But she was curious. A great man fallen from on high wanted to see her. It was worth hearing what he had to say. He knew a lot about her, too much.

"How are you?" she asked.

"I'm fine," he said. "Tired but OK."

They sat down, picked up the menus and studied them silently.

"Do you want to know why she fired me?" he said, as ever straight to the point. *Good*, she thought, there will be no meandering preliminary conversation. She could get the lunch over with quickly.

A waiter appeared as he spoke. Alison ordered the dim sum selection.

"I'll have the same," said Doxat. The waiter left.

"Well, do you?"

She looked at him, the wounded pride and the eagerness to tell his side of the story written on his face.

"The grapevine has it that you went to New York to get her fired and she beat you to it."

"That's only half the story."

"But it's true, isn't it?"

Doxat ignored the question and signalled to a waiter. He ordered a glass of white wine.

"Would you like something?"

"No thanks."

"Mind if I do?

"No, go ahead."

"This is one of the best Chinese places in town, a little secret known to the few," he said.

Typical, she thought. The man had to know the best restaurants, the barman who mixed the best cocktails, the tailor who ran up the best linen suits; the best of everything for Kennedy Doxat, one-time purveyor of dreams to gullible clients and creator of his own fantastic image.

The staff had loved him, his colleagues had feared him. You had to admire the way he pulled that off. But not now. The image and the job had gone. He would get another senior position, of course, probably a big one with a multinational.

But the dishevelled figure opposite had lost more than a job. His pride had been hurt, his ego dented. He had enjoyed power over people, playing the executive game. And he'd lost. She could see it in his face and the way he gulped down the wine the moment the waiter set the glass on the table.

This wasn't the man who kissed her in the rain outside Wiltons. He was a good kisser, she remembered, kisses soft as silk and sweet as honey, as the old song said. That man thought he could do anything.

A waiter appeared and asked if they wished to order more drinks. She ordered jasmine tea and a glass of water. Doxat remained silent. He fiddled with his chopsticks, finished his glass of white and ordered another without asking her. He cast glances around the room, as if fearing he was being watched. He looked like a man who wanted to say something but did not know how to start.

"So, tell me, is it true? she asked.

"Is what true?"

"That you tried to get her fired."

"Sort of."

"I take that as a yes. And you said that's only half of the story?"

"I'd rather not talk about it."

"All right. In which case, can you tell me what I am doing here?"

"I told you, I need help."

"How do you think I can help?"

"It's hard to explain."

"Perhaps you'd better try."

"You might be surprised."

She leant forward. "Trust me, nothing in this life would surprise me anymore."

The seesaw of the conversation had come down on her side. She was going to keep it there. Doxat finished his wine and raised his glass for a refill.

"I think you have a secret."

"We all have secrets," she said.

The food arrived in little towers of wicker baskets. The waiter lifted the lids and began explaining what each one was. Doxat waved him away.

"You know what I am talking about," he said.

"I don't, actually. Let's eat."

She used her chopsticks inexpertly, fiddling pieces of dim sum onto her plate. The taste and texture were delicious, the best she could remember. He had been right about the restaurant.

"Let me try and explain."

"I wish you would. I want to know why you asked me here."

"You seem to belong to another world."

"That's it, is it? You think I'm an alien or a witch or something? You said that when you barged in on me in Scotland, you said that in that swanky restaurant and now you're saying it all over again. Can't you think of anything else to say?"

The only reason she didn't walk out was because the dim sum was delicious, and she was suddenly hungry. She fiddled more pieces onto her plate.

"I'm sorry," he said. "Look, we all love mysteries, don't we? Human existence is one big mystery. Don't you sometimes feel that?"

"Oh, sure. I get out of bed every morning and ask myself how the Big Bang brought me to north London."

"All right, I asked for that. So let me try again."

"Good, but can you get to the point? I still don't know what I'm doing here."

"To me, you are a beautiful mystery."

"Is that all? I'm just a mystery to you. Maybe I'm a mystery to myself – so what?"

"You are a very special woman. There is something magical about you, mysterious, something hidden. It is not just that you are completely your own person or that I find you attractive."

That was the trouble. Even in his somewhat shabby, hollowed-out state there was a magnetism about the man. Shamefully, she found him attractive. She remembered the kiss.

"You seem to know more about me than I do myself."

"I'm not saying anything to you that you haven't said to yourself."

"How would you know? Tell me what happened. Why did she fire you?"

"Later."

"No, not later. Now!"

She rapped her chopsticks on the table. Doxat flinched slightly but said nothing. They finished the dim sum. He arranged the wicker baskets into a wobbly tower. A waiter came and cleared them away. She still felt hungry and poured more tea from a small iron pot. What did this man really want? As if intuiting her thoughts, he said, "I want to spend time with you. When I kissed you that day I felt something I had never felt before."

"Mr Doxat."

"Ken, please."

"Ken, I don't believe a word of this. You don't need help. You're using a silly kiss in the rain to persuade me that I have feelings for you. Well, I don't."

"But you don't know me. I want to show you who I really am."

She picked up her handbag, slung it over her shoulder and pushed the chair back.

"This is crazy, Ken. Listen to yourself. You're not making sense."

"What did you come here for?" he asked. "Curiosity? To gloat? To find out why I got fired – something to tell your friends in the office?"

She suddenly felt sorry for him. He seemed desperate, a man who once thirsted for praise now invoked pity. She leant forward and softened her voice.

"Of course I would like to know what happened. Everyone would."

"OK, but let me just say this."

"I don't want a speech, Ken."

"Don't worry, only a few words, and they won't bite. They're nice words; you can wrap them up and take them home with you."

"Or I can forget them."

"As you wish. You're on your own and so am I."

"I'm not on my own."

"I think you have something inside you that you cannot live with, that you want to share. I think you desperately need a way out of where you are."

"And what is this way out that I so desperately need?" She hoped sarcasm would bring the man to his senses.

"You need sanctuary…"

"Sanctuary?"

"Yes, someone to look after you, love you. Ahh! There's a word for you, Alison: love."

"Thank you." It was all she could think of to say. No man had ever spoken to her like that. She felt both flattered and repulsed at the same time. She got up.

"You keep running away, Alison. Sit down. Don't you want to hear the real reason she fired me?"

Get out of here, said a voice inside her. *The man is unstable. Go now. Get the bus. Move.* Doxat drank his third – or was it fourth – glass of wine in a long gulp and bent forward with a spluttering cough. She said nothing and waited.

"It was a long time ago," he said.

"What was?"

He stood up and threw some notes on the table.

"A mistake. A bad one. I should have known better." He turned and walked to the door. She pulled her chair back from the table but remained seated. He opened the door.

"Whose mistake?" she asked.

"Her mistake, my mistake. A man and a woman on different planets. It's an old story."

Doxat turned with his hand on the handle of the door and looked at her with the slight frown of someone waiting for a question. The man never changed, she thought, always demanding attention, posing as if he had something important to impart. He clearly wanted to tell her about whatever it was that had caused such a rift with his boss. She was curious. She wanted to hear it.

"Come and sit down. Tell me about it."

Doxat pulled the door open.

"No," he said, "I didn't behave well. It doesn't matter anymore."

"You mean you had an affair with her?"

"That was the problem. I didn't."

Doxat turned and walked off down the street.

CHAPTER TWENTY

Everyone has a favourite bus in London and for Alison it was the number 24, which lumbered its way from Pimlico, sandwiched between the Thames and Victoria station, through the West End and up to the heights of Hampstead. She always climbed to the top deck. The view was better and so was the air, especially when they left the traffic-choked streets of the city centre. Bus travel gave one time to think, slower by far than the sardine experience of the tube but a more reflective way to cross the city.

Doxat had been his usual maddening, provocative self, strewing behind him questions but no answers, yet cutting close enough to a disturbing truth. In his strange way he had said he loved her, hadn't he? Declarations of love, unrequited and uncalled for, are always an embarrassment, although not always unwelcome.

What had he said? What had he meant? Did he know or was he guessing? And then that strange admission, if it was an admission, of what? An affair, a casual fling, a promise made and betrayed. How could that account for such poison between two people?

Passengers got on and off at every stop. The young and fit coming upstairs, swaying and clinging on, while the old stayed down below. Children wearing hideous Halloween masks and costumes stamped with spiders and horned devils rushed to the back of the top deck. Downstairs, arguments broke out as mothers with babies in buggies tried to get on only to be told there was no room in the designated area.

"Driver! I've been waiting here for twenty minutes!"

"Sorry, love. There's another bus in ten. I've got my orders. Health and safety," said the driver.

"Get on with it," someone shouted to the driver.

London life in the raw replaced the lunchtime fantasies of a man with a broken ego. More than ever she wanted to get away, to put Doxat out of her mind. She wanted to go somewhere, anywhere. OK, she was running away again. Keep on running, said the old song. That was her all right. So what? Might she not find a way out of the maze in which was lost? But running to where?

Long hours in a hide, chilled to the bone and wondering whether to risk a pee behind a nearby bush while waiting for a female ruff to appear over the mudflats, did not appeal this time. She needed warmth and comfort: a long, hot, steamy bath with music, Beethoven's *Moonlight Sonata* for preference.

She would go to Brighton. It was close, only an hour on the train and beside the sea. She would go on her own without the pestilential Jed. He would only start lecturing her again. She didn't need that. There she would walk the seafront, breath the salt air, browse the antique shops, buy some new shoes and eat fish and chips.

She rebuked herself. Maybe Doxat was right. Maybe she wasn't running anywhere but just going around in circles. What was she afraid of? Why was she always on the move to somewhere else, destination unknown?

She was a woman with a shadow she could not shake off. Even at night, the shadow deepened the darkness around her. Someone in an old mythical story had sold their shadow to the devil for money in this world. The price was hell in the next life. She would take that deadly bargain. Anything to find a sanctuary from what she now knew. Doxat had been right. That was what she was looking for, sanctuary.

In Scotland, on that mountain, she had found the answer. There had been no memory loss, no blurred blackout from an epileptic fit. She had been confronted with, or rather had confronted herself with, a truth as hard and as cold as the granite peaks of the mountains in Skye.

She had wings. She could fly.

What would her father say if she had quietly explained this to him? She would make him tea and sit with him in the warmth of the sitting room. He would wait patiently, watching her with eyes bright as buttons while she sought the right words. The much-loved face, whose cheeks she had kissed a thousand times, would crease and lift in surprise. But he would say nothing. He would allow her to finish. She would say a final few words.

"Dad, you taught me to believe that the impossible was possible and you held up Gödel as an example of a man who not only believed that but proved it. Well, I have proved it, too."

He would say, "I have always told you to go your own way. Listen to those around you, of course, mark their advice, test it against your own knowledge, but above all trust your own instincts. You will know best what to do and where to go in life. Your own way, that's where you go."

That's why she was going to Brighton. She would go home, pack and take the next train to the coast. She would stay in a small hotel, a comfortable B&B, anywhere where she could be quiet and alone with her shadow. She would make sure Jed could not follow her. He would if he could, she knew that, despite what he'd said.

He would walk out of the office, tossing some excuse over his shoulder about a sick mother, and catch a train that night. No one would challenge him. He knew too much. Jed loved the stuff of other people's lives.

He pretended to be a cynic, affecting a world-weary view of the frailty of mankind. The real Jed was different and more appealing, a little boy lost, looking for something he could neither describe nor understand.

She turned her mobile phone off. He had told her once that he could track people's whereabouts via their phone.

"They don't have to make a call," he told her. "As long as their phone is on, I know exactly where they are. It still gives out a signal thirty-six hours after it's turned off. The police and the intel use that technology a lot."

*

She walked the boards of Brighton pier. Halloween had followed her here. The fake autumnal festival – dreamt up by marketing men to sell trash to parents and kids who should know better – was evident on every street. The sun was doing its best to throw glowing colours through a veil of dark clouds. It was getting dark, and the pier was full of shrieking children running around with luminous masks and other ghostly paraphernalia.

Doxat was right. She did have a secret. They both had secrets, his of a sexual collision with Tamara Morgan when both were much younger and powering their way up the ladder of success. It was obvious, when she thought about it. Lust and drink had taken them into a bedroom. Each wanted to control the other. She wanted a brief affair before she threw him aside. He had stripped her of more than her clothes and walked away. Her bruised feelings had turned to bitterness and bitterness to hatred. There were many worse secrets than that.

Her own secret was unbearable. It made her a monster; perhaps that's what she was, one of the masked myriads running around her with painted faces and black capes. She was a black magic woman possessed of the devil, gifted with an ability to spread her wings and fly.

She had known that since she and Jed came back from Scotland. The singular truth had been padding around in the back of her head like a kitten mewing for attention. How good we are, she thought, at keeping the unpalatable, the unreasonable and the painful locked away in an attic where kittens may mew and memories may bang on the door without being heard.

She needed a drink. It was cold, always a good excuse. Three blocks away she could see the Grand Hotel, famous or infamous for the bomb that almost killed Margaret Thatcher. There would be a cocktail bar lined with shelves of every known whisky in the world, a formally-dressed barman and an elderly crowd sipping sherry and white wine.

In a side street she saw a welcoming string of lights over a sign saying *Bar*. She walked in, squeezed to the counter through a throng of drinkers and ordered a glass of pinot noir. A young woman wearing a tight, cut-off T-shirt, with tattooed snakes climbing up her arms and rings in both her ears and her nose, looked puzzled.

"Pino what?"

"Noir. Pinot Noir."

The woman shook her head, turned and took an open bottle from the counter behind her. She poured a glass and pushed it towards Alison.

"House red," she said and moved down the bar.

Alison sipped the drink. It tasted like cough mixture. She pushed the glass away and left. She realised she had not paid for the drink. Good.

She walked to the Grand Hotel and sat on a stool in the cocktail bar. It was exactly as she had imagined it, except the drinkers were mostly younger than she had expected. The pinot noir was smooth and soothing. It was the only way to contemplate the impossible.

"Look life square in the face," her father had said, another of his many homilies that she had written down in a long lost notebook. How could she look life in the face? Her life didn't exist. She was a creature of someone else's imagination, a winged woman flying high in someone else's dream. Perhaps when they woke up she could come back to earth and find her real self again.

"Another one, madam?"

She nodded to the young barman and pushed her glass towards him. A middle-aged man with dyed brown hair and an expensive suit sat down on the stool beside her. He pretended not to notice her at first, then gave her a sideways glance.

"The lady is waiting for someone," said the barman, placing a glass of wine in front of her. "That's his seat."

The man eased off the stool, smiled at her and walked away.

"Thank you," she said. She wished she was waiting for someone. She sipped the wine, held the glass to the light, admired the rich red velvet colour and drank some more. She did not mind being alone, she never had. Her life had not been crowded with friends, family and children. It had been a contented existence, undimmed by any sense of loss or loneliness.

If the pleasures of her life, the joy of watching birds, the satisfaction of office work, drinking wine with an occasional friend, if these added up to happiness, then she was or had been happy.

But that had been taken away from her. Gödel always said that proving the truth of time travel brought him nothing but sorrow and despair. It wasn't that fellow mathematicians and logicians mocked him. They took care not to do so at first, because the great Einstein supported Gödel's work – or at least he acknowledged the purity of the logic behind it.

Gödel found he was unable to live with his discovery. His magnificent theory with its mathematically unassailable conclusion collided with reality. If you can go back in time, you can kill your own father, a growing band of critics pointed out. Gödel dismissed this as trivial. It simply wouldn't happen, he said. But the argument went on. If the secret of time travel lay in outer space, as Gödel insisted, how does anyone get there?

The Americans may have put a man on the moon, but those astronauts did not find on that silver orb a celestial chariot waiting to take them back in time to any of the great events that shaped their nation. That's what his critics said. Mocked, and abandoned by Einstein, Gödel chose the strangest way to die.

Right now in this bar with good wine to drink and a protective barman keeping an eye on her, it would have been nice to turn to someone beside her, Kath perhaps, or even Jed. She wanted to talk to someone, to share her secret and to persuade them she was not mad.

They would not believe her. Kath would say she needed to see a psychiatrist. She would write down the number of someone who knew someone who knew a good man in Harley Street. Jed would simply say, "Prove it, Ali. Go on, take wing and fly out of the door. Show us."

She would plead with them: 'I can't cope with this. I am at the end of my tether."

Jed would put his arm around her and say she was suffering emotional trauma after the death of her father. Kath would ask her to come and stay and repeat her suggestion of a psychiatrist.

Neither would understand the vortex into which she had fallen, a whirlpool that was dragging her down. No one in this world can hold the key to another world and survive. Gödel knew that. He struggled for years to reconcile what he knew to be true with what the world of science and physics always denied. No wonder the poor man starved himself to death.

CHAPTER TWENTY-ONE

The Last Post hotel described itself as an old-fashioned coaching inn but was more popularly known as the last resort for those seeking a bed in Brighton for the night. Faded carpets, peeling paint and wallpaper stained with damp told their own story.

She chose it because it was on the seafront, at the edge of town. There was another reason. Bookings were taken by telephone and written by hand in a ledger. Payment was by cash or cheque. The Last Post spurned the digital age, preferring to look back to the time when horse-drawn stagecoaches bound for London did indeed stop to pick up passengers. In the lobby, there was a large oil painting of just such a coach, its occupants huddled up in rugs on top while others peered from the window below. This preference for the past suited Alison. No one would find her here.

Her bedroom was small with just enough room for a single bed, a wardrobe whose door would not close properly and a desk by the window. The bathroom squeezed in a basin, a bath with rust-coloured stains beneath the taps and a lavatory with a long chain to the cistern.

She put her suitcase on the floor and unpacked it only to take out her binoculars. These she put on the desk. Pointless, she knew, but it added to the sense of order. She never travelled anywhere without them. She opened a bottle of cheap red wine bought from a local supermarket and placed it on the desk with the cork neatly alongside. A ballpoint pen, a spiral notebook and a small enamel box lay beside the wine, neatly lined up side by side.

In the bathroom, she found a plastic mug encrusted with old toothpaste. She washed it out as best she could, filled it to the brim with wine and placed it beside the bottle. The residue of toothpaste would probably improve the wine. She smiled at the thought.

These arrangements pleased her. Order and tidiness in the room allowed her to think clearly. Although it was a chilly night, she opened the window and leant out. A light wind blew a salt tang in from the sea. She breathed in deeply. There was rain in the wind and whispers of sailors and shipwrecks long since lost out there in the darkness.

She closed the window and drank the whole mug of wine. The faint hint of toothpaste did indeed make for an interesting taste. She sat down at the desk and looked out. The street lamps along the front threw a shadowy light on the waves rolling in from nowhere. There was something comforting in their sibilant sigh, the sound of childhood holidays by the sea, memories of sandcastles, candy floss and her parents paddling in the shallows or asleep in deckchairs.

Her mind wandered amid such happy memories, a walk in a field of wildflowers. She thought again of her father. He lay not in a cemetery mouldering to fleshless bones under a headstone, but as dust in a box in her mother's bedroom. The trouble with the dead is they do not go away. They intrude on your thoughts and dreams and stare out, often accusingly, from worn photo albums or images on iPhones. He would surely understand. He would recite a poem as he often did when she was a child, holding her on his knee and whispering:

When you are old and grey and full of sleep,
And nodding by the fire, take down this book,
And slowly read and dream of the soft look
Your eyes had once, and of their shadows deep;

How many loved your moments of glad grace,
And loved your beauty with love false or true,
But one man loved the pilgrim soul in you,
And loved the sorrows of your changing face;

It was his favourite poem. He never read her the last verse, because he said it was too sad for a young child. When older, she looked it up and learnt it by heart. Now she couldn't remember it. She sat down on the bed and began to cry. Rain pattered on the window. The street lights were blurred with her tears. She must be drunk. How could she forget? Then it came to her:

And bending down beside the glowing bars
Murmur, a little sadly, how love fled
And paced upon the mountains overhead
And hid his face amid a crowd of stars.

She repeated what she had said to herself many times that day. She was going to travel into the darkness of deep space where time was multi-dimensional. Here on Earth man has forever believed that time travels in a straight line from the Big Bang to the modern age. Gödel pointed out the absurdity of this concept. In space, time bends backwards and forwards. Somewhere out there would be proof that he was right. Even those eminent scientists who poured scorn on his theory of time travel recognised the mathematical certainty of alien life in a distant galaxy.

She had twenty minutes, maybe a few more. She had worked it out carefully. She opened the enamel box and took out two pills. She swallowed them with a quick gulp of red wine. She opened the notebook, picked up her pen, smoothed the first page and began to write.

To whom it may concern, she wrote and then she crossed it out.

To my darling father, who I know will read this, and to my Mother, Jed and Kath,

I want you to join me in the next few minutes of my life because they will be my last. I write this looking out to sea through the window of a small hotel. It is night-time. I find the sound of the waves as they foam onto the shingle very peaceful. And I am at peace. I want you to know that. I have taken this decision carefully and consciously.

It is now 10.00 pm. I have taken two pills and will take two more in five minutes. Fifteen minutes after that I will lie down on the bed and drift into unconsciousness. This gives me time to finish this letter and say goodbye.

I want you to take comfort from one simple fact: This is not an end for me – it is a beginning. I am bound for a different destination than death as we think of it. I don't just believe that. I know it to be the truth.

You will think me deranged, I know, and I fear that the coroner's verdict will be suicide while the balance of the mind was impaired. For the record, Mr Coroner, the balance of my mind is fine. But I digress.

Ask Tim and Xanthe, the friends who witnessed my fall from the mountain; ask that difficult, charming, talented and ultimately very sad man, Kennedy Doxat, what

*happened in San Sebastian; ask Jed about our stay on Skye –
they will all tell you the same story. They denied to themselves the logic of what they saw with their own eyes. Those
eyes were my witnesses.*

*I don't blame them. No rational human being can accept
that there are dimensions to life on this planet that defy reason,
logic and comprehension.*

*So bury me, stand over my grave and weep, allow the staff
newspaper to remember me kindly, but look up at the sky at
night, look beyond the moon and stars, look further into other
distant galaxies and further still, and take comfort from my
presence somewhere out there.*

*I know that sounds like the mawkish sentiments of those who
believe in ghosts, fairies and Santa Claus. I don't believe in any
of these things. But I do believe that there are forces we only
dimly understand in space which bend time backwards and
forwards – and sideways for all I know.*

*Once you look into deep space, you have to suspend belief in
the natural laws that govern life on earth. We believe in gravity –
there is no gravity in space. We believe in time as a single thread
that unreels from the past behind us into the future before us –
there is no measure of time in space. We believe in the sun and
moon, light and dark, but these do not exist in deep space.*

*Forgive me. I hope I am not boring you with these last thoughts.
As a deathbed confession they are perhaps a little too complicated.*

*By confession I mean that I confess what I have long hidden
from myself and thus from you. I am a woman with wings. I
can fly. I have no idea why or how this happened to me. I do
know that 150 million years ago – an unimaginable amount*

of time – small dinosaurs developed wings and thus began the evolution into birds. Sometime in the future, mankind will do the same thing and for the same reason – to escape. And that is my point: I believe I am in some strange way already in the future – I have long since left you. Gödel was right. That poor misunderstood man.

I feel the pull of the pills and am becoming sleepy. My handwriting is beginning to wobble. I hope you can read these very final words. Another glass of wine might steady me.

Lastly, and I promise you these really are my last words, because I feel my mind is closing down, I never believed there was any truth in love. I thought it a myth created long ago to tempt us into believing we could be happy. I have never been in love in my life nor have I ever reached that joyous state of mind that people call happiness.

But I am happy now. I have found love. I love you all.

Goodbye

Alis…

CHAPTER TWENTY-TWO

The first slap made a noise like a heavy door slamming. She only felt the stinging pain later. Head-swinging slaps followed and then the shock of cold water thrown hard into her face. A voice was shouting at her, screaming her name. There was a crash and a bump, and she was on the floor, at least that was where she vaguely thought she must be. The floor was cold: tiled, bathroom tiles, and then her head was pushed down into something hard and white. She smelt shit and disinfectant.

She began to open her eyes. All she could see was a hard white blur. She heard the clanking of a chain. More water surged into her face. The voice had put her head into the bowl of a lavatory and pulled the chain. She was sick, a great spout of vomit splashing the porcelain. There was a jerk and a flash of pain as she was pulled out of the bowl by her hair. The shouting grew louder, always her name, and then more slapping.

She wanted to go to sleep. This must be a nightmare. But the pain was too great; her face felt on fire, fingers were shoved down her throat and she was sick again all over the tiled floor or the porcelain of the lavatory, she couldn't tell which. Her stomach ached from vomit heaving.

Her clothes were coming off. The voice was ripping off her dress and blouse. She fought back, flailing at the attacker, flapping her arms at

250

him. A towel came from nowhere and was wound around her. She was rolled over and laid face down, her vomit-smeared face pressed into the floor. The voice was pressing down on her back, she coughed and drew in rasping breaths like the sound of a creaky door opening on rusty hinges.

Suddenly she was staggering around a room holding onto someone who had his arms tight around her waist. The walls swam back and forth. Everything was blurred. Her legs buckled. She had to sit down. She had to think. What was happening to her? Where was she? Someone held her up. Someone with a voice, shouting at her.

"Walk! Walk! Keep walking!" She began to see where she was, a room she vaguely recognised. She looked at the voice. The face was familiar.

"Let me sit down. Please!"

"NO!" shouted the voice. She was pushed towards the window and half-pushed out of it, her head hanging over the sill, the sea wind strong and salty in her face. Nothing ever smelt as good as the sea. She was dragged back and made to walk again on buckling legs. The voice slapped her backside hard and told her to straighten up.

"Stand up straight, you bloody fool," shouted the voice. Someone slapped her all over: face, backside, knees, everywhere. The towel was falling off her. The voice didn't care and kept her walking. Who was the bastard voice? She wanted to know. But more, much more, she wanted to lie down again and go to sleep. She was terribly tired. She looked at the voice, her brain clearing and eyes beginning to focus. Jed. John Edwards with vomit over his clothes.

He pushed her onto the chair by the desk. Her head sank forward. There was a long hand-written sheet of white paper in front of her. The letter. The letter she had written to say goodbye. She had not died. She was here in this room with John Edwards. She was naked. Where was the towel? How the hell did he get here?

She sat up slowly and watched Jed going to the bathroom with the mug. The mug from which she had drunk the wine that tasted of toothpaste when she was taking the pills. He handed her the mug, thrusting it at her face. She took it with shaking hands and drank thirstily. "More," she said, "give me more."

She drank more and was sick again, this time out of the window. Jed swore and gave her the towel. She held it against herself with one hand and ran the other through her hair. It felt like long strands of seaweed. She must look like a corpse washed up by the sea. She had seen one as a child, a blurred creature lying face down on the pebbles, fully clothed except for shoes. Never mind him. Concentrate. The whole room stank.

"We're leaving," he said. He put her a coat around her shoulders and opened the door.

"I can't go out like this."

"You can't go out in a towel either. I'll pay them for this mess. Let's go."

Sometime later that night – she had lost all track of time – she found herself in a hot bath. The water was steamy and smelt good. She craned her neck as the door opened. Jed came in, sat on the lavatory seat and looked at her. She was embarrassed and sank deeper into the water.

"Where are we?" she said.

"A nice hotel. Four star. I had to tell them quite a story to get a room. Said we'd been in a car crash."

"A hotel room?"

"Yes, last one left."

"I'm all right now," she said.

"No, you're not. You know what happened, don't you? What you did?"

She waved an arm at him. "Later," she said. "Leave me alone."

"There's a dressing gown on the door," he said "If you want to throw yourself out of the window, go ahead. I won't be there to catch you."

CHAPTER TWENTY-THREE

She woke up in a strange bed and swung her legs to the floor. She was in her underwear. Good. She thought back, trying to put the pieces together. She knew what had happened in that ghastly hotel, but everything after that was as if seen through a thick fog. He had wrapped her in a towel, put on her coat and taken her to this hotel, wherever it was. She had had a bath. Jed had come into the bathroom while she was soaking away the nightmare of the night – not so good. Now he was sleeping on the floor, wrapped in an eiderdown, his head resting on a neat pile of clothes.

He had saved her life, making her walk around that horrible room with vomit everywhere. How the hell had he found her? How could he have found her? It just wasn't possible. She had been so careful. And how did she know she wanted to be saved? Did she want to be saved?

Her stomach felt as if someone had punched her hard. She felt empty. She looked at her watch. It was early morning, 7.30 am. Jed was sleeping on the floor. Elusive thoughts rippled through her mind, the silver flash of a fish in a river. She felt hungry, she needed clothes. How the hell had Jed found her? The question wouldn't go away. She should have been dead by now. Should? Is that what she had really wanted? Right now she was glad she was alive. She needed breakfast. She sat down on a chair and began to shake. It was all too much. An arm slid round her shoulders and pressed her close.

"How are you feeling?" asked Jed.

"Bloody awful. I have been such a fool. How did you find me?"

"First things first. You need some clothes. There's nothing in your suitcase. There's a charity shop around the corner. Then breakfast."

They walked along the seafront, she wearing baggy jeans and an outsize jersey below her coat. Jed held her firmly, his arm around her waist. It was sunny but not warm. She felt a stranger in a strange land, but no one looked at her. They went into a seafront café and sat at a table by the window. Jed said not a word to her. A waitress appeared, pen and pad poised. He ordered a full English breakfast and asked the waitress what it entailed.

"Double fried eggs, bacon, sausage, black pudding, tomatoes and baked beans," she said. "Ketchup and brown sauce?"

Alison felt sick again. She looked at the back of the room and saw a sign saying *toilet*.

"What would you like, love?" asked the waitress.

Good question, thought Alison. She felt weak and shivery.

"Hot chocolate, please."

The food arrived, wafting a smell of fried fat over the table. Jed began to eat. He was hungry and looked tired. She felt a pang of guilt. The poor man had slept on the floor. He was waiting patiently for her to say something, to explain herself. The attempt to take her life. That is what she had done. There was no explanation that he would understand. It was too crowded to talk. The windows were steamed up. She traced a heart in the steam.

"It's for you," she said.

The café emptied as Jed drank a third cup of black coffee.

"Do you want to talk about it?" he asked.

"Not really. How on earth did you find me?"

He smiled into his coffee. "You really want to know?"

"Yes."

"Well, how about a thank you first?"

"Sorry. I'm being very rude. My head is still back there somewhere. Of course, I thank you. With all my heart, I thank you."

She pointed to the heart on the window pane and drew an arrow through it.

"You saved my life. That's just amazing. And obviously I'm just well… erm… deeply grateful. But please tell me how you knew where I was."

"You hid yourself away very well, didn't you? You were hard to find. You really meant to kill yourself, didn't you? Bloody fool."

"I don't want a lecture, Jed. Just tell me."

She could see he was going to enjoy this. Here was a techno-digital wizard about to show that, in the cyber age, there is nowhere to hide and no secrets that can be kept.

"You told me you were going to Brighton. And I had a pretty good idea of what you were going to do."

"I doubt that. I didn't know myself."

"I have been thinking about you a lot. It was like putting a jigsaw together. Suddenly I saw the whole picture."

"I still don't get it," she said.

"You booked tickets online, so that was easy. I checked the database of hotels held by the tourist office, but you hadn't checked in anywhere that I could see. So I knew it must be a very small place."

"You knew a lot, perhaps too much."

"Didn't you want me to save your life?"

"I suppose I must have done. I've told you I am very grateful – really. Go on."

"I hacked into the central police surveillance system and retrieved recent CCTV images. There are more cameras here than any other city except London, because of that bomb a few years back. It took time, but then I saw you leave the station and tracked you down the front. I saw you walking west past the big hotels. You didn't turn into town, so clearly you were going back to some small hotel or bed and breakfast on the front. Once I had worked that out, it was easy. I was lucky with the trains and got here in an hour – luckily for you."

Jed was so clever, and she was so lucky. Who else could have tracked her down like that? She would have been dead by now, on the way to the morgue probably, cold flesh on a marble slab. She felt ashamed.

"You must think I'm an idiot."

"Maybe. Tell me why you did it."

"It's a long story."

"Give me the short version."

"Can we leave it a while? I need to get my feet back on the ground."

They spent the morning walking the streets, skimming flat stones off the sea, bargaining for antique knick-knacks and playing slot machines on the pier. Desperately ill cancer patients are often given a blood transfusion that gives them a new lease of life. That's how she felt. But the respite is brief. Those patients die well before their time, in the end. That's how she felt, too. Their hands slipped into each other's as they walked.

He told her this was the first day of the rest of her life. She said that was a terrible cliché because, looking back, there wasn't a day she regretted except maybe just one. He had looked sad then and slid his arm around her waist. She nestled into him, her head on his shoulder as they walked onto the pier.

"You mean yesterday, the day you tried to kill yourself?"

The remark jolted her.

"That was stupid," she said, "stupid, stupid."

She thought back. The red wine, the toothpaste mug, the pills and the...

She broke away and looked at him.

"What happened to the letter?"

He took the folded letter from his pocket and shook it into a single sheet.

"I've got it here," he said. "It's really quite poetic – for something so stupid."

"Give it to me!"

She reached out. He stood tall and held the letter up high. She stood up against him on tiptoe, reaching up. He bent down, still holding the letter, and kissed her lightly on the lips, then more firmly. She put her arms around his neck, and they stayed like that kissing until an old lady passing close by started making hen-like clucking noises.

Other passers-by ignored them. Lovers come to Brighton pier to scream and laugh on the rides, hug and kiss, eat ice cream and candy floss, argue and fight; occasionally one or two have been known to jump over the railings and into the sea at high tide. Those that do so at low tide – and in the heat of a lovers' argument this has been known to happen – end up covered in stinking slime in the waiting room of a local hospital. They are made to wait a long time.

She broke away from the embrace and stretched up, saying again, "Give it to me!"

"No." He stepped back and folded the single sheet into a dart with swept back wings and a pointed nose.

"Watch this."

He threw the dart up in the air. They watched it dip and then float over the railings. Alison ran to the side, grasped the railings and leant with her arm out as if to catch it. He took her hand in his and squeezed it. They watched the dart lift in the breeze and glide further than seemed possible for such a flimsy piece of paper before falling into the water.

"I was going to put it in a bottle and chuck it off the end of the pier when the tide was going out," he said, "but I thought this was better."

"Thank you," she said and kissed him again. She had no idea whether they were going to stay or return to London. She didn't care. She was alive and, for the first time in a long time, perhaps for ever, she felt a sense of contentment, possibly happiness.

She had never been able to define happiness. When her mother asked her if she was happy with her work, with her life, with her birdwatching, she had never known what to say. Now she knew. If Jed had suggested they float out to sea in a beautiful pea green boat like the Owl and the Pussy Cat, with plenty of money and a lots of honey, wrapped up in a five-pound note, she would have agreed. That was happiness.

They went back to their hotel.

"Are we staying here?"

"Sure," he said.

"You'd better book yourself a room."

"I wish I could, but the hotel's full."

"Liar," she said and kissed him again.

Alison insisted they eat lunch in the most expensive restaurant in Brighton. Jed objected volubly. The receptionist recommended the Lorraine and pointed out the multiple stars and recommendations in the guidebook.

"I'd rather fish and chips or maybe a steak."

"You can eat what you like in the Lorraine. This is a celebration," she said. "I'm taking you and we're going there."

It was a mistake. The clipped tones and the deep frown of the maître d' told them they were not dressed properly for such a restaurant. The tablecloths were stiff and starched. The barman, vigorously polishing cocktail glasses, wore a gold-buttoned, midnight blue waistcoat with a white sash. He looked exactly like the barman in the Jermyn Street restaurant where Doxat had taken her. She wanted to forget that.

They left the Lorraine without even looking at the menu and walked along the seafront. They bought fish and chips wrapped in greaseproof paper. Jed had made no mention of the previous night, but enthusiastically described how he had neutralised the supposedly foolproof cyber security system on the local police database.

"Amazing what happens on that pier at night," he said, his words lost in a mouthful of chips. He coughed. "They've put in too much vinegar."

They sat down on a bench facing the sea. She knew the questions would start coming the moment he had finished his chips. An arcade full of slot machines offered no suitable distraction. He had read the letter. He would want to know what on earth she was thinking of. He would want answers. She didn't have them.

A line of gulls perched on the keel of an upturned rowing boat watched them. Herring gulls, she noted; fierce-looking birds with strong yellow bills and a well-deserved reputation for the aggressive pursuit of food. They would smash shellfish on rocks to get at the flesh, rob other birds of their eggs and their chicks and had been known to swoop on unsuspecting tourists and steal sandwiches and ice creams from their hands.

She opened her paper wrapping more widely and rested the battered fish and chips on her lap. Jed had finished his and was looking around for a bin.

The gulls shifted along the keel making space between them, their heads now firmly fixed on the two people sitting on the bench. You could look at gulls such as these and see beauty in their black and silver dappled colouring, the silken cream of their white bodies, and marvel at powerful wings that could take the bird miles out to sea following trawlers, or the curved bill that could rip apart a rubbish bag in minutes.

Then again, you could take the view of most people along the coast that ever-increasing flocks of the birds with their screaming cries and aggressive scavenging were as much a menace as rats. Myths grew that they had snatched dummies from babies in prams and even seized a silver purse from a woman, mistaking it for a fish.

Whatever their reputation, and Alison naturally preferred the former to the latter, she knew that this particular species matched high intelligence with a willingness to take risks in pursuit of desirable food. The herring gull never went hungry in seaside resorts. She watched as an older bird, larger and with more distinct colouring than the others, opened its wings, flapped and settled again. Alison raised her paper wrapper slightly, taking care not to attract Jed's attention.

The pink-rimmed eye looked at her, unblinking. She raised one piece of fish cautiously towards her mouth and held it there halfway. In one flowing motion from lift-off to flight, and without perceptible movement of its wings, the gull came towards her fast and low, the hooked yellow bill pointing forward. She thrust her head back and shielded her eyes as wings flapped in her face. "Go away," she shouted.

The gull did not take the fish in her hand but stabbed into the wrapping paper hard enough for her to feel the blow on her thigh before it wheeled away with a large piece of battered fish in its bill.

She screamed. The attack had been much faster and more frightening than she had imagined. Jed had one arm around her and was shouting at the bird. The gull swallowed the fish in flight and returned to the keel where the other younger birds shuffled up to make room.

They were probably that season's brood and his own young. Jed scooped a stone and threw it at them. The gulls contemptuously flew away and settled on another boat out of range.

"Bastard," said Jed.

"God, that was fast, it took the fish right out of my lap."

"Better than out of your mouth. Anyway, you asked for that. I saw you dangling that piece of fish in front of you."

"I was curious. Let's go back to the hotel."

She made him walk around the block while she had a shower and slipped under the eiderdown. She closed her eyes. She was exhausted. Gulls with giant orange eyes, wide open orange bills and wings like panes of frosted glass flew into her dreams. She shielded her face and shouted. A hand shook her awake.

"You shouldn't sleep in the afternoon," he said. "You'll get nightmares."

She leant up on one arm and rubbed her eyes. He was standing at the foot of the bed dressed as always in drainpipe jeans and a T-shirt.

"I've just remembered that you shoved my head into the lavatory bowl last night."

"I had no choice. Want to talk about it?"

"No."

She flopped back onto the bed and looked up at the ceiling.

"Know what?" she said. "You're a gull."

"What?"

"A gull. Remember you once asked me what bird I thought you were? Well, you're a gull. Of the herring variety. That's the answer."

"That's not very nice. You've just been beaten up by a gull. I've just saved your life."

"Jed, you're definitely a gull. I'm sorry."

"I'd rather be a hawk, perhaps a kestrel, fastest bird on earth."

No, Jed was a gull. He scavenged through digital data dumps. He would take risks for the most satisfying morsel of information: who was fiddling their expenses, cheating on their wives, downloading porn, lying about awaydays with the company when they were holed up in a motorway motel. She checked herself. This digital scavenger had saved her life precisely because he could hack his way into any encrypted password-protected system.

Anyway, gulls were creatures of power and menace with strong glossy bodies which hardly matched the pale skinny figure before her. Glossy, Jed was not. He had not shaved for a couple of days, and there were dark rings under his eyes. He looked frail and rather shabby. His power lay in knowledge. He knew all about her now. He had read her letter. Maybe he had cracked her shell on a rock and seen what was inside. It didn't matter. The shambolic, unwashed colleague who relished his role as an outsider wouldn't recognise the change in himself, but she saw it clearly. He had fallen in love with her.

"Close the curtains and come here," she said, opening her arms.

"Give me a moment to take my feathers off," he said.

*

Later, they walked to the end of the seafront and up a steep path along the top of the chalk cliffs. She had taken her binoculars, although it was getting dark. At the top they paused, breathing hard.

"How about we go back? I've had quite enough exercise for one day, and I could do with a drink," Jed said.

"No, I want to show you something."

They walked further up the hill, occasionally holding hands when the path allowed. Jed had been a surprise that afternoon. He had held her close, flesh on flesh, kissed her slowly, whispered silly things in her ear, made her laugh and reminded her that pure joy, the joy that pounds the heart and takes the breath away, should never be postponed. She shouldn't have waited so long.

It was dark now. The night sky was clustered with stars. Distantly the dim glow of Brighton could just be seen beyond the curve of the hill.

"Look up there," she said, pointing to the sky.

"Lot of stars. Very pretty. Can we go back now?"

"No. Look for five stars that make up a W shape. Here, take the binocs."

Jed looked up. He was cold. There was a gathering wind coming in off the sea. Find the stars that make a W and then back to Brighton and a large whisky. Good thinking.

"Got them," he said.

"OK. You should see a pale whiteish, fuzzy blob just to the left."

Jed moved the binoculars fractionally and refocused. There was the fuzzy blob.

"OK, I have it."

"Hold it there. You're looking at a galaxy called Andromeda. There are 500 billion, I repeat billion, stars in Andromeda and many if not most have planets circling them like we have the moon and the sun."

"Give me a break, Ali. I'm cold and there is a storm coming up the Channel. Can we do the astronomy lecture back in town? Then you can tell me all about Androm… whatever it was called. I really, really don't need to know right now."

She took the binoculars and kissed him, sliding her hands around his waist and then lower, feeling for his zip.

"Come on," she said, "a quickie under the stars."

He took her hand away and held it in his.

"Too bloody cold. I need a steak and chips and a large glass of red."

They ate in a steakhouse that advertised Scottish organic beef from pure-bred, milk-fed cattle without additives of any kind and killed with kindness in humane conditions.

"Killed with kindness! That's the sort of gibberish Doxat would come up with," said Jed.

They ordered steaks. When the food was on the table and the wine poured, he said, "Alison, you owe me an explanation. Skip all that galaxy stuff for a minute; can you please tell me why you – of all people – did that?"

"Did what?" she asked.

"Come on, Ali. No games. You tried to kill yourself."

"You read the letter, didn't you?

"Gobbledygook. I couldn't make it out."

"It was pretty clear to me."

"You said you had wings and could fly. That's not clear to me."

She reached for the bottle. His hands closed on hers. They held the bottle together for a moment, looking at each other, unsmiling. She released her grip.

"Every time I ask for an explanation you change the subject. I saw what you were doing with that gull. It was distraction. You were just playing for time. Why?"

"Because I can't explain to you something I don't understand myself."

Jed poured the wine, filling both glasses. A strong wind was tipping over plastic chairs on the terrace and rattling the front doors. Waiters were stacking the chairs and placing the tables on their sides. The curtains were drawn. Jed got up and opened the nearest curtain to their table. A waiter shrugged. Rain began to patter against the windows.

"Try," he said.

"It was all in the letter. I thought I had come to the end. There was nowhere else to go. That it was over."

"You said you could fly and that you had wings in the letter. Do you really believe that?"

"Don't you?"

"How would I know?" he asked.

"That's the whole point. I don't know either."

"So why write the letter? Why the pills? Did you think you were going to fly up to that Andromedidooda place and flit around the heavens like a fucking bird?"

"Andromeda," she said, "and don't say fucking."

Rain was beating against the windows. The drumming sound was comforting. Fishermen would call this a Channel blow. The squall would pass, leaving a heaving sea churning up sand in the shallows. Seabirds would sit out the storm in bushes and small trees along the shoreline, waiting a day or so before being able to feed again.

Only a hardy few, especially the storm petrel, would brave the open sea in such conditions. It was November now, and the petrel would be wintering around the coast of South Africa with other winged migrants. Would that she could join them, flying down over desert, jungle and savannah on the way to the warm climes of the south.

"I told you. I had come to an end. You cannot live with the knowledge that somewhere inside you is… is… well, I don't know what to call it… something beyond the understanding of science."

"Ali, this is all crazy. What you're talking about is not beyond science, it's beyond sanity."

She sliced into her steak and began to eat, pausing to drink some wine. The blood red taste of strong meat grilled pink with a thin ribbon of raw flesh in the middle was good. Jed watched her, knife and fork poised over his food, a frown on his face.

"Eat," she said through a mouthful of meat. He cut into his steak.

They remained silent, eating and drinking until a waiter swept their plates away. She wiped her lips with a napkin and finished her wine.

"You're right. It's crazy. So skip that and try this for a fact published in every scientific journal you care to name."

Jed grimaced and raised his hands palms outward in surrender.

"I showed you that galaxy for a reason. You didn't listen, so I am going to try again. It is a mathematical certainty that among 500 billion stars with their own planets there is intelligent life, maybe not as we know it, but life all the same."

"If you say so… but—"

"It is also highly probable, if not certain, that such life is doing what we are doing – looking out into space to see if they are alone in the universe. Man has been trying to work that out ever since he walked out of the cave with a stone tool in his hand."

"You're losing me," he said and raised an arm to attract a waiter.

"The problem is that light does not travel instantaneously. When you click a light switch in your room, it takes a millisecond for light to reach the wall. Magnify that millisecond by the vast distances of space that light has to travel to reach us, maybe trillions of miles, and you can understand that it might take millions of years for those eyes to see us. So…"

"If they do see us, it will be an Earth maybe way back in time," he said.

She had got him. He was suddenly interested. Sh e wanted to jump up and sing *I Think He's Got It* in a pastiche of *My Fair Lady*. The waiter came and Jed asked for the bill.

"So, what's this got to do with you?" he asked.

"Let me pay the bill and then I'll tell you. Pour us some more wine."

The waiter brought the bill and nodded to the window.

"Nice night outside," he said.

Alison paid, leaving a large tip. This was the difficult part. There was logic in what she was about to say, but she had to admit it would sound crazy to anyone else. If anyone could get it, Jed would. He had that sort of mind. He was half crazy himself.

"Suppose Gödel was right, that if you apply the logic of physics to Einstein's theory of relativity it is possible to show we can go back in time."

"Bit of a stretch, but go on."

"It wasn't a stretch for Einstein. He believed him."

"I'm listening."

"OK, hold that thought. Now accept the fact that there is a direct evolutionary line between dinosaurs and birds. Not the monsters we see in films but smaller versions that grew wings and learned to fly."

"OK, I'll buy that."

"Logically, therefore, it is possible that mankind will adapt and learn to fly in maybe a million years. After all, if dinosaurs did it, why couldn't we?"

"Millions of years, blossom, yes, maybe. Right here and now, no. I see where you're coming from, but I don't buy it. Let's drink up and go."

She tried to make him see that she was dealing in belief and instinct, not certainty, not proof but just a wild idea, indeed the only idea that made sense of her life: that if she could fly, and the evidence was there, then maybe she had emerged from, or dropped through, a chink in the space–time continuum.

"Space–time what?" he said.

The storm burst outside with crackles of lightning and fierce drumming rain. Jed opened the curtains further and sat back, allowing them to see the street lights swaying on their poles through sheets of rain.

"Tell you what," he said, "let's wait for a break in the storm and fall through the space-time whatever into bed. Your man Gödel would appreciate the logic in that."

"Bastard. You're not taking me seriously."

"I took you very seriously this afternoon."

"This is all a joke to you, isn't it?"

He laughed.

"Be fair, blossom. A man doesn't often find himself in bed with a woman with wings."

"That's all you can do, isn't it? Sneer and laugh."

The rain had eased to a light patter on the windows. The street lamps shivered in the wind. She got up and walked to the door. He got there before her.

"Sorry. I didn't mean that. Sit down."

"Go back home, Jed. There are plenty of late trains."

He took her arm, gripping it firmly.

"Ali, this is silly. Don't get angry with me just because I don't understand how time turns somersaults in space. I tracked you down and saved your life, didn't I?"

"Maybe I didn't want you to do that. Has that occurred to you?"

"Don't be ridiculous."

"I didn't take those pills and write that letter because I was being ridiculous. Get that? I thought about it, planned it and wanted it. Then, as usual, you barged in." She spat out the words.

"You really wanted to kill yourself, did you? Well, for someone with a death wish you certainly showed a remarkable appetite for life in bed this afternoon. They must have heard you halfway down the front."

She slapped him hard and walked out of the restaurant. He jogged after her and caught her up.

"Leave me, Jed. I mean it."

She quickened her pace along the front and turned into the neon dazzle of the pier. She had not realised the sheer size of the place. It wasn't really a pier at all. It was a giant fairground built a quarter of a mile into the sea. The big rides had all been halted due to the high winds. But the dodgems and arcade attractions were open, and they were packed on a cold and windy autumn night. If this was what it was like in November, Alison wondered how many thousands would squeeze onto the pier in the summer.

Queen of Piers, proclaimed a flashing sign, All the swagger of tradition balanced with the excitement of today. If the pier was feminine she was a gaudy lady indeed, striding into the sea decked out in a string of restaurants, bars and amusement arcades.

Jed walked beside her. She ignored him. He reached an arm out to her, but she brushed him away. They had almost reached the end when she stopped outside a small café, with flashing neon lights running around the door and along the roof and the sides. An illuminated cowboy picked out in fairy lights flashed a welcome to the End of the Pier Saloon.

He put his hand around her waist. She stepped back.

"I've told you I want to be alone. Just leave me. Please."

He stepped back, hands raised in surrender.

"You seemed so happy back there. This afternoon…"

"Things change, don't they?"

"OK. At least come in and have a coffee. It's freezing out here."

"No thanks. Just leave me alone."

He growled at her, a back of the throat growl that a dog might make to an unwelcome stranger.

"Have it your own way. Come in when you have calmed down."

"I'm perfectly calm, thank you."

She watched him go into the café. He looked back once, then went through the door. She walked to the end of the pier and leant over the railing. Beyond and on either side, waves rose and fell, the bristling crests just visible in the dim light from the illuminations.

She looked back at the café. Slatted shutters had been closed over all of the windows except one. Jed was sitting at a table by that window, staring into the darkness. He looked pale and drawn. Behind him, a few middle-aged couples sat drinking. In that well-lit room he would be able to see nothing in the darkness outside. He wouldn't be able to see her.

He had not understood anything she had said, which was hardly surprising, since she didn't really understand it herself. *You cannot understand what doesn't make sense, can you?* She smiled and shook her head.

She pulled her coat around her tightly. The temporary lull in the wind and rain would not last. Another squall was blowing up the Channel, the deep sigh of a distant Atlantic storm. It occurred to her that the strange man in the café staring blindly into the night loved her. The thought surprised her. She should have known that long ago.

Women were supposed to have antennae to pinpoint incoming male emotions, distant signals of love; not that men understood love, its meaning was as remote to them as a distant star in the Andromeda galaxy. Perhaps there was a love star up there beyond the storm clouds hurtling through space towards them – except, like love, it was an illusion.

It wasn't the star we saw but the light from a mass of molten rock and gas, that had imploded into nothing long before microbes formed the first life on earth.

The love star was a fraud, a deception, its twinkling light an intergalactic fantasy in the immensity of space. That was Gödel's point, wasn't it? A shimmer of white caught her eye further up the beach. She turned to see a gull blown in from the sea, flighting low over the front. It was a large bird, probably twenty years old, and would not live to see many more storms. Weary from a life on the wing, it would just fall to the ground from wherever it had perched for the night. Some birds, the lucky ones, were said to die in flight.

Would that the human race had such a set time on earth, a sixty-year span that would end peacefully at a given hour known to all, she thought. It would make life so much easier. The long loving goodbyes could be carefully prepared and loved ones folded in a last embrace. Death would be but a pause in the long green grass.

She wanted to turn, look back at the café and see Jed again, but decided against it. He had thrown her letter into the sea. He had turned her words into wings and made them fly into the waves. Somewhere in those churning waters that paper dart had disintegrated into nothing. Like the love star. Now, nobody would ever understand.

The scream was blown away by the wind. Those in the café heard something out there, a halyard snapping against a flagpole, maybe electric cables loosened by the storm rattling on the roof.

The second scream was louder this time, a woman's strangulated voice pitched against the wind and clearly heard in the café. People got to their feet and moved towards the door, fearful and curious. Jed ran outside and saw two old people, a man and a woman, holding the railings on the far side of the pier, he with a rubber-tipped walking stick raised forwards, she with one arm outstretched facing the sea, about to scream again.

The two figures, motionless as if in a photograph, were pointing at the end of the pier. Alison was standing on the third and final rung of the railings facing the sea. Her arms were outstretched and she was bending forward to balance against the wind.

Jed knew why the couple had not moved. They knew what he knew: never approach a jumper whether from a cliff, a bridge or a building – or even the end of a pier. Engage them in conversation, ask simple questions, make them take their mind off what they are about to do, remind them that there is hope and keep using that word.

Hope. That wouldn't work with Alison. This was the second time in twenty-four hours. He made a quick calculation. The long drop to the sea was survivable, but wearing those clothes she would quickly be sucked down by the waves or be dashed against the support pillars of the pier.

He ran, shouting her name, his feet slipping on the wet planks. He saw her quite clearly look back at him. Later, he would tell those who asked that in that final moment she smiled, whether at him or the couple or just a smile of happiness, he did not know.

Then she went, jumping forward, arms outstretched, her overcoat flaring in the wind, a figure lost in the misty spume of the wave tops. Jed ran to the railings and looked down. She had vanished. There was not a sign of her, not even a flailing arm or pale face amid the brutal blue-black waves. Someone threw a life buoy into the water. Others ran to phone the lifeguard. The old couple joined him at the railings and stood peering down, as if not able to believe what they had seen. Jed turned and walked back through the fairy land of lights and music.

Somewhere ahead a siren was wailing.

CHAPTER TWENTY-FOUR

A sergeant at the local police station took Jed's details and asked about Alison's nearest relatives. Jed told him her mother was on her way. The officer assured him the body would be washed up a few miles east along the coast within a week. There would be an inquest once it had been found.

"On an ebb tide at this time of year that's where the sea takes them, just down the coast. Plenty of beaches that way. Drops them off at high tide. Not very nice for the swimmers in summer. Identifiable, but not a pretty sight for the family. Clothes mostly gone. I take it you are family, sir?"

"No, just a friend. Did you say *them*?"

"Yes, all sorts get themselves in the water round here. Mostly damn fool weekend sailors, the odd fisherman and stupid kids. Most are rescued, but a few always get taken. No one lasts long in these waters at this time of the year. But the good news, if I can call it good news, is that we always get them back. That's important for the families, sort of rounds it off."

Jed watched as the officer filled out several forms and then looked up.

"Cause of death," he said, "we will leave that to the coroner. But I assume death by drowning following an unfortunate accident. People do silly things in a storm – run along the beach and see how close they can get to the waves, that sort of thing."

"She jumped," said Jed.

The sergeant looked up. He was used to dealing with the bureaucracy of death and took a certain pride in guiding grieving relatives through the tedious formalities.

"What – from the pier?"

"Yes, we all saw her."

"Are you sure she didn't fall? It does happen, especially when drink has been taken."

"No, she definitely jumped."

"Well, that's a new one on me, and I thought I had seen it all. The jumpers normally go up to the clifftop, although we did have one from a hotel bedroom last year. Nasty business that, went straight through an awning onto a table at lunchtime. Luckily—"

"Thank you for your help, sergeant."

*

Alison's mother listened carefully to Jed's account of her daughter's final day. The rattle of cup against saucer was the only sign of emotion. Jed described the time they had spent together. He said nothing about the events in the hotel nor the leap from the pier. Mrs Spedding asked only one question: "Were you her boyfriend?"

Jed paused, sipped his tea and said, "Yes."

"I'm glad about that. She was very lonely. It's nice that she finally found someone."

There was no reason for Jed to remain in Brighton. He was due to give evidence at the inquest, but that couldn't take place without a body. But he stayed on in the town, blaming himself for not having stopped her, forgiving himself because she did what she was determined to do, cursing himself for their argument in the restaurant.

He spent hours every day in the public library researching the facts and theories about the Andromeda galaxy. The vast field of science devoted to the study of space astonished him. Nothing he learnt about the closest galaxy to Earth helped, neither did his research into Kurt Gödel, the Austrian mathematician and logician who had meant so much to Alison. Jed could not begin to follow the complex web of theories that linked Gödel to Einstein, and both men to the concept of time travel. Books, printed lectures and talks on the subject were impenetrable. Nothing made any sense of Alison's death.

In the evenings he drank in seafront bars and hotels. Always about 11.00 pm, because that had been the time, he went to the end of the pier, past the noise and glamour of the attractions, and stood at the railing. The sea was calm now. Anyone jumping off, or falling from, the pier would survive if they kept afloat until a boat picked them up. If they wanted to be picked up, that is.

For a few days Jed delayed replying to Kennedy Doxat's emails and text messages. Finally, he agreed to meet him at a hotel in the centre of Brighton. Doxat wanted to make it 6.30 pm in the bar. Jed said 4.00 pm in the lounge for tea. They met there, shook hands briefly and sat in a corner with a low coffee table between them.

Jed ordered tea. Doxat asked for a large vodka and tonic. The waitress looked a little surprised and said she would ask the manager if they could serve alcohol to non-residents at that time of day. Doxat waved her away impatiently.

"Can you tell me what happened," he said.

"You know what happened. It's been in the papers."

"I want to know what really happened."

"So do I," said Jed. "The answer is, 'I don't know'. She jumped. Into a very rough sea. At night. Without hope of rescue. Suicide. End of story."

"Why?"

"You tell me, Mr Doxat. You knew her better than most."

"What's that supposed to mean?"

Doxat's drink arrived with the tea. Jed pushed the tea aside and asked for a large vodka as well.

"It doesn't mean anything. I'm just saying. You knew her well, didn't you?

"What are you insinuating?"

"You dropped in on her out of the blue in Scotland, took her to lunch at Wiltons, had a nice Chinese meal together. I am not insinuating anything Mr Doxat. Just saying."

"She was an extraordinary woman. I'm just shattered by this. I had no idea she was so troubled."

Doxat sighed, shook his head and took a large gulp of vodka. Jed's drink was placed on the table. He swirled the ice around with a teaspoon.

"Did you see her jump?"

Jed raised his glass and drank. "Yes."

"Straight into the sea. Just like that?"

"Yes. It was very rough. She just vanished."

"Can I ask what you two were doing here?"

"No, you can't."

"Were you lovers?"

"Mr Doxat, let me be as polite as I can. Mind your own fucking business."

Doxat lunged at him across the table. There was a crash of glass and china. Cries of alarm arose from others in the lounge, punctuated by a single shout of "Call the police!" The two men grappled briefly until Doxat pulled himself back to his own side of the table. He was breathing heavily. Jed was brushing the remains of his drink from his trousers.

"I'm sorry. Out of order. I apologise," said Doxat.

"Fucking idiot," said Jed.

A hotel manager came bustling across the room.

"Pay the bill and leave now or I'll call the police," he said and turned on his heel.

Outside on the forecourt of the hotel, Doxat apologised again and offered his hand. Jed took it and they shook hands.

"One last question," said Doxat. "You spent the last hours of her life with Alison. Was she very depressed, possibly traumatised by something?"

"No, not at all. I think she was happy for the first time in a long while."

"Happy enough to kill herself?"

"Maybe she didn't."

"Didn't what?"

"Kill herself."

"What are you talking about?" Doxat's words trailed after Jed as he walked away.

*

Two weeks after Alison's disappearance, Jed got a call from the police sergeant in charge of the case.

"There's no sign of a body, which is unusual," he said. "But we are going to keep looking. Sometimes the bodies get taken out into deep water and it can be weeks before they get washed up again. But she'll be back sooner or later. Don't worry."

Jed thanked the sergeant. They would never find Alison. He knew that. The sea would never give up its dead. A high tide would never return her body to shore. There wasn't a body to return. There never had been.

Jed knew something else. Deep in his heart he knew with a binding certainty that he would see Alison again.

Acknowledgements

I am grateful to those who helped me in the research for this book and many more who offered advice and criticism – and occasional counselling in the shape of a large glass of Pinot Noir.

My friend and colleague Karen Robinson loved the story and was indefatigable in giving her help and advice.

To Dotti Irving, Chief Executive of Four Culture, I owe heartfelt thanks for her wise counselling and friendship.

Mark Finn, who runs bird watching tours from his home on the Black Isle in Scotland, took me to Skye in search of the white tailed eagle.

Members of the Kent Ornithological Society, too many to name here, allowed me to join them for a chilly morning on the estuary marshes near Faversham.

My agent, Annabel Merullo, patiently pursued the steep and stony path to publication and somehow managed to put up with my constant bleating.

I am grateful as ever to the advice and editing of Sue Robertson.

Thanks also to Sophie Moorsom, executor of her mother, the poet Sasha Moorsom, for permission to reprint the fine poem *The Company of Birds*.

Tim Clifford made small but important changes in a brilliant final edit, and to Mrs Deborah Keegan, my part matron part mother superior, my love and thanks as ever.

Above all I record my thanks to Matthew Lynn at Endeavour Media and his enthusiastic team: Alice Rees, Cate Bickmore, Rebecca Souster and Rufus Cuthbert. It was a pleasure working with them as with the Four Culture team of Natasha Monroe, Chloe Davies and Kate Klevit.

Finally, to Sally Davies who refuses to be called a partner and prefers the status and nomenclature of lover, my thanks and my love.

Having graduated from the University of St Andrews, James MacManus enjoyed a successful career in journalism and is currently the managing director of the *Times Literary Supplement*. He has written several novels, including *The Language of the Sea*, *Black Venus*, *Sleep in Peace Tonight* and *Midnight in Berlin*.

jmacmanus1x@gmail.com
jamesmacmanus.com